Bert and Norah

MURDER
IN THE
OZARKS

Bernard H. Burgess

Bert and Norah: Murder in the Ozarks
Copyright May 2020 by Bernard H. Burgess
All rights reserved.

Inquiries should be addressed to
Bernard Burgess
2975 Shelton Road North
Bee Branch, AR 72013

E-mail: bb2975@hotmail.com
www.bertandnorahmysteries.com
Facebook: The Bert and Norah Mysteries

Cover designed by Kristy Kennedy-Black of Idea Creative Services
Kristy@ideacreativeservices.com

This book is a work of fiction. Names, characters, places, and incidents are products of the author's imagination or are used fictitiously. Any resemblance to actual persons, living or dead, or locales is entirely coincidental.
Printed in the United States of America

First printing: June 2020

Kindle Direct Publishing
ISBN: 978-0-96-00069-2-2

DEDICATION

I dedicate this book to three people who went missing from my region of the Great Plains states: Jonelle Matthews, Serenity Dennard, and Chance Englebert. They are among the approximately 600,000 annually who go missing across the United States of America. When I read that shocking statistic from namUS, I decided to dedicate my latest book to what this organization calls "The Nation's Silent Mass Disaster."

Jonelle Matthews disappeared without a trace from her home in Greely, Colorado in 1984 at the age of twelve. Her remains were discovered by coincidence in July of 2019, 34 years later. The case is again under investigation.

Eleven-year-old Serenity Dennard hasn't been seen since she walked out of her Children's Home in Rockerville, South Dakota, in February of 2019. The case is under investigation and unsolved.

Chance Englebert, 26, of Moorcroft, Wyoming, disappeared without a trace from Gering, Nebraska on July 6th, 2019. He is married, has one child, and was visiting relatives when he vanished while walking downtown. Active searches and investigations are ongoing but unsolved. Any and all legitimate help is welcomed. At this writing, he is still missing.

Despite the magnitude of this crisis, many of us have not been touched personally by the unexplained loss of a loved one or friend. My hope is that this fictional story can touch all who read it in such a way as to embed this national crisis in your consciousness.

If you have any information which might be of benefit to the ongoing investigations and searches, please contact the appropriate authorities or visit the pages on Facebook: "Serenity Dennard Missing" and "Let's Start with Chance."

TABLE OF CONTENTS

CHAPTER ONE: ANNABEL

The sun was slowly sneaking over the eastern mountains and peeking through the dense forest of pine, oak, hickory, sweet gum, and cedars, made the more impenetrable by the brushy mix of greenbrier, Virginia creeper, and poison ivy. The quarter mile-wide and two-mile-long valley of Bobcat Hollow was nestled in the still-shadowy dawn of this fall morning in November of 2016. Heavy dew covered the grasses and low shrubs of the valley, leaving telltale trails where the several whitetail deer had been grazing. That Friday before the start of deer rifle season was a clear one; chilly, without a cloud in sight.

The secluded hollow was ten miles and twenty-minutes-drive from Mountain View, Arkansas, accessible by a partially graveled and paved county road. The end-of-the-road, three-bedroom, wood-frame house was situated along the north side of the Bobcat Hollow valley. The quarter-log siding and forest-green metal roof caused the house to blend into its deep forest background. A heavy, homemade, wooden door provided a secure barrier from the unknowns of the night. That fall morning, interior lights illuminated the kitchen and provided glimpses of the female inhabitant as she prepared coffee and breakfast.

Annabel Leery scurried around inside the house shared with her husband, Izack Leery. She was a petite brunette, with beautiful blue eyes, slim, and down-home pretty. The exposed skin of her arms and face bore the tan of a woman who spent several hours of an average day outside, tending to the farm livestock and garden. Her hands were small and lady-like yet were abnormally strong from the days of wholesome outdoor labor. Annabel had one of those personalities that made almost everyone like her. The only times she was ever down was when

Izack was in one of his many moods.

Her husband was a good-looking man, with sharp facial features, brown eyes, and dark hair. He was the life of the party as a young man, but married life did not agree with him. The slender and muscular fellow could turn on a dime into an angry and self-serving jerk. While he had never hit his wife, he was often verbally abusive toward her. At home! Out in public, he put on the persona of a loving husband. The public was fooled for a while, but word gets around in a small Ozark Mountain community of just under 3000 people. Most knew that Annabel was increasingly unhappy at home.

Annabel and Izack were both in their early thirties and, despite having been married ten years, they had no children. While they had never been medically tested, it seemed obvious that one of them was infertile. Izack assumed it was him and that added to his jealousy when he noticed the looks that his wholesomely attractive wife would get from other guys. He was increasingly entering fits of jealous outrage whenever they returned home from the occasional trips into town. That Thursday night had been no exception.

Thursday nights in Mountain View had evolved over the years into a social night for many of the locals. Being a unique and interesting little mountain town, nestled at the confluence of two valleys, quite a few artists had moved there, either for a permanent residence or as a part-year getaway. Many of those musicians started getting together on Thursday afternoons and evenings to jam and create a free performance for anyone wanting to listen. The handful of cafés, coffee shops, and fast food places did a thriving business on those nights.

Annabel and Izack had gone in during the late afternoon to hear some of their favorites play. As the music blossomed like an Ozark Mountain dogwood, they followed a couple of friends to the increasingly crowded town square. Annabel reveled in the strains of banjo, fiddle, harmonica, and dulcimer music and had her customary one hot dog. Izack, on the other hand, had several alcohol drinks, snuck in with the other two guys. Stone County was a dry county. He became his loud and increasingly obnoxious and jealous self. At one point he began to threaten a guy who seemed to be eyeing Annabel from a nearby hamburger and lemonade stand. She became both self-conscious and upset and told her husband she wanted to go home. Izack was beyond using much common sense by then, and he refused. He wanted to continue having fun and the idea of a fight didn't dissuade him.

The fight didn't happen, though there were a few heated words exchanged with the guy seated at the counter of that stand. That fellow wasn't into backing away. His brash boldness helped Izack refrain from taking a swing. Finally, Annabel, with the support of the other two wives, convinced Izack to take her home. That didn't make her night much easier, though.

"I can't believe you, Annabel," Izack had blurted out as they left the lights of the town behind. The twenty-minute drive wound up the side of the narrower northern valley, into increasingly dense forest. "What were you thinkin' to be flirtin' with that ass? What a jerk."

"Honey, I wasn't flirtin' with him. I wasn't even lookin' at him. You're the one makin' mountains out'a molehills."

* * *

"Don't give me that crap," he had yelled. "You knew he was looking at you all night. I knew he was looking at you. Hell, everyone in the square knew it. I've half a notion to make you walk home from here."

"Izack, please don't be like this. I'm sorry if I gave that guy any reason to be lookin' at me. I wasn't tryin' to; please believe me. I'm sorry." She was aware of the pitch darkness of this county road for the last five miles. The thought of having to walk it was terrifying. She was scared to walk it in daylight, much less at 11:00 at night. Although close to town, it was very isolated and wild. The rough, rocky terrain insured that the length of the road was almost completely undeveloped as it wound through the rugged and heavily treed mountains.

Her apology seemed to settle Izack a little. He had driven in stone cold silence until their cabin began to appear through the breaks in the trees as they approached the only significant valley along the road.

"Who was that guy, Annabel?" He'd growled. "I've never seen him before."

"Izack," she had pleaded, "please believe me. I have no idea who he is. I've never seen him before, either. Far as I know, he's from way out yonder somewhere. He sounded like a city guy, so maybe he's from Little Rock. Just passin' through, I'd guess."

"Well," he'd snarled, "you remember this, Annabel. If I ever catch you doing anything with that guy, somebody's fixin' to get hurt bad. It ain't going to be me, neither. Now get your butt out of the car. I'm going back and meet up with the other guys at Jimbo's. I need another drink. I'm supposed to go huntin' with Jimbo tomorrow up on his property, so I won't be back until afternoon or maybe tomorrow night." He then led her inside their cabin and stormed around, gathering his hunting clothes, equipment, and gun. Grabbing two boxes of 30-06 rifle cartridges, he slammed the door as he stomped angrily out of the house and drove away.

Annabel had quickly moved around the cabin, locking the doors and windows. She didn't mind being alone in this secluded place during the day, but she really hated being alone at night. The night was absolutely black if the moon and stars were obscured by clouds. You couldn't see your hand in front of your face without a light. At least tonight it was clear, and the sky was filled with the brilliance of the twinkling stars. The moon had disappeared behind the western mountain. However faint, there was some comfort in the dim starlight. She had to take some comfort in it, because Izack had taken their only means of transportation. She had been abandoned and left stuck at home. Just her and the night sounds of the Ozark Mountains.

One who knew her situation was her sixteen-year-old nephew, Billy Joe Magnus. Annabel's only sister had died in a car accident just a couple years after the birth of her one son. So, Annabel took it upon herself to become the surrogate mother as well as doting aunt to Billy Joe. She practically raised the cute, sandy-haired, boy and it was a rare day that he didn't visit his aunt. As he became a teenager, he even had a mild crush on her for a while. He was a short but stocky and muscular lad and he loved his life as a country boy in the Ozark Mountains. On that day he stopped in to have an early morning coffee with his aunt before scouting the surrounding valley and woods for the big bucks. He intended to be in his first hunting hide by that time the next day. He'd been hunting with his father, Jim Magnus, since he was ten, but this was to be his first time going alone.

When Billy Joe knocked on the door about 6:00 that Friday morning, Annabel was very happy to see her nephew. He was always such a bright light in her life, and on that morning his bright blue eyes and big smile lit up her kitchen.

"Hi, my sweet nephew, how y'all doing this morning? Let's

have a cup of coffee and some breakfast before ya head out in the hills. Those big bucks can wait a while."

"Hi, my favorite aunt," Billy Joe replied. "For sure, let's have some breakfast. You can tell me how you're doing."

She didn't reply but poured him a coffee, then turned her attention to fixing some sausage, eggs, and toast. He noticed that she was trying to suppress tears.

"What's wrong, Annabel?" he asked. "I know you're upset about something. Tell me."

She looked at him through tear-covered eyes. "He got very mad at me last night and threatened to make me walk home. I was so scared, Billy Joe."

Billy Joe's face reflected his immediate anger. "Annabel, I wish you'd divorce that S.O.B.; he's a jerk and always gonna be a jerk. If he'd done that, I'd clean his clock."

"Honey, I'm okay so please don't get involved with him. It'll only make matters worse and I don't want ya to get hurt."

He replied, "Well, I won't do anything this time, but mark my words. If he hurts you, Aunt Annabel, I'll make him regret it."

She knew her nephew meant every word and he'd attempt to take on Izack. She also knew that her husband had been in a lot of fights and knew how to handle himself in a brawl. His quick temper was exacerbated by a mean streak. He was not one to take lightly. She also knew that Billy Joe was a crack shot with a rifle.

"My dear nephew, I know you'd defend me against Izack or anyone else. I love and appreciate that loyalty about you. I always feel safe when I'm with you, Billy Joe, and happy. Whenever I think about it, my heart breaks for my dear sister who never had the pleasure of watching her son grow into such a good young man. I try to change my thoughts to those of gratitude that I was able to stand in for your mother in her absence. It's been my honor and happiness to watch you develop into such a good man. I'm proud of ya."

He now wiped away his own tear. "Aunt Annabel, I don't know what I'd have done without you as my aunt and standin' in for -mom. You've always been here for me. My mother would be right proud of ya."

"Okay, enough of all this gushy stuff," she replied. "Let's eat this breakfast before it gets cold. You can tell me about this buck you're fixin' to get."

He bowed his head while his aunt said a blessing. He dipped his toast in the egg, followed it up with a bite of deer sausage, and nodded approvingly. "Oh my God, Aunt Annabel, this is soooo good. Great way to start the day. That buck can wait a few more minutes."

She nodded in agreement. "So, where is the big fella that you're scouting? I think I may have seen him a couple mornings out in the far meadow while gathering eggs." The very ones she was now devouring like a starved fox, she thought.

"This guy hangs out down here occasionally early in the day to feed on grass. But he spends most of his time way up near the top of that west peak, in and around a couple of little clearings. There, he has plenty of shrubbery, leaves, and nuts to eat. Some cute little does running around up there, too. I've been scoutin' him all summer and so far this fall, so I know his habits pretty well. I think he's about five years old; in his prime. Got a nice rack, six points on each side."

"Oh, wow, that sounds like a great buck. I'm going to be praying that you take him. You deserve a trophy like him, and there will be a lot o' good eatin' to go with it."

"When I get him, I'll call on ya to come up and help me dress him out and carry him back down here. Maybe we can get a quarter and some of the best cuts in your freezer."

"That'd be great. I love venison as you know, and I sure won't turn any of it away. Just let me know when you need the help. I would love to carry some of the meat down."

"If you want, throw on your cammies and go with me. You can help me find him."

She shook her head. "No, sweetie, I can help dress and carry, but I'm just not very good at stalking. I like gawkin' at the scenery and critters, too much. I'd probably scare him away. You just go and let me know when you need help. I'll be here. I can't go anywhere until Izack gets back and that could be late today. Heck, if he doesn't get one on opening day, he might stay out another day. I have a lot of work to do around here, anyway."

"You be careful and keep your eyes open, Annie. Have you heard about what happened at the Watson's last night?" he asked.

"Why, no, what happened?" she replied.

He went on, "About 2:00 this morning, something tried to break into their house. It made some weird noises and scratched their door up pretty good. Mr. Watson drove down to our house right before I left a while ago."

She shivered. "Oh my, did they get a look at it?"

"No, they couldn't see it," he said. "Only heard it. They think it was probably a bear, but not sure."

"That seems a little out of character for a black bear, but I guess you never really know," she replied. "Of course, you know it will stoke the fire of those other rumors."

He nodded. "Yeah, once this gets around, the Sasquatch hunters will get even crazier than they already are. Who knows, maybe there's something to it. Just because I haven't seen it, doesn't prove they don't exist."

"Well, you be careful out there in the woods, my nephew. If they exist, you'll be out in their territory. Keep your eyes open."

He pulled his vest back to expose the sidearm carried in a belt holster. "This 44-magnum will take care of Magnus." He laughed. "Nothing out there is going to take a slug from this baby and keep walking. So, don't worry. I'm on full alert when I'm in the deep woods."

She stood up and gathered their empty plates for washing later. He was pulling his jacket off the back of his chair. "Good luck up there today, Billy. Hope you find him. Be careful. Stop by on your way back out if you want. I'm going to be here."

"Yeah, I'll stop by on the way home if it isn't too late. Either way, if you're up early on opening morning tomorrow, I'll have a coffee with you."

"I'll have coffee ready by 5:00 in the morning. Just come on in," she said.

With that, the young man gave his aunt a strong hug. He kissed her on the forehead and waved silently as he was opening the door to leave. As he entered his truck, he remembered virtually every word of their conversation. At the time, he didn't know just how important their talk would become. And how imprinted it would be on his mind.

Annabel pulled on a light jacket and stepped outside into the chilly morning air, watching as her nephew drove his old

Dodge pickup to the far end of the valley. Then she turned her attention to the chicken coop and the waiting eggs. Their eighteen hens kept them in a good supply. Her cap filled with a dozen of the brown and ivory ovals; she went back into her house.

Having done the dishes and cleaned up the kitchen, Annabel scurried around the house, making beds, gathering laundry for washing, and doing general cleaning. She would gather any remaining produce from the garden a little later. Her immediate chores done, Annabel sat at the table, thinking about her nephew, and her jealous husband. Then there was the mysterious attack at the Watson house. What was that all about, she wondered.

She sighed deeply. For a few seconds, she sat very quietly, listening to the sounds outside. It was strange only in the complete absence of sounds. Rarely was there a time in these mountains when it was totally silent. She wondered why. Sometimes, she knew, the wilderness would go silent in the presence of an apex predator.

Standing up, Annabel Leery, of Mountain View, Arkansas, walked to the front door, donned her jacket, and stepped outside. Closing the door, she vanished without a trace.

CHAPTER TWO: PREPARATIONS

Norah knelt beside Missy, taking in the beauty of their coywolf's soft, silky coat. Even as a spirit, Norah nevertheless stroked the animal's fur and observed a noticeable reaction by Missy. The female tracker and companion animal laid onto her side, yawned, and stretched, completely relaxed. She opened her eyes momentarily and then closed them. Norah knew that Missy sensed her presence and knew who she was. Though she'd been gone, physically, for nearly two years at this time, Norah had almost eighteen months as a living entity in the young animal's life. Long enough to bond together. Long enough for their spirits to intertwine and each to sense the other. The adult, forty-pound, female hybrid twisted onto her back, and lay momentarily in the unashamed pose used frequently for the purpose of eliciting a belly-scratch.

Her husband, Bert Lynnes, was outside, tending to the yard on this late-summer day. She left Missy to her immodest daydreaming and moved to the picture window, overlooking the yard and the North Fork Valley leading from Cody to Yellowstone Park. She watched longingly as her shirtless, retired, army man guided the mower over the sloping ground. For a middle-aged guy, Bert was still in good shape and held her attention. She might be a ghost, but she still felt the love and lust so often given into on the other side. She held onto the precious memories of their bodies intertwined in the pleasures of lovemaking. At times like this, her emotions ranged from love and happiness to intense sadness and yearning. It was so hard for her to know and want the touch of this man, while knowing there could be no physical exchange between them. She knew it was difficult for him, too. He loved her, wanted her, and missed her warm body, yet she could not fulfill his needs, or her own. Was it a mistake to choose to stay connected to his dimension? Should she have followed the light?

The ringing of his cell phone interrupted her melancholy soul-searching. She recognized the ring tone as that of their business number. Bert had both his business and personal calls routed through his one cell phone, which he'd left on the kitchen table. Maybe the month-long drought of business was about to break. Her husband was getting concerned that the case load had dropped significantly this summer. The few cases that did come in were given to Becky, so she could continue to cover her expenses at the new apartment she'd rented in town. Norah went to Bert and told him of the phone call. He turned off the mower, thanked Norah, and went inside to retrieve his phone.

Bert listened to the voicemail left by the caller. He lowered the phone with a half-smile and told Norah they might have a case. The caller, a young-sounding man with a southern accent, had said he wanted to discuss hiring them to investigate a missing person.

"He asked me to call him back around 6:00 this afternoon, Norah. I have just enough time to finish mowing if I get back to it."

Blowing a kiss to her, he went back outside to his mower. As he resumed the task, his mind wandered. It wasn't too long ago, just back in January, when they finished the case in Nebraska, one of their most perplexing, yet satisfying, cases. It had been a challenge to help bring those poor women back into the light of day from their watery tomb. The following months brought a variety of cases, from several more regional missing persons, mostly lost or runaway children, to a spattering of surveillances for divorce, custody, and the like.

July, though, was one of those lull months. The only two jobs were given to Becky. She had proven to be a valuable addition to their team. Her always cheerful and positive attitude was like a constant cool breeze on a hot day; simply refreshing. Yes, she was very attractive for sure, but she was also a very good member of their team. What she didn't know or naturally perceive, she was more than willing to learn. It amazed him how much she was like Norah. It amazed him even more that Norah's spirit showed no sign of jealousy. Norah was a psychic. She knew he was attracted to Becky.

As for Rebecca Abigail Thompson, Becky as she preferred to be called, her position as a private investigator with B & N Investigations was indeed her dream job. She loved the challenges of sifting through the clues and seeking the truths which would lead to resolution for their clients. Bert was a model boss for her; very professional while also a warm, witty, caring, and charming good guy. She couldn't ask for a better man to work with and for. And Missy. Missy was a joy to be around. Like man's best friend, the little canine was very devoted to Bert, but Becky knew that she, also, held a special alpha female place with this friendly and energetic animal. Missy would wriggle from head to tail with delight every time that she saw Becky, and there was no bending down to greet her without the expectation of a good licking of the chin and cheek.

Norah was another matter. Becky accepted the relationship with the wife of her boss, although she was still occasionally entertaining the questions. She'd been with the company now for eight months, since beginning in early January of 2018. Yet, she still had not met the lady of the house and business. Bert seemed uncomfortable talking about Norah, so Becky had quickly learned to avoid the subject. She always sought Norah's opinions and inputs about her cases and appreciated the fact that both her questions and Norah's inputs were quickly relayed by Bert. The one thing which Becky noticed above all others, though, is that she usually felt Norah's presence anytime that she talked with Bert. While she felt an increasing desire to meet Norah, Becky felt a growing realization about why that might never happen. She was beginning to understand why Bert was having a hard time really explaining the situation. If she was right, it would not be an easy explanation.

On this day in late August, Becky was enjoying the drive from Billings, Montana, down to Cody, Wyoming. She'd just completed the child custody surveillance and paperwork for their client on the outskirts of Billings and was headed back to home base. Bert had just relayed by text message that they might have another, bigger, case coming in. He'd asked if she would call after she was settled back at her apartment this evening, so they could bring her up to date on whatever might be coming. Regardless of the status of the case, it was another opportunity to talk with Bert, a man she felt increasingly close to with every passing encounter. She felt a little guilty about it, but Becky knew that she liked Bert a bit too much. She forced herself to focus on and enjoy the scenery of the plains to her left and the mountains to her right. This was not the time to behave like a giddy teenager over the hot guy in the class. She drew a deep breath and made herself revel in the power and handling of her black, Dodge Ram Hemi, truck. She chuckled to herself as she recalled the many stunned looks she received from men when they saw a pretty woman driving a muscle truck.

Back at their log cabin west of Cody, Bert had finished his lawn mowing chore and was inside, preparing to return the call of the young man from the South. With Norah and Missy on the floor nearby, basking in the sensations of closeness, he dialed the number. It rang four times before it was answered.

The same young fellow from the voicemail gave a very southern, "Evening, this is Billy, what can I do for ya?"

Bert introduced himself as the owner of B & N Investigations, returning Billy's call to his company. He answered several questions about his company and asked where Billy was calling from. The answer surprised him, even given the lad's southern accent. To Bert, Missouri was in the deep South, so when Billy said "Arkansas," it was almost a shock. "Do people live that far down there?" he jokingly replied.

Billy obviously had a good sense of humor. "Oh, you better believe it. Where do you think Daisy Mae and the rest of the Clampetts came from? We pity all you northerners who have to wear so many clothes all the time."

"Well, you do have a point there," Bert laughingly replied. "So, how may we help you, Billy? I'm sorry but I didn't catch your last name."

The young man became serious. "Mr. Lynnes, I'm Billy Magnus. Everyone calls me Billy Joe or just Billy. A good number of our family have pooled our money in the hopes of finding a P.I. company that can help us put a killer where he deserves to be. We've been looking online, and your company seems to be what we need. A relative of ours has been missing for about two years now, the case has grown cold, and the killer is running around free as a bird. We want to find her, and we want this . . .. person, put away for good."

"Just call me Bert," he replied. "Can you tell me a little about the woman who's missing?"

"She's my aunt, but really more like my mother. She raised me after my own mother died, since I was about two. Her name is Annabel Leery. I had breakfast with her that morning and she was gone that afternoon. She'd be 34 years old now."

15

"How old are you, then, Billy?" Bert asked.

"I'm eighteen," he answered. "I was sixteen the last time I saw Aunt Annabel. For a long time, I referred to her as mom, although she was my aunt. She finally trained me to call her aunt. Bert, she was, is, a wonderful woman. We love her, I love her, very much. Sir, we want to know what happened to her and see that justice is served to the person responsible."

"You seem to think that you know who's responsible for her disappearance," Bert said.

Billy didn't hesitate, "Hell yes, we all know who did it, Bert! Her no-good husband. He was never good for her and she often was afraid of him. The night she disappeared, she told me he scared her in one of his jealous drinking fits."

Bert replied diplomatically, "Well, we'd just have to try to prove that theory, if possible. From my experience, Billy, things are not always as they seem. There are a lot of jealous and drunken jerks out there who haven't committed a crime, so we must be open-minded. If you hire us, that's how we must proceed. We'd want to find her first, then find the person who took her, whoever that might be."

"Yes, sir. I kinda figured you'd say something like that. I understand and appreciate what you said. It confirms my thinkin' that you guys are the ones we need. I'm aware of your fees, Bert, and my family and I are ready to pay ya. When can ya start?"

Bert glanced at Norah, and their minds met. She nodded in agreement. He returned to the call and told Billy they could begin the two-day drive by Monday, August 27th. That gave his team the weekend to get ready to go. He proceeded to get all the necessary information from their new client. With the formalities out of the way, he hung up the call and returned to

Norah, who waited patiently alongside Missy.

"What are your perceptions, Sweetheart?" he asked her.

After a minute to collect her thoughts, she replied. "This young man is understating his love for his aunt, Honey. She is probably the most important person in his life, and he's been completely heartbroken since she vanished. He truly believes his uncle did something to her, and there is an underlying hatred there that we'd need to be aware of and ready to deal with, Bert. I received one vision, Honey. I see the barrel of a rifle aimed at a man, maybe more than one. I see the smoke and feel the recoil. The target is hit. If we can't determine who took his aunt, I get the feeling that he could kill her husband, his uncle. I feel that someone else is going to die in this case. Possibly several people. If we take this case, you need to be very careful."

Bert thought about that for a bit. "So, Sweetheart, we need to determine the real criminal or killer, in order to prevent what may or may not be a justifiable homicide by our client. We must find a killer to stop a killing. Is that about how you see it?"

She nodded.

Bert wanted to do some research online about the national scope of this missing person status. He'd been wondering for some time just how big this situation was, and he decided to let the present case be his catalyst for digging into it. He first opened the NamUS website and began to read about "The Nation's Silent Mass Disaster."

"Norah, listen to this," he said. "About 600,000 people go missing every year across the US. It says that tens of thousands remain missing for over a year. About 4,400 unidentified bodies are recovered each year."

"Oh my, Bert, I suspected it was bad, but I had no idea it was that bad," she replied.

He did the math quickly. "Honey, that's an average of 12,000 missing persons per state. Despite the efforts of the various state and federal agencies, this is still a little-known tragedy. The FBI has a long list of pictures of current missing people, mostly women and kids, as you would expect. However, there are men there, too."

Norah moved closer to Missy and stroked at her back. Missy whined softly.

Bert went on. "I'm just looking at the website of the National Center for Missing and Exploited Children. Oh my God, Norah. There are kids listed here that've been missing for over ten years, some over twenty. This is even worse than I thought."

Norah pulled her legs up and sat forward with legs crossed. "Honey, what this tells me is that you had the wisdom and intuition which makes our business a very successful one. You said from the beginning that we are suited for finding missing people. Your insight is not only on the money from a business standpoint but is creating another resource for heartbroken families to turn to. I'm very proud of you and proud to be on your team."

He rubbed his hands together as he sat staring at the floor, taking it all in. "Thank you for that, Honey. The truth is that you played the larger role in our direction. It's your psychic abilities which make the difference. You, and Missy's nose. Without the two of you, I'd just be another P.I. doing divorce and custody surveillances. Nothing wrong with that, but not what I want to be focusing on. I always wanted to make a real difference in the lives of my clients. I want them to become our friends."

"You have already made a difference in many lives, Bert. Don't doubt that, Honey. Becky is another one for whom you've made a big difference. She loves working for us, especially you, and is doing a good job. Will we be able to take her with us to Arkansas?"

Bert realized that this was at least the second or third time that Norah had campaigned on Becky's behalf. Maybe his fear of jealousy was unfounded. He told Norah that she would be calling very soon to discuss this upcoming case.

"You do know, don't you, that you have to tell her about me, soon?" Norah said.

"Yes, I know that's coming. I think she already has suspicions, Honey. I just don't know how to bring it up with her. How do I tell her that my wife and partner, also her partner, is a spirit?"

Norah's answer was intuitive. "You'll figure it out, Bert. It will come to you. Maybe you're worried about what she'll think, but I have a feeling that you don't need to worry."

Bert nodded and walked to the kitchen for a glass of milk. He hoped Norah was right, but he had to admit that she was also right about him being worried. As he walked back to the den, Becky called.

She was bubbly and excited to tell him about the case she'd just finished in Billings. She felt like she'd nailed it for that client. Bert got a kick out of listening to her. He knew that Norah enjoyed her enthusiasm, too. They knew that hiring Becky was one of their best decisions. After telling them about her case achievements, Becky then asked about the possible new case.

He proceeded to bring her up to speed on the known details of the Ozark case, as they'd start calling it. "Becky," he said, "I think this is going to be the first case that will likely take all our

19

resources to solve. That means that I think you should go with us on this one. What do you think about that?"

"Oh wow!" she exclaimed. "I'd love to go and help with this case. It sounds interesting and challenging and I've never been south of Missouri. Mostly, though, this sounds like a family that needs to know what happened to their loved one. If I can help with that, it will be worth it. That's exactly why I got into this line of work."

Bert replied, "That's what we figured you'd say, Becky, so we've already begun our plans with you included. We have one request, though."

"Shoot," she said. "What do I need to do?"

"Well, we have no idea what we might find down there once we start digging into this case. We think it could be helpful, maybe even necessary, to have a second vehicle. So, would you have any problem with driving down in your truck? It will take us at least two days to get there. It's almost a twenty-hour drive."

"No problem with that," she said. "I do have one small request of you, though."

"Name it," he said.

She laughingly answered. "For such a long drive as a single woman, I'm going to need some security. So, I'd like to have Missy ride with me at least half the time. Please!"

Bert looked at Norah and saw her smile and laugh. He laughed as he gave Becky an affirmative answer. He didn't tell her that he was already thinking of that. Missy would enjoy the change of scenery every now and then on such a long trip. Becky and Missy had formed a strong bond over the months, anyway. He drew a deep breath. It was time to address the issue and get it over with. He asked her if she could meet him at the Irma in an hour for a short chat. She could. He looked at Norah, again. She just smiled and nodded. She also knew it was time.

The next hour and its short drive to the Irma Hotel in downtown Cody was an apprehensive one for Bert. He was more nervous about this meeting than he'd been about doing building sweeps in Iraq, looking for the bad guys. That made no sense to him, and he tried to figure it out as he drove. Pulling up to the Irma, it still perplexed him. He saw Becky's muscle truck and grinned. What a woman she was. Maybe he was afraid of running her away.

"Hi Boss Man," she said from her table overlooking the street, "sure good to see you again. I'm so excited about going with you guys on this next case. I feel like I've had twelve cups of coffee today. I almost can't wait to get on the road."

Bert couldn't help but smile at her as he sat down across the table. "Can I buy you a beer, Becky. I don't think I've ever had a drink with you. Guess it's about time."

She wasted no time answering. "You bet, Bert. It is about time. Make mine a Moose Drool."

He couldn't help but chuckle. "Moose Drool, huh. How does a sweet little gal like you know anything about Moose Drool?"

"Hey, I wasn't always a sweet little gal. I have a sordid past with a few skeletons." She laughed. "This is actually one of my favorite microbrews. The fact that it's from a local brewery is all the better. It fits my drinking style, too, because I can't drink more than one."

He ordered two bottles of Moose Drool. It was secretly one of his favorites, too. He wasn't sure if he should tell her that or not. They engaged in some small talk about her cases and college football. He was pleased when he found out some time back that she also liked watching football. He remembered asking himself if there was anything about this woman that he didn't like. Nothing had come to mind.

The beer was delivered, and they clinked bottles and took a sip. His sip was a couple seconds longer than her's. He sat the bottle down, drew a deep breath, leaned forward on the table, and looked her in the eyes. "Becky, I've been meaning to tell you something for quite a while. Ever since you joined us. I haven't been sure how to go about it."

She leaned forward, smiled, and looked back at him. "If it has something to do with Norah being a spirit, don't worry about it. I think I understand. And I don't mind. We'll figure it out."

Bert sat in stunned silence. He looked down at his beer, trying to hide the tears that suddenly welled up. He realized that there are special challenges when dealing with psychics and empaths. They can always surprise you if they choose to. What will we figure out, he wondered? No sense in trying to hide the tears, so he wiped his eyes with his hand. "Well, you are more complex than I realized. When did you know?"

"Just now," she smiled. "But I've wondered about it for quite some time. Nothing was really making sense until I sensed her presence so much whenever I talked with you. What else could it be?"

He looked out the window at the traffic on the street, gathering his thoughts, and reining in his emotions. The past two years of memories flooded his mind like a raging river. Was he struggling more with those feelings, or the ones from the pretty, blue-eyed, blonde woman sitting across the table? A woman who did not get up and walk away in disbelief and disgust. She was still there, waiting patiently for him to come back.

"I'm glad you know about the situation now," he said. "It makes it easier going forward. Especially when we work this coming case together." He reached out his beer again and clicked it to her bottle. They both tipped their bottles and took a drink to that.

She took a second slow sip from her bottle. "So, I guess Norah knows that I'm aware of the situation, too?"

"Yes, she knows I came here to tell you," he replied. "She felt it was time that you knew; that we owed that to you."

"Thanks for that. I've never had to rely upon anyone to tell me the thoughts of someone else before. We've been functioning that way for eight months now, so I know it's possible. I sense Norah's presence when she's near you, but I can't hear or see her. So, I guess we keep using you as the go-between for her and me. That puts you under a lot of pressure, doesn't it?"

He gave that a second before replying. "Well, no, I don't see it as much pressure. I just keep doing what I've been doing, only now without the worry of you not knowing."

"Oh my, Bert, you really must be a man!" She said. "Only a man wouldn't recognize the danger of being caught between two head-strong women." She laughed and took another sip.

He laughed at that, but inside a big question was brewing. "Was she right about that?" He wondered.

It was time to get to some business, he figured. So, he discussed his plans to meet again the next afternoon at his cabin, work on the details of communication and what they could surmise about the Ozark case. They could finalize their travel plans, which he thought tentatively should begin around 7:00 Monday morning, August 27th, 2018. That would be day one of the case. Becky was okay with all that.

"Anyway, Boss, I'm about Moose Drooled out, so better get back to my bachelorette pad while I can still drive. Thank you for coming clean with me." She laughed that playful little laugh. It was still fun to tease him a little, even if he was the boss. She knew he was buying the beers, so she tossed down two dollars for the tip, said good-bye, and headed for the door.

Bert watched her go. He noticed that half a dozen other men in the joint were watching her as well. "We're all alike," he thought to himself, "easily mesmerized by a pretty woman."

With that, he downed the last of his beer, paid the tab, and left for the doghouse. Was it a sign, he wondered as he entered the vehicle, that he called his SUV the doghouse? Maybe it was pre-ordained that he was going to be spending a lot more time in it. Not because of traveling, either. "Okay, Mr. Army officer, get your head out of the clouds and get down to understanding how you're going to make this situation work," he said aloud to himself. He proceeded to drive back west on the Yellowstone Highway toward home.

As Bert drove back to his cabin, his spirit-wife Norah, and Missy, Becky drove to her small apartment on the south edge of town, went inside, and decided to get ready for bed. She was just realizing how tired she felt. The rigors and excitement of her recent case, the exhilarating drive home to Cody, and the emotional meeting with her boss, all combined to suddenly make her very tired. The Moose Drool provided an extra kick. Although it was nearly 8:00 P.M., the sun was just sliding behind the mountains to the west. The summertime sun would hang around a lot longer at these northern latitudes, she knew.

She thought about putting on her pajamas for just a few seconds. Then she decided they were for colder times, undressed, and slipped under the covers, naked. As she turned off the light and studied the darkening room, she thought of the irony of it all. She had finally found a man she knew she could fall in love with, and he was still in love with the spirit of his dead wife. A spirit he could communicate with and who was usually with him.

"What can I do about that?" She said aloud to the darkness. "What should I do about that?"

* * *

The Saturday meeting began in early afternoon. Bert had asked Becky to stay for supper later and watch the Wyoming Cowboys football game with New Mexico State. Until then, they discussed, with Bert acting as go-between, how to handle communications among themselves. Becky could sense Norah, although she could not see or hear her. She had decided that morning to try to ignore her feelings for Bert and just keep it professional. There was just no way that she could see to compete with a spirit. Especially the spirit of a woman whom she admired, respected, and liked.

They all agreed that it was necessary to protect Norah from the clients and public. Most people simply would not understand the relationship even if they believed it. So, the party line would remain that Norah's medical condition and psychic abilities required that she remain in the background and away from other people. That was all true, if not the entire truth. Bert noted another as-yet unused, potential benefit of Norah's psychic and paranormal status. Because others could not see or sense her, except those few mediums they might encounter, she could literally eavesdrop on select characters and see what they were saying and doing. This had to be tempered with the knowledge that anything learned would not be admissible in their reports or in any court.

Norah reminded them that she was primarily attached to Bert. Therefore, she went mostly where he went. However, she said, there was a risk for her if she strayed too far. There are spirits who are attached to places that are evil and those spirits are sometimes evil. It was possible for a good or benevolent spirit to become trapped by such an evil and unable to escape. Bert didn't realize that and was not reassured by the knowledge.

Norah could see and hear Becky, so Bert didn't have to relay her inputs to Norah. He could see that Norah enjoyed the conversation with their investigator. She seemed to like Becky, just as before yesterday's revelations. He could see that Becky was trying hard to build a relationship with Norah, even if it was an indirect one.

They shifted the conversation to discussing the upcoming case. Because of the distance from home and the added expense of motel rooms, Bert felt they needed to hit the ground running and give themselves the best chance for satisfying their clients quickly. None of them had ever been to the Ozarks of Arkansas, so they'd have a pretty steep learning curve at first, just getting used to the terrain and the summertime heat. He also thought it might be a good tactical move to appear removed from Becky, initially. There could be a situation where a person might be inclined to open up to her if they didn't perceive her connection to Bert's business. The opposite could also be true. So, when they got to Arkansas, they would initially give the appearance of discreet unfamiliarity. They would arrange similarly discreet meetings to update each other and make plans.

"So, any theories on what happened to Annabel?" Becky asked.

Bert replied, "Well, besides the obvious and prevailing one that her husband killed and hid her, I've been thinking about all the other possibilities. The more I think, the more I come up with."

Norah replied to him, "Maybe you'd better quit thinking, then, Honey." She laughed. "Besides the husband, it's possible that someone else may have killed her. Then it becomes the question of a new motive and suspect."

"Right," Becky said after Bert relayed Norah's comment. "There's also the possibility that she wasn't killed at all. What if she was abducted? She might even still be alive. That brings up a different set of who and where questions."

"I'm also a little concerned about the apparent attack on the nearby family's cabin the night before Annabel disappeared. It seems unlikely to have anything to do with Annabel's disappearance. But what if it did?" Bert wondered aloud.

Becky added, "That family thought it might have been a bear, Billy told you. Do you think a bear might have grabbed her?"

Bert answered her, "It would be unusual black bear behavior if that happened. And, a bear attack would be messy. There'd be blood and other evidence of the attack. She vanished without a trace."

"Since we're brainstorming," Becky said, "what if an abominable snowman took her?" She laughed, seeing this as half serious and half funny.

Bert and Norah both chuckled at that. He replied, "I suppose we could even consider an alien abduction. There is credible evidence that this has happened to some people. On the scale of possibilities, though, I think it should probably be down the list a way." He snickered, although his logical mind was reminding him that even this might be a possibility.

They all were getting a kick out of the humorous brainstorming. However, all knew that they could rule nothing out for certain. However improbable something might be, when someone vanishes without a trace an investigator must keep an open mind and methodically rule out the improbable along with the probable. The truth was likely to be somewhere between the two extremes.

"How should we divide our focus, then?" Becky said.

Bert had been thinking about that also. "Norah, what do you think about you and me trying to get close to where Annabel lived and see if you pick up anything psychically? Then we'll start with the husband, Izack, and see what we can find out about him. At some point, after we've done our homework, we'll try to sit down with him and question him face-to-face. Maybe we can rule him out as a suspect in her disappearance. Or confirm that he might be behind it."

"Yes, I agree with that approach, Bert," Norah replied. "At the same time, Becky might float around the community and see what the locals have to say about Annabel. Someone may have a theory that should be considered.

Bert agreed with that and so did Becky. "When we first get there, we'll arrange a private meeting with Billy and have him go over the police report and any newspaper articles that seem relevant. Let's try to leave at 7:00 on Monday morning and we'll plan to stay overnight in Kearney, Nebraska, which is about halfway. I'll make reservations at a couple motels around Mountain View beginning Tuesday night. Hopefully, Billy can meet us someplace private for breakfast Wednesday morning.

They couldn't think of anything else to discuss now, so decided it was time to get ready for supper and the game. Norah remained in the den with Missy while Bert and Becky moved to the kitchen. They talked while he grilled a couple of steaks and shared a bottle of wine with her. Bert enjoyed listening to her talk. Being from Minnesota, she had a bit of that regional dialect to go with her smooth voice. He was glad she had never been a smoker, because she didn't have the raspy voice so common with long-term smokers. As he tended to the food, he periodically smiled at her wit. Boy, she was so much like Norah in many ways.

"You are a man of many talents, Mr. Lynnes," Becky chuckled. "When you aren't solving mysteries, you're a chef. When you aren't being a chef, you're being an animal trainer. When you aren't training animals, you're breaking hearts." "Oops," she thought to herself, "maybe that's going a bit too far."

He laughed. "Well, maybe you're giving me a little too much credit. You haven't tasted the steak yet." The heartbreak comment wasn't lost on him.

"If it tastes anything like it smells, it will be wonderful," she said. "I'm about to drool, I'm so horn..... hungry."

"Oh my God, Becky," she thought to herself, "get under control. Two glasses of wine and you're about to turn into a slut." She knew her face was turning red, but he was tending to the stove so maybe didn't notice. Change the subject, change the subject.

"Who do you think will win the game?" she asked quickly. "The Cowboys seem to have one of the best teams in years, but New Mexico State is undefeated, too."

Bert was trying not to laugh at her embarrassment. "Yes," he said, "I think the Wyoming running game is going to be the difference in our winning. I expect it will be a good game, though. Come and get it, everything is ready, and you can just get what you want from the stove."

They both filled their plates and ate quietly, savoring the tenderness and flavors of the meat and vegetables.

Norah, in the meantime, reclined next to Missy, softly stroking the hair on her back. Even though the hair didn't move, she could always tell from the body language that Missy sensed her presence and her affection. It was rewarding to know that she hadn't been forgotten by this beautiful animal. As she petted her loving companion, Norah listened to the banter from the kitchen between her husband and Becky. Most of the time, she viewed Becky as the professional and talented investigator that she was. Listening to their conversation, though, Norah realized that Becky was also a woman, a beautiful and sweet woman, and she was now acting like a woman, not an investigator. It was somehow comforting to know that a woman like Becky also found Bert to be a good and attractive man. Rather than feeling threatened or jealous, Norah felt that it was a validation of her own attraction to Bert, and her feelings for him. She was happy that he enjoyed Becky's company as well as her help. Norah sat up, pulled her knees up to her chin, and nodded silently in approval for her choices.

Wyoming went on to defeat the New Mexico State Aggies by the score of 29 to 7, with their running game playing a major role in the victory. Becky had traded places with Norah during much of the second half, lying on the floor next to Missy with her arm over the coywolf. Norah smiled at Bert at one point when they both realized that Becky was sound asleep with her face tucked against the top of Missy's head.

"She obviously feels relaxed around us," Norah mused. "I'm glad she likes us all enough to feel that way."

Bert nodded and smiled. It was nice to see that. It was nice to hear Norah say that.

Becky had woken up for the last quarter of the game. She smiled sheepishly at Bert, knowing that Norah also saw her, and sat back against the couch. Missy stood up, moved near Becky, and dropped down heavily beside her, placing her head on Becky's lap. She turned her eyes up to Bert for a second and then closed them. Content.

After the game, Becky gave Bert and Missy a hug, said her good-bye, and drove back to her apartment. There were still quite a few cars on the road at the late hour, just after midnight on this Saturday night. As she arrived at her apartment and prepared for bed, she acknowledged the mixed emotions she was feeling. There was always the loneliness at bedtime, but it was tempered by the warm feelings from her visit with Bert and Norah. Then again, it wasn't helped by the frustrating attraction she felt toward Bert. Why couldn't she just see him as her boss and leave it at that? Why was he getting into her heart? For the second night in a row, she decided to sleep nude. She wasn't sure why.

"I need to find someone else," she said aloud, as she turned out the light and pulled up the covers to her chin. Tomorrow she had to get her clothing and investigative gear packed up and in her truck. She also needed to inventory and update her emergency and survival equipment for the trip. Monday morning would arrive sooner than she might expect.

CHAPTER THREE: ON TO THE OZARKS

Sunrise came shortly after 6:30 A.M. that Monday morning, August 27th. The red-orange glow of the eastern sky slowly gave way to the brilliant ascent of the solar king, as it climbed above the horizon. The first rays spread in broken rivulets between the trees, leaves, and low buildings of Cody as Bert, Norah, and Missy pulled up to Becky's apartment. She was already at her truck, securing the last of her gear in the truck box, stowed in the large waterproof toolbox behind the cab. She looked up with her big smile and an excited wave.

"Hey there, Miss Private Eye," Bert blurted as he exited the doghouse. "You're chomping at the bit to hit the road, it looks like."

"Hi there, Boss Man," Becky shouted back. "How are you, Norah, and my critter this morning?"

Bert and Norah both laughed. "Your critter?" he said. "Are you trying to illegally adopt our coywolf?"

"No, not adopt!" she replied. "I'm merely demanding joint custody."

They all got a good laugh at that, as Bert helped her get the last bag stowed. "Okay, you drive a hard bargain, but joint custody it is."

Bert noticed that Becky had kept the back seat of the truck clear and had a blanket tucked neatly over it. She was ready to exercise her custodial rights, apparently. He chuckled. Then he noticed the chest harness and seat belt attachment. That's a good idea for a valuable animal like Missy, but she had never worn a harness. He wondered how that would go. Might as well find out.

"Would you like to have custody of the tracker for the first leg?" he asked.

She was quick to answer. "Absolutely! This is a tough road and a girl can use some security. Would you put the safety harness on her? I would hate it if she got hurt in a fender bender or who-knows-what."

He shook his head in mock disgust. "Oh yeah, make me be the first to put a harness on the wild wolf. She'll take my hand off."

"Don't be a sissy," Becky grinned. "That's just a sweet puppy there. Piece of peach pie."

Bert called Missy to him and began to introduce her to her new safety equipment. She didn't take his hand off, but she wasn't cooperating, either. She squirmed away, pulled her legs away, and wanted nothing to do with it. She almost pulled him off balance with her last escape.

"Let me try," Becky said. Taking the harness, she called Missy over and put the harness on without a bit of trouble. Missy stood obediently through it all.

"Oh my God," Bert exclaimed. "Are you kidding me? You won't let me do that, but you stand like a statue for the pretty girl. Good to know where I stand." He was still laughing as he watched Becky hook Missy to her new safety strap in the back seat. With that, he returned to the doghouse, minus the dog, and both vehicles pulled out simultaneously for the drive to Arkansas. Norah laughed at the recent antics for the first ten minutes, to add to Bert's sense of betrayal. After a few minutes, as Cody faded in the rearview mirror, Bert began to laugh, also. It really was funny. He kept glancing at Becky's Dodge truck in the mirror, the sunlight glinting off the windshield. Settling into the seat, he began to pass the time by watching for antelope as Wyoming Highway 120 streamed ahead of them and studying the various options and questions they expected in Mountain View.

After a couple hours had passed, they arrived at one of Bert's favorite watering holes along Highway 120, the Storyteller bookstore and coffee shop, in Thermopolis, home to the world-renowned hot springs. Norah browsed unseen in the shop while Bert and Becky chose a favorite drink. They made a trip to the bathrooms, then led Missy back to Becky's truck. As soon as they found a stopping spot outside the town, they'd give her a short break, too.

They Stayed on point for the bulk of the day, not stopping again until reaching Scottsbluff, Nebraska. A brief bathroom break and short walk for Missy was rewarded by the view of Scotts Bluff Monument and glimpses of Chimney Rock. Both these natural promontories are products of erosion, so the experts say, and Bert recalled. Becky and Norah were always interested in the surrounding history, so he continued a quick research on his phone.

He read that Chimney Rock towered almost 400 feet above the valley and the North Platte River. Scotts Bluff was 800 feet above the River. The Native American tribes of the Sioux, Cheyenne, and Arapahoe used the vast area around the two landmarks as their hunting grounds for buffalo. They were among the most recognizable landmarks for pioneers on the Mormon, Oregon, and California Trails. The journals of travelers often referred to Chimney Rock, the most used name of several, as an optical illusion. It was said that it was "unapproachable" since no matter how long you drove toward it, it always seemed to be as far away as when you began. The surrounding 80 acres and the landmark were designated the Chimney Rock National Historic Site in 1956.

Scotts Bluff and its surrounding 3000 acres became a National Monument in 1919. It sat largely untouched until the depression of the 1930's, when the works programs of the Civilian Conservation Corps, Works Progress Administration, and Civil Works Administration carved in some of the roads, tunnels, and parking area. The Native Americans referred to the Bluff as "Me-a-pa-te," or "the-hill-that-is-hard-to-go-around."

For the next 30 minutes, as their two-vehicle caravan continued down US Highways 385 and 26 toward Interstate 80 at Ogallala, Bert, Norah, and Becky continued their glances toward the two spectacular points to the south. As they passed through the Ash Hollow State Historical Park, just past Lewellen, they took another quick pee break for Missy while drinking in the natural beauty of this historic Native American and westward-expansion watering place along the North Platte River.

At Ogallala, they proceeded east on Interstate 80. A couple more hours and the last rays of the setting sun lit up the Arch over the Interstate, the Great Platte River Road Archway Monument, like a beacon calling them to stop and rest awhile. This amazing museum at Kearney, Nebraska, celebrated 170 years of regional history in westward expansion and development. Interactive displays and audio systems led visitors across the Interstate on a lower pass to the south and then back north on an upper level. You could progress in time from buckboard wagons drawn by mules and oxen to trains and the development of the roads, which linked Kearney to the eastern cities of Lincoln and Omaha. One could easily spend an entire day there. Unfortunately, Bert's team arrived after hours and they didn't have the time on this trip. Someday, however, he promised himself that they would take the time to do justice to a thorough visit. It would be a dream stop for a history buff like Bert.

This evening, though, as the sun disappeared behind the western horizon, the team ate a lunch from the cooler at the parking and picnic area of the Arch Monument. It was a fast chow since darkness was rapidly replacing twilight and a few mosquitos were making their presence known. Then they headed off to the nearby Holiday Inn and their separate rooms.

Becky negotiated successfully for overnight custody of Missy, prevailing with the argument of being a little, single, defenseless, female in a strange town filled with big, cornhusking, farm men. Bert had no counter to that argument, that he could get out past the belly laughing, and Norah was no help. She was laughing too hard, also. So, Missy licked him on the chin and politely followed Becky to her nearby room.

Bert and Norah were still laughing about the abduction of their companion animal as they laid in the bed. Bert looked at her one more time with the love he felt in his heart. She was there with him, but she wasn't there with him. Her blue eyes and red hair seemed to shimmer in the overhead light of the room. Even as a spirit, she was beautiful. The strange set of mixed emotions led him to express his love in words before he turned out the light. Then, in the darkness, he felt the tears slowly running down his cheeks with the knowledge that she was there, but untouchable.

Norah reclined in the darkened room and knew the pain her husband was feeling. She felt it also, as she always did when she faced the reality of her existence in the spiritual plane. Her love for Bert was endless. From the first day they met until her unexpected death, they were inseparable. They shared his military career, hiked the mountains around their cabin, camped overnight under the stars, hunted deer and elk, parented two children, and founded a business, all together as husband and wife, as business partners, and as lovers. When she could have followed the light, she instead chose to stay with him, a perfect attachment to a perfect relationship. Lying in the darkness, she listened to his increasingly heavy breathing and wondered if she was doing the right thing. Was it the right thing for him?

Three doors down the hall, Becky sat on the floor with Missy, loving on her. Missy, of course, enjoyed every second of the attention from her fledgling alpha female. As she gently stroked Missy's head, Becky's joy in her furry companion slowly gave way to that nagging sense of loneliness and longing, which so often plagued her nights. It was becoming another of those nights when the absence of a man in her life seemed to flow over her like the shadow from a dark cloud. Missy's presence both comforted her and yet, at the same time, reminded her of the man she increasingly wanted but could not have.

* * *

Bert met up with Becky and Missy at the side door of the motel just as the first rays of the sun were peering into Kearney from the golden glow on the eastern horizon. He had called to ask if she wanted company while she gave Missy her morning outing.

She was very happy to accept his offer and looked forward to sharing one of the early morning strolls she'd heard so much about. With her hair pulled back in a ponytail, she wore her workout shorts, top, and hiking shoes partly to deal with the morning temperature, still in the mid-sixties on this summertime date. There was also the matter of showing off her trim figure and legs, she had admitted to herself with a smile. She took pride in the way she looked. It wouldn't hurt if the boss noticed.

Bert couldn't help but notice. He liked this woman and found her very attractive. He also had elected to wear his workout clothing, having some pride in his own fitness. For a man in his fifties, he had good looking legs from years of working out, and it was a nice morning for a walk. Missy seemed very content to have this joint custody arrangement.

"Are you looking forward to getting to Arkansas and the case?" he asked.

"Oh, you bet," she said. "I'm really anxious to see the region and this sounds like a very big challenge for us. It's a chance to help a family with a personal crisis. That's why I got into this business and why I like the direction you've taken it."

"Becky, we're very happy to have you with us. Norah and I both believe that hiring you has been our best decision."

She walked quietly for a minute, before replying. "I'm very glad you did, Bert. I feel like your company is perfect for me. You're the perfect boss for me." To herself, she thought he was the perfect man for her, too.

He replied, "When we get there, what do you think about you devoting your time, initially, to finding out all you can about the victim? Annabel."

"I think that's a great idea, Bert," she said. "The reality is that we have to consider whether she may have just been fed up with her life and taken off. Maybe she wanted to disappear and start over. There's always the possibility that she had a secret lover and left for a new life with him. Or, I suppose, with her."

He thought about that. "You're right about all that, Becky, we have to be aware of all possibilities. I'm thinking this must be a process of elimination. The more we can rule out, the closer we'll be to what really happened."

"I haven't given a lot of thought to having someone disappear without a trace, Bert. In most crimes, you have clues, a body, a trail to follow. But in a case like Annabel's, you have almost nothing to go on, just suspicions."

"You're right," he said. "Suspicions are often like opinions, everyone has one. The problem with suspicions, just like opinions, is that they can become preconceived notions which trap you into trying to prove your opinion and not looking for the facts. Facts which might disprove your opinion."

"You're a smart guy, Boss," she said. "I see why you're so successful with this business."

They continued to walk silently with Missy, pausing to let her sniff areas of interest and look for the ideal spot to pee. She enjoyed checking out the clumps of grasses and searching the bases of the fence posts. No vermin this morning.

"Why don't you guys take Missy from here for a few hours, and I'll let her ride with me when we make the next stop," Becky said. "I'll be content to float along behind you."

"Sounds good," Bert replied. "There's a park at the south edge of Lincoln along highway 2. We can make a brief stop there to stretch our legs. Another possible rest just past Nebraska City at the junction with Interstate 29. St. Joseph is just a couple more hours south before Kansas City. Judging by my map, we could be to Mountain View around 6 PM tonight, depending upon how long we stop. So, we'll be hitting it pretty hard to get there."

Becky nodded her understanding. "I'm good with a bathroom break every three or four hours, usually. So, press as much as you wish, Bert."

They had returned to the door to her room. Bert told her to keep and take care of Missy until they were ready to go. He paused awkwardly for just a few seconds. Becky took that cue and stepped forward, giving her boss a warm hug for just a couple seconds. Then, she unlocked the door and led Missy inside. Bert watched the door close, before he walked down the hall to his room and Norah. He wondered why he had such a feeling of guilt, just because he liked Becky. He was in love with his wife, with Norah, but he was a widower. He held her spirit but otherwise he was alone, and lonely. The only thing which held him back from acknowledging his feelings for Becky, was himself. He entered the room.

Norah's spirit sat on the bed, leaning against the headboard, looking stunningly beautiful with her shimmering red hair and blue eyes. She looked at him with total love in her eyes. "How was your walk, Honey? It looks beautiful outside. How are our girls this morning?"

"Our girls," he said with a smile, "are doing just fine. Missy is really taking to Becky, and vice-versa. They're getting ready to go just as soon as we're ready. We'll try to get to I-29 in Iowa before we take another short break."

"Sounds like a plan," Norah said. "I'm ready to go when you go, Baby." She smiled.

"Norah," he said, "I love you. I've always loved you from the day we met. I will always love you, Sweetheart. Nothing can ever change that."

She looked at him with her lovely smile and the look of wisdom. "I know that, Bert. I always feel your love. Don't worry, Honey, I understand you." She was a psychic, after all.

* * *

They left Kearney at 8:30 as the sun was high enough to not be directly in their eyes. Before long they followed I-80 past the city of Grand Island. This modern city of over 48,000 residents was founded in 1857 by 35 German settlers from Davenport, Iowa at La Grande Isle, an island formed at the junction of the Wood and Platte Rivers. It became a last stop supply point for the gold rush at Pike's Peak. In 1868, the Union Pacific railroad came to town, and thus began the transition to a modern city. Grand Island was now the location for the Nebraska Law Enforcement Training Center, as well as a popular junction with the Sandhills Scenic Byway.

As they bypassed Lincoln, the capitol city of Nebraska, Bert had called Becky to make sure she noticed the state capitol building, which loomed straight ahead just before they exited I-80. The third of three capitols and two territorial capitols, the 400-foot domed tower watched over the city, with its 19-foot-tall statue of "the sower," adorning the top. Built between 1922 and 1932, the structure is considered by many to be among the most beautiful of state capitols.

They continued around the south side of Nebraska City, home of Arbor Day Farm and Foundation, entered Iowa, and proceeded south on Interstate 29 toward Kansas City. Always the history buff, Bert proceeded to tell Norah about the alluvial flood plain they would be traveling in for a while. I-29 paralleled the Big Muddy, the Missouri River, south in this southwest corner of Iowa and into northwest Missouri. The highway flowed south within the one-to-three-miles wide valley on the east side of the River. He told Norah that the almost flat and level valley would occasionally flood with the spillover water from the Missouri. The flood of 1852 was one of the worst recorded floods, but there had been numerous others. While these floods were often catastrophic for the farmers, they also brought the nutrient-rich silt from the watershed to the north, which helped make rich farmland when the water was gone.

Norah was quiet for a little while and Bert could tell she was lost in her mind. Finally, she turned to him. "Bert, as you were talking I began to receive a strong vision of water along and on this road; lots of water, Honey. I'm getting an almost-overwhelming feeling that this area, perhaps for many miles, is going to be underwater soon. I don't think it's a past vision of floods that have happened. It feels like something in the future, the near future. I can't be certain, but I feel like another big flood, maybe even an historic one, may happen next year.

"You're feeling like a big flood could happen in 2019 sometime, Sweetheart?" he asked.

"Yes," she answered. "I'm sensing a great deal of destruction and even death, Honey."

"I don't know anyone down here to warn, and even if I did, how would we convince them? he replied.

"That's one of the problems with being psychic, Honey," she said. "People don't want to believe you. I guess we have no choice but to just see what happens and hope for the best."

They drove along in silence for another hour until passing St. Joseph. Back in the expansion days of the West, this Missouri town was a crucial supply stop and hub for the Mormon, California, and Oregon Trails, as the sometimes-foolhardy settlers headed toward the setting sun for a new life. Some would only find death along the harsh trails. Injuries, sickness, disputes, and occasional conflicts with the Native Americans, would leave a few in often unmarked graves near the wagon roads.

Today, St. Jo is a bustling city with at least four exits from the interstate.

Another couple of hours and with Kansas City faded from view in the mirror, the caravan of two angled across Missouri on highways 7 and 13 to Springfield, the queen city of the Ozarks. As they picked up highway 65 south toward Branson, Becky called Bert to make sure he knew that she was exercising superior discipline to keep from calling for a quick shopping trip to the regionally renowned Battlefield Mall.

"Might need some new shoes for this Arkansas adventure," she said. "But, I'll suffer along with my combat boots, Boss, so don't feel guilty about slighting me. I bet Norah understands me."

He looked at Norah. She smiled and nodded in agreement. He thought to himself, "Dead or alive, these gals do stick together, don't they?" He chuckled silently.

Branson, Missouri, was just a quaint little mountain town when one of Bert's buddies told him about it many years earlier. Then it began to transition into a Nashville-to-the-west. Now as Bert's team passed through, it was a mecca of billboards, shops, restaurants, and home to dozens of musical acts, predominantly country. The billboards flew by them, proclaiming the reasons to stop and see everyone from Dolly Parton to the Judd's and even Elvis impersonators. The sun was sinking in the western sky as they entered Arkansas.

The winding mountain road rose and fell from valley to mountain crest as they worked their way to Harrison. There, they took a short break to walk Missy, hit a restroom, and grab something from Bert's cooler. Becky rubbed her fanny, and asked Bert if workman's comp covered numb-butt syndrome. He confessed that he didn't know but it should if it didn't. After they all had a good laugh, it was back in the vehicles for the final push to Mountain View, Arkansas.

While he still had phone reception, Bert called their client, Billy Joe, and updated him on their travel. He wanted Billy to have the option of visiting tonight after they got into their motel rooms. Billy declined, since he knew they'd had a long drive and just wanted to relax for a while. They arranged to meet over breakfast at 8:00 in the morning at Ma's Diner. Billy Joe also told Bert that his uncle, Bobby Joe Haskins, Annabel's older brother, would be with him. Mr. Haskins, Bert discovered, was a major part of the money which was paying for B & N Investigations' service.

After the call, Bert glanced at Norah as he drove down the two-lane, increasingly darkened, highway deeper into the mountains. "I'm wondering if everyone down here is named something-Joe. What's with these folks that they use so many double names? We're dealing with Bobby Joe and Billy Joe. Who's next? Jimmy Joe and Johnny Joe?"

"Well, be thankful that we're not looking for Annabel Joe, Honey." They both laughed. But their laughter was tempered by the gravity of the task ahead, and the unknown plight of the victim.

Bert called Becky to ask how she was doing, along with Missy, now riding with her. Becky started to reply but they lost reception just after her attempted "We're doing just . . . ."

He assumed she was okay, so he pressed on down the winding road. Several switchbacks slowed them to 20 MPH and even that felt too fast in the dark. The "steep road" signs and lost-brake turnouts for truckers kept his focus entirely on the road. The lack of a significant shoulder and all the deer-crossing signs made his hands nearly numb from gripping the steering wheel. He wondered how Becky was handling it. That thought made him drive even a little slower. It was almost 9:00 when they rolled into the sleepy town of Mountain View.

The Dogwood Motel didn't look very fancy as they pulled up to the front, but it was sure inviting after their thirteen-hour trek. In keeping with their strategy, Bert went in first to get a room while Becky sat toward the back of the parking lot. She went in after watching him unloading his bags into an end room with outside entrance. Fifteen minutes later, she and Missy moved her gear into a room four doors down from Bert and Norah's.

A few minutes later, Bert called her and asked if she'd like to come down the inside hallway to their room and have a glass of wine. He wanted to discuss the plan with their client. Following her knock on the door, he invited her in, along with Missy. As he handed her a glass of red wine, he said that both he and Norah were wanting them all to be on the same page with Billy Joe in the morning.

"I want our client to meet you and be okay with our strategy," he told Becky. An approving nod from Norah told him she agreed.

Becky nodded her understanding. "Great, because I'd like to meet them and hear everything they have to tell us. Where are we meeting? It must be someplace pretty private, right?"

"Top secret!" Bert replied. "Ma's Diner. How's that for a cover?"

"Oh, I like it," Becky said. "Who would suspect that?" They all had a good laugh.

Becky knew that Norah could hear her. "Norah, I'm really looking forward to working with you on this case. It will be interesting to work together in figuring out what happened to Annabel."

Bert answered for his wife. "She thinks so too, Becky. She knows you sense her presence even though you don't hear her. We'll have to look for opportunities to use your empathic abilities, if they present themselves."

"That'd be great," Becky answered. "Whatever it takes. I just hope we can determine what happened to this poor woman."

Bert became businesslike. "At first, we'll just introduce ourselves. Tell them a little bit about yourself when that time comes. Then, we'll let Billy ask whatever questions that he, and his uncle, may have. We'll ask if they have any new information which might be helpful. After that, I'll run our plan by them." He continued to run over the list of questions he'd developed in his head.

Becky sat quietly, listening to her boss. She studied his face as he talked. He had a good face, she concluded. Caring and honest. His middle-aged lines just made him look wise, like a guy you could believe in. She found him to be a very attractive man. A guy easy to like. Maybe a guy easy to love.

They had finished their glasses of wine. Bert noted the time and said they should get some sleep. It would be a long day tomorrow.

Becky said good-night and she and Missy departed for her room down the hall. Bert watched her shapely figure until she was in her room and closed the door. It might be a small town, but he still felt responsible to make sure she was safe. He closed his door and returned to Norah.

"They're safely in their room, Babe, can you think of anything that's I've missed?"

Norah smiled back. "No, Honey, you're very thorough. You've only missed what I've missed."

"What's that, Sweetheart?" he asked.

"Making love," she said softly.

Her words reverberated in his mind for minutes later as he lay in the darkened room. Sleep took its sweet time coming to him this first night in the Ozark Mountains of Arkansas.

CHAPTER FOUR: BILLY AND BOBBY

Day one in the Ozark Mountains of Arkansas promised to be warm. As the sun peered above the eastern mountain horizon, it was already nearly eighty degrees. The clear blue sky was interrupted by only a few scattered cumulus clouds, like puffy balls of cotton tossed randomly upon a blue sheet. There was no hint of the danger they could pose if they developed into the infamous cumulonimbus thunderstorms, all too common in this part of tornado alley.

Mountain View is a small town but the largest town and the County Seat of Stone County. Formed in 1873, it has a history of tourism centered around mountain culture and folk music. It claims the title of "Folk Music Capitol of the World." The population of nearly 3000 included many artists and musicians, some very well known. James Corbitt Morris, known by his professional singing name, Jimmy Driftwood, had his "Barn" at the northern edge of his home town. This rustic performance hall was a fitting tribute to the singer and songwriter's 6000-plus songs and his numerous Grammy's and platinum albums. He was instrumental in establishing the Ozark Folk Festival and Ozark Folk Center, both in Mountain View. The Jimmy Driftwood Barn remains a popular attraction for locals and visitors, alike, who want to hear the mostly local performers sing the songs of the Ozarks. During most performances, one will probably hear at least one of Driftwood's most recognized songs: The Tennessee Stud, Wilderness Road, and The Battle of New Orleans.

Postponing their desire to take in such sights as the Driftwood Barn and the Ozark Folk Center, Bert left Missy in Becky's truck after they had both driven the few blocks to Ma's Diner. On this increasingly warm and partly cloudy morning, Becky had managed to find a nicely shaded parking place. They went separately into the restaurant. Once inside, she sat at the table just beside his. He pretended to strike up a conversation with her, while waiting for the clients to show. It wouldn't look unusual when he invited her to join them. Until they knew differently, it still seemed prudent to maintain the appearance of separation. Norah took up a chair at the corner of Becky's table, close enough to hear. Unseen by all except Bert.

Billy Joe Magnus and his uncle, Bobby Joe Haskins, joined Bert just a few minutes later. Bert motioned for Becky to come to his table and introduced her. The waitress took their orders for breakfast and departed for the kitchen.

Bobby spoke first. "I'm anxious to see what y'all can do to help us find Annie. It's been a bitch having no idea what happened to her but knowing the son-of-a-bitch who did it. All I can do to not gut him like a deer."

Billy added, "That makes two of us. I've had him in my scope many times but know I don't dare pull the trigger. Keep hearing innocent until proven guilty in my head, so I pull off him and watch him walk away."

"I assume you think her husband, Izack, did something with her," Bert said. "You've done the right thing by holding back. For the reason you said. As much as you suspect him, there still isn't any proof that he did anything with her, apparently. Is there?"

"No, that's the damned problem," Bobby retorted. "The sheriff says he checked him out but hasn't been able to find anything to pin on him." Finally recognizing Becky's presence, he added, "I'm sorry, Miss Becky, don't mean to cuss, but this has been a big strain on all of us."

Becky smiled back at both. "I understand, guys, don't worry about it. I can only imagine how difficult this has been for your family."

She studied Billy Joe for a few seconds. He was a handsome young man; nicely built with the strong, stocky body of a football fullback. She'd seen from Bert's notes that he was nearly nineteen. He would've been almost seventeen when his aunt disappeared. His thick, tousled, sandy-brown hair accented a round-ish face with vivid blue eyes. If she was a young woman, she'd set her sights on him. Right now, though, she could sense the deep anguish, despair, and anger which flowed from him. He was truly tormented by the loss of his beloved aunt, and she knew that he really was on the verge of pulling the trigger. It wasn't just bravado talk. The only thing keeping Izack Leery alive was the absence of clues or proof, and Billy's sense of honor. She reached out her hand and placed it on Billy's hand.

"Billy," she said. "Just be patient and keep your cool. It won't do your aunt or her memory any good if you spend your life in prison. Especially if her husband is eventually cleared by proof. Let us try to find out what really happened to Annabel. Bert is an exceptional investigator and has a good team. If anyone can figure this out, he can."

Billy seemed to relax a little. "Yeah, ma'am, I know you're right. That's why I never could pull the trigger. I want to know for sure. Aunt Annabel deserves to have the truth come out."

"Okay," Bert said. "Let's focus on getting started, folks. My team is ready to go. So, what else can you tell us that we haven't already discussed about Annabel's disappearance?"

Uncle Bobby also calmed down some. "The last time the sheriff did anything on this case was to do another interview with Izack. I'd reckon that was about the first of the year. Nothin' came of that. Izack keeps denyin' everything."

"Was anyone else considered a witness or potential suspect.

Perhaps someone from the day or two prior to her going missing?" Bert was recalling Billy's description of the last hours before he left Annabel that morning.

Billy answered him. "They've questioned everyone who saw her and Izack the night before. They all knew that Izack had too much bootleg liquor and was being a usual ass before he left to take her home. But Jimbo Elliot, Izack's huntin' buddy, gave him an alibi. Said they hunted together all that day, and Izack stayed at his cabin the night he left her at home."

Becky chided in. "Who was the last known person to see her?" She was sure she already knew the answer to that question.

Billy replied quickly. "Oh, it was me. Believe me, I've been questioned dozens of times. But, I can't tell them any more than I've told you guys. They interview me because they have nobody else. They all know that I loved her like a mother and had nothin' to do with this."

Becky had listened intently and opened her mind as much as possible, allowing her empathic abilities to read the young man. She could sense sincerity and honesty in his words; she was certain that he wasn't involved in whatever happened. Norah was also using her psychic abilities as she watched Billy. Like Becky, she wasn't picking up on any deception from him.

Bert was watching Becky and reading her expressions. He also cast glances toward Norah and saw her nodding in agreement. It was unanimous. All three of them believed Billy. Unless some clue surfaced to change their minds, Billy was not a suspect.

Norah passed a question to Bert, which he asked of the two men. "Could there have been anyone in town that night who might have taken an interest in Annabel? Someone who didn't make the interview list?"

Billy repeated what he'd told the police. "The only unknown person was some guy having a burger and soda at the food stand that Thursday night. He was a stranger to everyone. Izack had a few words with him and the guy left before my Aunt and him left to go home. Nobody saw him again. The Sheriff doesn't see him as a suspect so hasn't made much effort to find out who he is."

"Why did Izack confront him?" Bert asked.

"Izack was a jealous jerk," Billy replied. "Plain and simple. He thought the guy was looking at Annabel too much. She was a pretty woman; every guy looked at her if they had a chance. A friend of mine who was there said the guy was minding his own business and seemed embarrassed by it. He left at the first opportunity. He must've been from out-of-town and just passing through, because nobody saw him again up here."

Bert asked, "What do you guys think? Is he someone you might suspect or wonder about?"

"Not really," Bobby said. "Like Billy Joe said, the guy seemed to just be a stranger having dinner at the wrong time and place. I agree with the Sheriff."

Bert thought for a minute. "So, all we know for sure then is that Annabel left her cabin that Friday morning, fully clothed, wearing her jacket and outdoor boots. We can assume these things because they also vanished. There were no signs of forced entry, any struggle, or foul play in or outside the cabin. Anything else?"

"No, sir," Billy answered. "I've gone over all this a hundred times in my head. We've all sat around and discussed it until we're blue in the face. That's all we can come up with."

"Was the cabin locked when it was first entered after she

vanished?"

"No, sure weren't, Bert," Bobby interjected. "The door was closed but unlocked and a couple of windows was partly opened."

"So, it seems like she intended to return to her home, shortly, after she went outside that last morning," Bert surmised.

Both men nodded in agreement.

Becky asked a question. "This part of Arkansas is known for rugged mountains, wilderness, lakes, rivers, and streams. I suppose those have been searched?"

Billy looked at her with a nod. "Oh yeah, hundreds of volunteers searched everywhere we could think of. It became the largest search effort in this area, one of the largest in the state. It wasn't called off until a few days before Christmas. Nothing!" His voice cracked just a bit, and he looked away.

Becky could feel the deep sense of grief, despair, and frustration, emanating from the young man. She couldn't think of him as an almost-nineteen-year-old. He was much too mature and composed, despite his broken heart, to be thought of as a teenager. The tears welling up in his eyes made him more manly, in her view. He had heart; he had a heart.

Norah looked at Bert and passed her thoughts to him. He nodded almost imperceptibly. This case was likely going to rely heavily on her psychic abilities, Becky's empathic qualities, and Missy's nose.

"Bert, do we get to meet your psychic?" Bobby Joe asked.

Bert went through his usual explanation about her need to work behind the scenes and out-of-sight; how they needed to shield her from the "psychic noise" of outside influences. Both men accepted his justification without question.

"How close can we get to where Annabel lived?" Bert asked. "Also, can you find us something personal that she used regularly, like a hairbrush, which would still have her scent. We may need that so Missy, our tracking animal, can know who to follow."

Bobby was first to answer him. "Their house is right at the beginnin' of their property, so you can legally drive to within a hunnerd feet of it without trespassin'. Now what's with this tracker? Billy said you have some kind of a wolf?"

Bert happily gave them the rundown on his cherished, furry buddy. Both guys sat back, listening with great interest and sipping their coffee.

"Be sure you keep her close at hand around these parts," Bobby said. "There are lots of hillbillies out here that'll shoot her in a heartbeat, just because. Our coyotes can be pesky if you have chickens or goats. Many goat herders have guard dogs. Mostly Great Pyrenees. Them critters are bred to kill anything that might take their goats."

"Thanks for that bit of advice," Bert said. "We'll keep her close by." He was beginning to get the feeling that Missy wouldn't be allowed as much freedom in these parts as she was used to in Big Sky country. He was familiar with the Great Pyrenees. Beautiful and friendly animals to the people they know. However, not even a wolf or mountain lion can match the ferocity of a Pyrenees, when guarding its flock. "When we leave here, I'll take you by my car and introduce you to Missy."

"I'll tell my cousin about her," said Billy Joe. "He's a dog nut and loves all animals. I know he's going to want to meet her, too, when we have the chance."

Bert replied, "Just bring him along next time we get together. Or, have him call and we'll arrange a time to get together.

What's his name?"

"Jimmy Joe Haskins," said Bobby. "He's my brother's boy. He's about sixteen.

"Another something-Joe," Bert thought amusedly to himself. "That must be a family tradition." He couldn't suppress a smile.

"Annie J. thought highly of him, also," said Bobby Joe. "She just had a mother's instinct."

"Annie J.? Bert said.

"Yeah, Annabel Josephine Haskins, my sister, Annie Jo." Bobby reflected sadly. "Too bad she married that Izack jerk. She was a great gal. Couldn't ask for a better sister."

Bert glanced at Norah and saw that she was laughing. When his eyes met Becky's, she also was trying not to laugh. Her eyes twinkled as she smiled. It was a full sweep. Everyone they were dealing with was a something-Joe. He smiled back and asked for the check from the waitress. Time to get to work on the "Something-Joe" case.

Out in the parking lot, he and Becky introduced the men to Missy. She was excited to get out of the car, barely containing herself as she followed his hand signal to sit. She sat, but she fidgeted a little. Once she got over the thrill of being outside, she allowed the new guys to let her sniff their hands. She was comfortable with Billy Joe but voiced a barely audible deep growl when Bobby Joe reached out. She became more relaxed when he slowly kneeled to her level, turned his hand over, and reached the back of his hand just close enough that she could lean forward to smell him when she wanted. After a few seconds, she carefully leaned out to meet him and get familiar with his scent. Maybe he wasn't so bad.

Bert watched the introductions with interest. It was obvious that both men knew animals. He was impressed that Bobby instinctively knew how to gain Missy's trust. It would make their working relationships easier if she knew and trusted them.

After ten minutes with Missy, Bobby Joe suggested that he and Billy Joe lead them out to Annabel's cabin. Both men said that Izack should be at work at least a half-hour away. Bert made it clear that he wasn't yet ready to meet personally with Izack. He was just interested in getting Norah's initial perceptions in the vicinity of the cabin. Also, he wanted to see the lay of the land. Since Annabel was housebound without a vehicle the day she vanished, then was it possible for someone to be close without being noticed. They drove from the parking lot with Bert following. Becky left her truck and rode in the back-passenger seat with Missy. She wanted Norah to have the best view, though she knew that Norah could just go out there and look around if she wanted to.

The twenty-minute drive to the cabin was on increasingly rough, gravel roads. Bert noticed how quickly they left the town environment and entered what felt like pure wilderness. The dense forest came to within a few feet of the road on both sides, and the terrain was often rough and rocky. There were a few pull-outs where a vehicle could pull off and park. He surmised that these were primarily for hunters to leave their trucks and head into the woods. They did pass a couple of roads that led off into the woods. Those apparently led to a few neighboring homesites.

Their leader vehicle slowed down after twenty-some minutes, apparently because they were close to the Leery's cabin. A narrow valley came into view as the road split. The right fork wound its way out of view toward the western end of the long valley. There appeared to be several properties down that way. A left fork ended abruptly at a small log cabin with a green metal roof. There were numerous out-buildings and a garden on past the cabin and behind it. The cabin looked to be two-bedroom, with a couple of windows looking south across the valley. The property seemed to be generally well-maintained.

Bert and Becky stepped out of the doghouse and talked with Billy and Bobby for a few minutes, discussing the terrain, road, and possible surveillance positions. He asked them about what appeared to be a rocky ledge about two-hundred yards to the left rear of the cabin. That spot would also be close to the road coming into the valley from town.

"You're pretty perceptive," Billy replied. "You have a pretty good view of parts of the cabin, including the front door, from there. I would know because I've been up there with a rifle several times. The trees are spaced just right so you can see between most of the lower trunks all the way to the valley."

Bert didn't have to ask Billy why he was at that position with a rifle. "So, guys, it's possible that someone could have been keeping an eye on the cabin from there. Probably wouldn't be detected."

Billy nodded. "Yeah, and there are other places closer to the cabin, too. But you're a little more exposed. They might see you if you're not a hunter."

As they discussed hunting techniques and how similar those were to military stalking, Bert glanced at Norah. His spirit partner and wife had moved near the cabin and was slowly taking inventory of her perceptions and psychic clues. He knew that she was on duty, doing her part to the extent that the spiritual lines were open to the past.

When he knew that Norah was done, Bert put his hand on Becky's shoulder and told her and the two men that they'd better be going. He didn't want to press their luck and risk being here if Izack came home unexpectedly. He was also anxious to hear what, if anything, Norah might have picked up on. They returned to their vehicles.

On the drive back to town, Bert again followed his clients as they traversed the narrow, winding road with its often-overhanging canopy of trees. It seemed almost claustrophobic in the daytime. He could only imagine how dark and foreboding it would be at night. He glanced at Norah as she spoke.

"Honey," she said, "I'm sorry but the trail seems cold. I didn't pick up on much, I'm afraid. Near the house, at one time I felt a sudden burst of fear hit me. For just those few seconds, I felt paralyzed, unable to move. Then it was gone."

Bert passed that to Becky. They all were quietly thoughtful for the next couple of miles.

Finally, Becky asked, "Norah, did you see any glimpses or visions which might be clues?"

"No," Norah answered to Bert. "Just the feeling. I'm not certain, but I think the fear likely relates to whatever happened to her. It felt like something sudden and totally unexpected happened. Whatever it was, it elicited a very strong fear response from Annie. The fact that it was gone so quickly might mean that she was drugged, knocked unconscious, or killed. Quickly. Since I have no visions right now, that might mean that she didn't know what happened to her. If there was an attacker, maybe she didn't see him. Or them, or it."

"It?" Becky said, after Bert relayed the feelings.

"Yup," Bert answered for Norah. "This part of Arkansas is known to have black bears, mountain lions, coyotes, and maybe even coywolves, wolves, and panthers. Any of those could take a human if they wanted to. Rarely, though, because usually they fear us."

"And, there would undoubtedly be signs of such a struggle, with a lot of blood," said Becky. "She vanished without a trace, so such an attack seems very unlikely to me."

Bert nodded. "I agree, although the larger predators are capable of grabbing and dragging someone away before killing them. In that case, there might not be much blood nearby and it could have been overlooked by the searchers. Still, not very likely, though. These are country people and hunters out here. They'd probably find signs of such an abduction."

They were almost back into Mountain View, and they waved to their clients as they turned back toward the restaurant and Becky's truck. At the parking lot, Bert parked near her Hemi, turned off the doghouse, and turned in his seat to look more at both Becky and Norah. He reached behind the driver's seat and scratched Missy's ears and under her chin as he talked with the ladies.

"Well, we have some interesting clients to work with," he said. "Good people, though. For the rest of the day, I think we should go with our earlier plans, unless either of you has another idea?"

Both Norah and Becky nodded in uncanny unison.

He smiled. "So, Becky, Secret Agent number one, let's have you check around and find out all you can about our victim. Secret Agents two and three will do likewise with the prime suspect, Izack. Let's pool our knowledge back at our room this evening around 6:00. I'll spring for something to eat while we talk."

"I'll grab something to wet our whistle," said Becky.

"Sounds good," Bert replied. "What do you guys think about the wild predator theory?"

Norah shook her head negatively. Becky shook her head similarly as she told him she didn't put much stock in it. "I think it's much more likely that a two-legged predator took her than the four-legged kind."

Bert agreed. He then said they'll just keep it on the very back burner. Not impossible but not likely. Unless something comes up, they won't spend any time on it.

Becky wanted to see if Bert and Norah had any ideas for looking into Annabel's history. She had her own thoughts but knew that she could always use other inputs.

Norah asked her husband to relay that coffee shops and bars might be a good source of people ready and willing to talk about someone else. She said you'd get a lot of chaff, probably, but might also find some grains of wheat. On second thought, she remembered that Stone County was dry. There were no bars. Maybe restaurants or diners.

Bert suggested finding some of her teachers and associates from any other organizations she might have been affiliated with. She could call the clients and ask about those. Such people often have inside knowledge about their students and friends. Newspaper articles might provide some valuable insights, too.

Becky entered her truck, waved to her teammates, and headed toward the library. She had already planned to research all the articles she could find about Annie. However, she noted the time, shortly after noon. Good time to catch a coffee shop, first, and see if she could strike up a conversation over a sandwich. She blasted the AC on her as she located a place called "Lotta Koffee." She was sweating in the 94-degree heat of the late August day, while wondering if the humidity was 94%, too.

Bert and Norah, along with Missy, drove to a gun and hunting store down on the main street. Such places would likely be frequented by a country hunter guy. There'd be a good chance of someone knowing Izack well enough to talk about him. He decided that being mostly up-front was the best course of action. He would tell them that he heard about the case and wanted to try to solve it independently. It would soon get back to Izack, and that was okay with Bert. The quail sometimes flushes itself out of the brush before the dogs get there. Izack would probably flush from the brush and get in touch with Bert. However it happened was irrelevant, he would eventually talk with Izack, which was his main objective for now.

CHAPTER FIVE: ANNABEL AND IZACK

Becky entered the "Lotta Koffee" café, surveyed the interior, and decided to take a seat at the counter next to one man and with just a seat separating her from another. She knew that it might seem a little flirtatious or suggestive, since there were other seats available.

She ordered a coffee with honey and cream, smiling at the irony of liking her coffee the same way her boss did. Was that coincidence, she wondered? Or, a sign? Of what? Either way, it was time to get to work. She was wearing khaki, mid-thigh length, shorts and a button-up khaki shirt with no sleeves to counter the heat. She crossed her legs while getting more comfortable on the bar stool, knowing that the men were bound to notice her trim legs. Might as well use all the assets, she surmised. Whatever it takes to get a man to talk.

The man to her right was probably in his sixties, she guessed. He seemed to be some kind of businessman judging by his pressed slacks and polo shirt. He was a decent looking guy and seemed friendly as he smiled at her while taking another sip of his coffee.

"Good morning," he said to her. "How are you today? Since I've never seen you around here before. I'm guessing you're from out-of-town."

"You guess correctly, Sir," she said, using the title both out of respect but also to let him know she considered him much older than her. "I'm from Wyoming. I came up here yesterday to research a story about one of your residents."

He was curious. "Oh really, that's a long way to come for a story. Must be something pretty big?"

"I heard about this woman who's been missing for a long time" she answered. "I want to find out about her and write her story."

"Which woman?" he asked.

Becky was taken off guard by his question. Which woman? Was there more than one? "Well, Sir, Annabel Leery is the only one I know of. Is there another? I'm Becky, by the way. Becky Thompson." She extended her hand.

Shaking her hand, he nodded. "Yes, Becky, glad to meet you. I'm Tom Brock. I own Brock's Insurance here. Yes, there was a woman who disappeared from here about five years ago, if I remember right. She's never been found, either."

Becky was curious, now. "What was her name; the first woman? Do you remember the circumstances?"

Tom thought for a few seconds before answering. "Her name is Debra Trayner. She went missing in early October of 2012. Shortly before the Mayans were supposed to end the world. She was the cousin of one of my best friends. She lived with her husband and two kids in a farm valley west of town about fifteen miles. While her husband was at work and the kids in school, she just vanished. Just like Annabel Leery. No trace and no clues."

Becky sat forward and sipped her coffee, thinking. Was this another situation like the case in Nebraska City, she wondered. Do they have to solve the case they're not working on in order to solve the one they're paid to work?

"Tom, are there any similarities between the two women and cases, that you know of?"

The younger man to her left had been listening. He now chimed in. "I couldn't help but overhear you guys. I went to school with Debra and we graduated together. She was a good friend. I knew Annie well, too, though she was a grade ahead of us. They were both very nice gals, friendly, and attractive.

Debbie was stockier and more muscular than Annie, but still pretty. She was a jock; played every sport she could. Would've played football if they'd let her."

Becky introduced herself to this fellow, identifying himself as Jake Rogers, and asked him the same question.

Tom answered now. "We found it odd that both disappeared in broad daylight and on Fridays. Several of us think there might be some connection because of that."

"That's if someone abducted them. A stranger, maybe," said Jake. "If it's a local crime, maybe by a husband, then the timing might be irrelevant. Just a coincidence. They disappeared three years apart, so makes a case for being just a coincidence."

"I've heard that Annabel's husband was a possible suspect. What about any of Debra's family? Becky asked.

Tom replied to her question. "Annie's husband was a bit of a jerk, and there was reason to suspect him. But Debra had a good, loving home life and family. Nobody could find any reason to seriously consider any of them."

Becky had her note pad out and continued to take copious notes. "What was Annabel like," she asked of both men. "You know, as a person?"

Jake replied first. "Besides being nice, she was a popular girl in high school and after. Everyone liked her. I can't think of a single person who didn't. The only one who ever had a problem with her was her dip-shit husband. Oh, I'm sorry for talking like that, ma'am. Just have no respect for him."

She smiled and told him not to worry. She'd heard worse than that.

Tom added, "Jake's right in that characterization of Izack; I agree. Also, of Annie. She was a sweetheart. Everyone I knew loved her."

"So why do you think Izack had problems with her, then?" Becky asked them.

"She was cute and half the guys in the county had a crush on her at one time or another," Jake responded quickly. "He was jealous and couldn't handle it. Guess he thought she was fooling around."

"Was he right about that?" she asked.

"Nah," Jake said. "If she was fooling around, I would've been one of the lucky guys. I had a crush on her, too." He laughed.

Tom nodded in agreement. "Yes, there were plenty of guys and opportunities for her to be unfaithful, if she wanted to be. I think she was so devoted to that boy, her nephew, for so many years that she just wasn't interested in other relationships. She essentially was his mother for most of his life after his mom, Annie's sister, was killed. Annie didn't have any kids of her own."

Becky realized that she had about as much information as she was going to get from these men, right now, so she checked the time on her phone and said she had to be going.

Tom said he had to get back to his office, also, and said his good-bye. Jake was a little slower to leave and asked if Becky would like to get a drink or have supper sometime while in Mountain View. She thanked him and said it would depend upon her schedule. Jake was probably telling the truth about being willing to have a fling with Annie. She figured him to be a ladies' man, always looking for a score.

As she drove away from the coffee shop, she began to second-guess herself for giving Jake her phone number. "What are you doing, Becky?" she thought to herself. "Well, no harm in having a drink or dinner with someone. But, that's all."

After arriving at the local library, Becky was shown where to find the old newspapers and articles, pertaining to Annabel. The first article in this weekly, Friday, newspaper was on November 7th, 2016. Under the headline: "Annabel Leery Still Missing," she read that 28-year-old Annabel continued to be missing without a trace after almost one week. Dozens of volunteers had been searching the surrounding woods, valleys, and waterways within the county, to no avail. Divers had been called in to do dive searches in some of the lakes. At the time of the article, the local Sheriff had conducted several interviews of "persons of interest," but no suspects were yet identified. Becky took note of the information that Annabel was one of the leaders of the local chapter of 4-H and that she sometimes worked as a substitute teacher at the elementary school. She looked for other following articles.

Over the ensuing two years, articles about Annie tapered off. The lack of leads and suspects seemed to generate many theories, but there was nothing but speculation upon which to base continued investigation. Her disappearance eventually reached the cold case file.

One article in the spring of 2017 caught her attention. It referenced an interview of Izack Leery by the author. It talked about how distraught Mr. Leery was at the mysterious disappearance of his wife. Leery was asked if he knew anything at all about that, and he absolutely denied any knowledge of her whereabouts. He said that he spent the night before and the day she vanished with his hunting buddy, Jimbo Elliot. Mr. Elliot confirmed this alibi. When asked if Annabel might have just left on her own, Izack said there was no reason for her to leave. While he wasn't always a model husband, he said he loved her and wanted to continue making a life with her. He felt sure that someone abducted her. Leery said that he would never lose hope in finding his wife alive.

Becky had to admit that she didn't yet know what to think about Izack. Like Bert said, just because he's a jerk it doesn't mean he's a murderer. From what she'd heard, there were plenty of reasons to be suspicious of him, and just because he had an alibi there was always the chance that he had someone else take her. So, he remained a "maybe" with her.

It was after 4:00 in the afternoon, so Becky made a few quick inquiries about the 4-H club, hoping to contact one of the leaders. Hopefully one who knows Annabel. Thanks to a couple of helpful librarians, she managed to reach one of the men, a guy named Anderson McCreedy. He was nearly 40 years old and had three kids in their club, one was an eighteen-year-old daughter and a leader with her dad.

She reached Anderson on the phone. He was still at his work but listened to her reason for wanting to possibly talk. Saying he knew Annie well; he was willing to talk with her. If she wanted, he said he'd buy her a drink at "The Wing Shack," and they could discuss her questions. He could meet her there about 5:10 after his work. Becky agreed.

She waited outside the popular and rustic restaurant, admiring the charm of cedar chairs and tables under the overhanging porch with its log purlins and corrugated roof panel walls. The ambiance and cuisine were purely Americana. It wasn't long until a man drove up who looked like he could be Anderson. Upon confirming it was him, she went into the establishment with him and proceeded to a table away from most of the handful of others, mostly couples or teens, already there. While she waited for him to get a couple of ice teas at the front counter, she studied her host. He was a stocky, square-shouldered guy, very muscular, and looked like a farmer and sports fan. There was a nice charisma about him that she found comforting, and his southern dialect was very pleasant to listen to. When he returned and introduced himself further, she found him very likeable.

After a few minutes of small talk about Mountain View and Wyoming, she explained why she was seeking information about Annabel. He seemed to understand. Confessing that he only knew Annabel from their time together at the 4-H Club, he said the eighteen months there gave him a very favorable impression of her.

"She was warm, friendly, intelligent, and very much a country girl. All the kids loved her," he said.

"Were there any qualities or habits which stood out to you?" Becky asked.

He smiled. "Well, aside from being very cute and just plain nice, she was really great to work with. Dedicated to the qualities we want to instill in our kids. A shame that she never had kids of her own, because she loved working with them. As for habits, she loved being out in the woods, around nature. She would often go hiking for hours out in the woods by herself. She usually led our nature hikes."

"Okay, very interesting," Becky replied. "So, Annabel was comfortable going out in the wilderness by herself. She apparently wasn't afraid of anything out there. Would you agree with that?"

"Oh, yeah," he answered. "She knew about the predators and other dangers we have, but also knew they very rarely interacted with humans as long as you were careful."

"Off the record," Becky asked, "Annie was attractive and noticed by the men around her. Do you think she might have gotten involved with the wrong guy, leading to her disappearance?"

Anderson was quick to respond. "Oh no, Becky, I don't believe that. It's true that a lot of guys found her appealing, but I'm not aware of any involvements with anyone. I think she was dedicated to her marriage and the boy she helped raise, and to our kids here."

"That's good to know," Becky said. "I hoped to hear that. Anderson, do you know any other people, maybe another woman or two as well as men, who knew Annie fairly well and might share their experiences with her?" She took her last sip of the tea he'd bought her.

He seemed to think about that for a bit while he drank another swallow of his lemonade. "The main one who comes to mind is Jill Jones. She volunteered here, at 4-H, once in a while, but was a long-time friend of Annie's. I have her number, I think." He scrolled through his phone's contacts until arriving at Jill Jones.

Becky took down Jill's number, added the name and number to her case notes, and put it in her phone. "Thanks a lot, Anderson, I appreciate your inputs and thoughts. For now, though, I have a dinner date so need to be going." It was 6:05 already. "May I call you if I need more information?"

"Sure," he replied. He gave her his phone number. Becky thanked him for the drink, said good-bye, and headed out the door. She needed to get to the motel and meet up with Bert and Norah. But first, she headed for the local Walmart to get the wine so they could "wet their whistle."

* * *

Earlier, after leaving with Becky from the diner parking lot,

Bert and Norah pulled up to the "Bucks n Ducks" hunting store. Bert elected to be totally up-front with his desire for information. With Norah following silently and unseen beside him, he introduced himself to the on-duty manager as a private investigator looking into the disappearance of Annabel Leery. He said he would like to talk with any of the employees who knew Izack.

"Why Izack?" said the manager. "He's been cleared by the law a dozen different ways."

"I've heard that," replied Bert, "but I'm starting from scratch and retracing all steps. Annabel is still missing without a trace. Right?"

The manager, Josh, had no answer to that. He motioned for one of his employees, a middle-aged man with greying hair, to come forward from doing inventory in the back corner of the store.

"Mr. Samuels," Josh said, "this gentleman is a P.I. looking for Annabel Leery. He wants to start over with the case and wants to find out about Izack. You probably know him as well as anyone here, would you take about fifteen and share your knowledge?" Josh laughed.

Bert introduced himself to the man, Bucky Samuels, who'd worked his way up over a ten-year span to become assistant manager at the store. Bucky wasn't the most driven man on the planet, so he was very happy just having the title of assistant. He didn't want any more responsibilities. His first love of life was deer and turkey hunting. The sporting goods store was a perfect match for him.

"So, Bert, wha-da-ya need to know bout my nephew, Izack?"

"Nephew!" thought Bert. The manager had set him up with a relative. It wouldn't be very long before word got back to

Izack. That interview would probably be sooner rather than later. Well, he had to roll with the flow and go where it took him.

"Okay, so he's your nephew. All the better, because you know him very well." Bert stretched the truth a bit; he really didn't want to be talking with a relative just yet. "I just want to get to know Izack as a man. What's he like, what're his interests, how's he handling his wife's disappearance. Stuff like that. I'd like to know his habits, his rubs, scrapes, scent markings, and so on before I talk with him." Bert knew the analogies to deer wouldn't be lost on this man and might make him relax a little. Sometimes it was a good strategy to gain some rapport with the subject of his interview.

It seemed to work. Bucky grinned through his greying, salt-and-pepper, beard and mustache, disclosing a set of coffee-stained teeth surrounding one missing incisor. "Well, Izack is a lot like me. We're hunters, fishermen, outdoors people, ya know. We've spent a lotta good days tellin' stories and drinkin' beer in deer stands and duck blinds. Every now and then, we'd shoot somethin' too. Always bagged our limit. Usually, the first day."

"He's doing okay then with Annabel gone?" Bert asked. "I know that had to be hard on him, especially with so many suspecting him, at first."

"Yup, you can bet your ass on that, Buddy. He was under the gun fer a while. Her asshole family were sure he'd done somethin' to her. They still think that, even after the law shot holes in all that crap. Won't give it up."

Bert asked, "Why do they think Izack had anything to do with her missing?"

Bucky shook his head in disgust as he thoughtfully rubbed

his bearded chin with a weathered right hand. "The bastards never did like my nephew, our whole family for that matter. It didn't matter to them that he was huntin' the whole time; they had him convicted, anyway."

Bert persisted. "Why would they keep thinking he was guilty, then?"

"He was a hot-head, quick to fight; could be a prick, sometimes. He and his wife argued a lot. They had a big blow-up the night before she left. He spent the night and next day with his other huntin' buddy, Jimbo."

Bert picked up on Bucky's words. "You said before she left. Do you think Annabel just packed up and left, without a word? Does Izack think that?"

"For a while, Izack was sure she'd done that. Just grabbed her coat and took off. We all thought that, at first."

"At first?" Bert inquired. "Do you guys still think that? Or do you now think something else might have happened to her?"

Bucky was slow to answer. Finally, he said, "We aren't sure, Bud. Some of us are starting to think maybe somethin' did happen to her. Nobody thought she could stay away from here this long. She did love Izack, though she also hated him. And she loved that nephew of hers, Billy Josephine, or whatever his name was. Another pompous little ass. He's threatened to fight Izack and me, several times. He's damn lucky we haven't taken him up on it. Yet!"

Bert changed the subject. "You said he liked to fish, too. Does he have a boat? I suppose he knew the lakes around here pretty well."

"Damn straight," Bucky replied. "We fished a lot, too. I have a great bass-boat, and I let him borrow it any time he wants."

"Did he use it a lot during the time that his wife disappeared? Being depressed and under the gun, I would think he'd like to get away whenever he could to drown some worms."

Bucky replied emphatically. "Absolutely, Hoss. Fishin' was better than goin' to a shrink. Izack was like me; we could both veg out when on a lake. Like makin' love to a purty woman who keeps quiet and doesn't give you any crap."

Bert was beginning to see why Annabel was unhappy with her choice of a man. "Did he like to go to the big lakes, or to the smaller ones?"

Bucky smiled. "When we had the time, we'd go to either Bull Shoals Lake or Greers Ferry Lake; sometimes to Norfork Lake. White River was a good place, too, could usually get yer hook in a trout's mouth. Mostly, though, we didn't have that much time. Those were day trips, or overnighters. We'd usually hit one of the small lakes closer to home."

"Sounds like he knew the local area pretty well, then. Could go to one of several lakes around here," Bert said.

"Yup, sure could," Bucky replied. There are probably two dozen decent lakes within an hour drive of Mountain View."

"How well did you know Annie's family and friends?" Bert interjected.

"Not real well," said Bucky. "We didn't do much with them. Just when the families got together once or twice a year because of Izack and Annie."

"Did Annabel have any close friends?" Bert asked.

"I think she did," he replied. "One gal about her age lived north of town a few miles."

"What's her name, if you don't mind," asked Bert.

"Daisy, Daisy Long."

Bert thanked him for that as he made a note of the name.

"Did Izack think Annabel was playing around?"

Bucky was quick to answer. "He thought so, sometimes, but never did ketch her at it. I figgered she prob'ly was but had no proof of it. A good lookin' gal like her, good chance she was. Izack thinks she might have run off with one of the studs."

"Does he still believe that?" Bert asked.

"Yeah, sometimes. Most of the time, maybe. He just isn't sure. The night before she left, she was flirtin' with some strange guy at the square. That's what led to them havin' a blow-up that night."

Bert contemplated what he thought he knew about the case. "If she didn't have a vehicle at their cabin, how could she have left. It's quite a ways from town.. ... Isn't it?" He quickly added.

"Yeah, Bud, it's out a ways. If she ran off with someone, guess he must have drove out and got her. I ain't a P.I., but I can figger that out."

"Yeah, you got me there. You must be right," Bert replied with a grin. "So, if Izack thinks she ran off with someone, does he have any idea who the guy is or where they went?"

"Nope," Bucky snorted. "If he did, they'd both be pushin' up daisies somewhere. Ain't no way he'd let them get away."

"He's still angry enough to kill them both?" Bert asked.

Bucky almost glared as he answered. "Hell yes, wouldn't you? He don't talk much about it, but I know it eats away at his insides all the time.

Bert had a belly full of Bucky and wanted to get away from the guy. "Bucky, thanks for talking with me about your nephew. I'm sorry for what he's been through. Regardless of what happened, I know it must be tough to deal with. Take care and good luck this coming season." With that, he turned without waiting for a reply and headed back to the front counter.

He thanked the manager for his help, without giving him the satisfaction of looking disgusted. He wouldn't be talking with Bucky again soon, if at all.

As he walked toward the door, the manager followed him and said, "I know Bucky's a bit rough around the edges, but he's really a good guy. He was in the Army in Vietnam and came home pretty calloused. Though he received several medals, including the Purple Heart, he doesn't talk about his service. The only thing I've ever heard him say is that there were good people there and some not so good. He said they had their way of getting rid of the bad ones."

"So, he's an Army man," thought Bert. "Not all bad, then. Just rough around the edges."

As he got in the doghouse and gave Missy some love, he looked at Norah. "Boy, I hope that guy isn't typical of men down here. What do you think, Sweetheart?"

"I'm thinking I was even luckier than I knew to find a man like you, Bert. A rather disgusting sort of chap, I'd say. However, I have the impression that he's being truthful with you. He just has a warped view of things. While he was talking about his nephew, I kept getting a vision of a younger man sitting alone at the edge of a bed, crying. I assume it was Izack, although I've not met him yet. I got the feeling that he's genuinely tormented, as if he really doesn't know what happened to his wife. Right now, Honey, I don't get the sense that Izack did something with Annabel."

"Thanks, Honey, I have the same feeling, too. And I just realized that I didn't see her spirit around the cabin earlier. I think that if she was killed there, her spirit would possibly be there still. That seems to support the notion that either she wasn't killed at the cabin, or she may not have been killed at all. Maybe Izack is right; maybe she did run off."

"Maybe," Norah said, "but I had that feeling of stark fear hit me out there this morning. That doesn't suggest running away intentionally."

Bert nodded his agreement. Looking at his phone, he noted the time. Two-thirty in the afternoon. Still time to do more before they met Becky for some supper. Speaking of supper, he thought, maybe they could order a couple pizzas and possibly make another contact with someone who knows Izack. Norah nodded her understanding, and he followed his phone's map function to one of three pizza shops in Mountain View.

Ten minutes later, the doghouse was parked at the Pizza Inn a block off main street near the Walmart store. Bert went inside to order a couple of pizzas from an extensive menu. After ordering, he asked the cashier about Izack. The young man said he didn't really know the guy. He asked another of the kitchen group. One of the older members of the staff, a woman looking to be around forty, said she knew Izack. She was about ready for a 3:00 P. M. break, and said she'd be able to talk with Bert for ten or fifteen minutes.

Mildred Jones introduced herself to Bert as she took her break and sat down with a cup of coffee at a corner table. The somewhat portly, middle-aged, brunette told him she went by "Mildy" most of the time. She had been a neighbor of the Leery family for over twenty years. Her cabin was about half-a-mile from their homestead.

Bert introduced himself and explained his reason for inquiring about Izack as a prelude to looking into the cold case disappearance of Annabel Leery. He didn't disclose his clients

76

but left the impression that he investigated cold cases around the country.

"What do you think happened to Annabel?" he asked her.

She answered without hesitation. "Oh, she was abducted, Mr. Lynnes. I have no doubts about that."

"What makes you think that?" Bert asked.

"First, I've known Izack for a long time. He's a hothead and can act like a jerk sometimes, but I just can't believe that he'd do anything to harm Annie Jo. He was shocked when she agreed to marry him. Thought he was beneath the desire of a woman like her."

"I can relate to that," Bert said. "I married way above my pay grade, too." They both laughed. His quick glance at Norah confirmed her agreement as she nodded her head vigorously, with a smirky smile.

"I don't think Izack ever totally realized that Annie J. really did love him. He was a wild spirit while she was loving and dependable. But, you know, opposites attract. Right?" Mildy looked at Bert for his acknowledgment.

"Yes, Ma'am," Bert nodded. "I know that, too. My wife was, is, a warm and delightful woman, married to a guy who can be scatter-brained at times."

Mildy smiled. "I read people pretty well, Mr. Lynnes, and I don't think you're all that scatter-brained. I suspect that you're quite intelligent and driven to succeed."

"Well, thanks for that vote of confidence, Mildy," he replied. "However, I want to stay on Izack. It sounds like Izack might have been jealous of his wife, especially if he wasn't confident in her love for him. He apparently had a confrontation with a stranger the night before she disappeared. You really don't think Izack was capable of doing something to her?"

She didn't hesitate. "No, Sir, he loved Annie Jo. There's just no way that he'd harm her."

"So, what do you think did happen to her, then?" he asked. "Could she have just run off?"

"No! Annie wasn't one to give up on anything, including her marriage. Even if she did give up on it, she would never have walked out on Billy Magnus, her sister's boy. Annie was like his mother. No, Mr. Lynnes, Annie didn't run away."

"Then who would have taken her, Mildy?"

"That, Sir, I don't have an answer to," Mildy said. "There are plenty of local men who were attracted to her, but I couldn't name one who'd do something like this to her."

The only stranger I've heard mentioned is the guy Izack confronted that night. Do you know who he might be?" Bert asked.

She shook her head. "No, he was just alone at the jam session that night, best I can tell. Nobody I've talked to seems to have any idea who he was or where he went. Just left after the confrontation and wasn't seen again."

Bert rested his elbows on the table, his fingertips touching together and thumbs supporting his chin. "Is that stranger a possible suspect, Mildy?" Bert said.

Again, no hesitation by this woman. "Yes, Mr. Lynnes, my friends and I all think that guy is maybe the one who took her. Unfortunately, our suspicion might be mostly driven by the fact that we have nobody else to consider. There's no evidence that he did anything."

"Mildy, can you think of anyone who might have some idea about that guy? I'd sure like to learn more about him."

She clenched her lips and shook her head. "I wish I did, Sir. For months, my friends and I tried to figure this out. We didn't find even one person who knew anything about the guy."

Bert leaned back; his hands briefly clasped behind his head. "I really appreciate you talking with us, with me, about this, Mildy." He glanced at Norah. "Do you know anyone else who might have knowledge and be willing to discuss any of this with me?"

"Rhonda McFadden lives here in town with her family. They've been close to the Samuels family, that's Izack's mother's family, for a long time. She's an interesting lady."

Bert took down Rhonda's number and thanked Mildy again. It was time for her to get back to work and he was ready to head for the room with the pizza's, which were now done.

After getting in the car and getting the AC on to beat the heat of Arkansas in late August, Bert turned to spirit wife, Norah.

"Well, babe, you heard all that Mildy had to say. What kind of impressions are you getting?"

"The strongest sensation I got while listening to her was that feeling of dread that I had at the cabin," Norah replied. "And feeling like I was being grabbed from behind."

"Oh really," he said. "You don't think she ran away. You think she was abducted?"

Norah answered quickly. "Yes, Dear, she didn't run away. I keep getting these feelings like someone, or something, accosted her."

"Something?"

"Well, yeah, I guess it could be anything, Honey. Or anyone. It's just that startled feeling and fear you'd get from being unexpectedly grabbed from behind by a stranger. I don't get any impressions of her running away, Bert."

"What about Izack?"

"I'm just not sure about him, Honey. I got that same vision of someone, a man I think, sitting on a bed, crying. I don't really see him clearly; it's as if I'm in his place, both seeing and being him."

"Can you get any idea of why he's crying, Sweetheart?"

"I have a heavy feeling," she said. "Like the sense of loss, you feel from a death."

"Is it Izack you're seeing, Norah?"

"I think so, maybe I'm assuming so. Once we've met him in person, I'll have a much better idea. Hopefully, I'll know."

"If it's Izack you're channeling, he might be saddened by his wife's disappearance. But he could also be feeling remorse because he did something to her. Can you tell which might be at play?"

"No, Honey, just an intense sadness. Because he's sitting on the edge of a bed, my guess is that it's because she's gone, not guilt. But I really can't tell."

With that, Bert drove in silence to the Dogwood Motel. It was only 5:00 and Becky wouldn't be along for about an hour. He decided to take the time to go online and dig into Izack's social media presence. It wasn't a big surprise to find only a Facebook account under his name. He went back in time as much as possible. It seemed that Izack hadn't created an account until nearly three months after his wife's disappearance. The little bit of chatter was about what you'd expect. Requests for help and information, suggestions, theories, and such dominated the discussions. All in all, Izack's posts and replies gave no indications other than a man trying to find his wife. The various theories were all over the map. One guy even suggested an alien abduction. For validation, he claimed to have seen an unusual set of lights in the sky the night after Annie vanished. Most of the chatter slowed to a trickle after a year-and-a-half.

Bert looked at his phone. It was almost a quarter-after-six. Becky would be there any minute, so he signed off the internet and arranged the chairs to accommodate their agent. He was doing so, when the knock at the inside door told him she'd arrived. Her bubbly personality and smile entered, followed by her outstretched hand with a bottle of a local red wine.

"Hey there, bosses," she said, "how ya doing? I hope you had a great and productive first day."

As Bert took the bottle from her, he smiled back as he looked into her bright, blue eyes. For just a second, he almost forgot what to say. Her mix of shining eyes, infectious smile, energetic personality, and attractive looks sometimes almost took his breath away. This was one of those times. "Ah, hi Becky. Yes, I think we had a pretty good day. How about some wine and pizza?"

She smiled and looked around the room, knowing that Norah and Missy were there. "Oh, you bet. I'm famished. Going around in this heat has taken it out of me and worked up a serious appetite. My truck said it got up to 96 degrees this afternoon. That's too dang hot for a northern girl, guys. I bet Missy's been miserable, right, girl." Missy had come to the door to greet Becky, turning in an excited circle as she rubbed against Becky's slim legs.

Norah nodded in agreement with that and Bert said, "Yes, I don't think she likes this kind of intense, humid, heat. It saps you and makes you fall in love with air conditioning."

Becky nodded in agreement and asked if they would mind if

she kicked off her sandals. Bert shook his head.

"So hot out there that my feet are almost sticking to them," she said as she kicked off each sandal and lined them up beside the door. She wriggled her bare toes on the carpet and let out a sigh. "Wow, sure feels good to be barefoot for a bit."

Bert nodded. "Yes, I understand." Glancing at Norah, he added, "we both do."

Bert poured them both a glass of wine and motioned for her to sit on the chair he'd placed next to the bed. It would double as a table for the plate of pizza and let him see Norah where she reclined against the headboard. He pulled his chair up near the foot of the bed. They began to sip the wine and discuss the things they'd learned during the afternoon. Missy opted out of the conversation and sought refuge in the bathroom on the cool tile floor.

"Well, special agent number one, did you learn anything interesting this afternoon?" Bert asked as he raised his glass for another sip. She'd chosen a good wine.

Becky smiled and took a drink herself, savoring the taste as she watched her boss, enjoying his anticipation. "Do you remember Nebraska City?" she said.

Bert was surprised by the question and its obvious answer. "Sure do, what's that got to do with here?"

Becky leaned forward, holding her glass securely in her hand. "We might have a similar situation," she said. "There's another woman, missing without a trace for about five years now."

Bert looked at Norah, noticing her change of expression to one of surprise and great interest. He nodded in understanding of their silent exchange. "That's very interesting, Becky. What'd you find out about her?"

Becky had already laid her notebook near her on the bed. She opened it to her daily notes. "Her name is Debra Trayner. She's a mother of two who disappeared about three years before Annabel. No clues. Broad daylight, just like Annabel. Both on a Friday, if that means anything."

"Any theories?" Bert asked.

"More or less the same as with Annie," she replied. "Allegations of an affair. Maybe she ran away because she got caught in a compromising situation. Abduction seems most likely to me, because of her children. Without a trace, guys, just like Annie."

Norah passed a question to Bert, which he relayed to Becky. "Was Debra similar in age and looks, was she attractive, also?

Becky understood Norah's underlying meaning. "Yes, from the guys I talked with, both these ladies were, are still, I hope, attractive women. Annie is a year older. Like you're suspecting, Norah, I also get the sense that sex probably played a role behind the abductions."

"Yes, that sure sounds like a factor," Bert said. "Did you find out anything else about Annie?"

Becky leaned forward, putting her pizza down on the bed. "Yeah, sure did, a few things. For one, Annie was cute, and a lot of guys were attracted to her. However, there doesn't seem to be any evidence that she played around. All indications so far are that she was loyal and devoted to Billy Joe and to Izack. My impression is that infidelity was not a factor behind her disappearance, guys. In addition, she was an outdoorswoman. She would lead kids on nature hikes and liked to just go out in the woods on her own. While she was comfortable and skilled at being out by herself, that does leave open the door to something happening to her out there, somewhere."

Bert looked at Norah as he digested what Becky said. "We

bumped into someone who said much the same regarding possible motives. This lady is adamant that Annie was abducted. Said she'd never leave on her own. The long hikes by herself are some concern, though. What if she got hurt, lost, or something happened while on a long hike into the wilderness? She might still be out there somewhere."

"The large searches that took place would surely have covered much of that ground, wouldn't they?" Becky offered.

"You'd think so," replied Bert. "But there is a lot of mountainous terrain out there. It'd be nearly impossible to cover every bit of it. Given what you perceived, Norah, this seems an unlikely option."

Norah nodded in agreement and reiterated that her feeling of fear and panic seemed more aligned with an abduction than an accident out on a hike.

"I agree," Becky said. "My impression right now is that Annie was abducted. And I can't help but wonder if the other woman's disappearance isn't somehow related."

"It does make you wonder, doesn't it," Bert answered. "This is a small rural community of only about 2000 people in the town and surrounding area. What's the likelihood of two women being abducted in a three-year period in such a sparsely populated area?"

Norah told him, "You're right, Honey, even though the Arkansas share of the nationwide disappearances averages 12,000 per year, it still seems strange for two women to vanish in similar fashion in such a small community three years apart.

Becky was listening with great interest. "So, it seems that we all think Annie, and probably Debra, were taken by someone. If that's our belief, then the question is who would do that. Was it the same person?"

"Yeah, Becky, I think that's the first question that we have to answer. Until we know who, it will be almost impossible to determine where she might be."

"The first question to settle is that of Izack," Norah said. "Was he responsible for Annie's disappearance?" Bert relayed her input to Becky.

"And if so, could he also be behind Debra's vanishing?" Becky said.

Bert silently digested their thoughts for a minute. Finally, he said, "I think none of us are convinced that Izack did something with Annie. However, we need to somehow rule it out, if possible. Even if he did, what reason would he have to do something to Debra?"

"Since we weren't hired to find out what happened to Mrs. Trayner," said Becky, "how do we handle that? The cases could possibly be related, so can we afford to ignore her?"

Bert acknowledged Norah's thought on that. "Becky, good question. Norah and I think we have no real option but to treat Trayner as possibly related to Annie's abduction. From that standpoint, let's stay open to any information about Debra that could have any relevance to Annie. Annie will be our focus, though."

Becky nodded. "Okay, understood, bosses. So, should I continue to stay focused on learning what I can about Annie?"

"Norah, are you getting any other connections which could give us some direction?" her husband asked.

"So far, I'm not getting much, guys," Norah said. "Just a strong feeling that she was grabbed by surprise. And fear. An intense fear."

Bert leaned back in his chair, thinking. After a minute, he

said, "I think you should continue to learn all you can about Annie, Becky. See if you can identify who she ran with or was friends with. Somehow, we must identify anyone who might have taken her. We'll keep checking out Izack and getting a feel for his motives and actions. Let's all look for anything we can find out about the stranger, or anyone else who seems a possible suspect."

Becky nodded in agreement as she took another bite of her pizza. Bert followed her lead and took another mouthful of the savory, spiced, delight. That shop really had an interesting mix of spices.

Secret agent number one washed down her last swallow with a final sip of wine. "Oh my gosh, Bert, that was very good pizza. We need to go there, frequently, while we're here. I'm beginning to think we may be here for a while. This case seems very perplexing."

"That might be a good lead-in to make a quick review of what we have, so far," Bert responded. "Right now, we sort of know how she disappeared. Evidence seems to support the theory that she was taken by surprise and abducted, probably alive. We don't know who took her, or where. Virtually every guy in the region had the methods for doing something with her. The big question is motive. Who had a reason to do this? Currently, the only person with a possible motive is her husband, Izack. We don't know who might have had the opportunity to take her in broad daylight that day. If Izack was, in fact, with his hunting buddy all that night and the day she vanished, he, personally, wouldn't have had the opportunity. That's unless he hired someone to do it. As popular and well known as Annie was, I can't imagine being able to hire someone locally to abduct her. It's likely that he'd have had to get someone from outside the area. That almost guarantees that he'd have to pay for that service."

Becky chided in, "They have a cute but rustic little property out there in that valley. But it doesn't speak to me of a lot of money. My guess is that he wouldn't have been able to pay very much."

Norah nodded in agreement and relayed via Bert that she thought that was unlikely. "I don't get the sense that he had that kind of anger or hatred toward Annie," she said. "Even if he had the money or the ability to persuade someone to take her. I doubt both."

"Becky," Bert said, "are you comfortable getting hold of the hunting buddy, Jimbo, and seeing if you can get him to validate Izack's alibi?"

"Yes," she replied. "Do you think he'd be more likely to talk with me than you?"

Bert nodded. "Yeah, I have the gut feeling that he'd be more likely to open up to you. In your presumed role here, you would seem more disarming and less threatening."

"Okay, I'll see if I can get in touch with him tomorrow. I also have a couple of other leads to follow up on."

Bert added, "Great, and we'll be doing the same with Izack. If we can either rule Izack out as a suspect, or confirm him as the chief suspect, it'll help us get some direction for our investigation."

Norah relayed through Bert, "Once I've had the chance to meet and hear Izack in person, I hope I can channel more of him into the equation. I'm anxious to do that."

"Well, guys, and Missy, I think we've gotten a good start on this for our first day in the Ozarks. The priorities and direction are starting to take shape. Let's continue meeting here at 6:00

in the evenings, for now. Assuming no other priorities get in the way, of course." Bert paused. Then he added, "Becky, we're very glad to have you with us on this case. With this team, I think we have a good shot at finding out what happened to Annie, and maybe to Debra, as well. We need to keep in mind, though, that the odds are against us. Thousands of the missing are never found. While we want to succeed, we need to recognize that we might fail, and be mentally prepared to deal with that disappointment."

Becky stood up, tossed her paper plate in the trash basket, and walked to Bert, giving him a warm hug. The enormity of their task was hitting her hard. She found it overwhelming right at that moment. She was glad that she was part of this team. Stepping back from her boss, she smiled, opened the door, and left for her room.

Bert could sense the conflict in Becky's heart. He turned to Norah. As she sat near the head of the bed, her auburn hair flowed to her shoulders like crimson fire, waving and shimmering. The motel room lighting made her stand out even more, with her charming face, blue eyes, and a mouth that always seemed ready to smile. Even in the spirit world, Norah was beautiful and warmed his heart. He was irrevocably attached to her. And, she to him.

"You like our new girl, don't you?" she said.

Her question surprised him, and he awkwardly said, "Yeah, she's great, Norah, who wouldn't like her."

She moved closer to him, her face just a foot from his. "It's okay, Honey. You don't have to be embarrassed, ashamed, or feel guilty about liking her. I don't mind, really. You will need a living person in your life, Bert, and I like her, too."

"I'll never stop loving you, Norah. You have always been and will always be the light of my life."

"I know that," she said. "But I also know that I can no longer be everything to you. I wish and yearn that I could. Death took that away from us."

Tears rolled down his face, as he tried in vain not to give in to the intense emotion that was suddenly engulfing him. He could only nod.

"We must make do with what we have, Sweetheart. Life isn't always fair. Perhaps we can seek fairness in death."

He didn't know what she meant by that. As he struggled to regain his composure, he just nodded. Finally, he spoke. "I don't know how to make anything about this fair, Honey. I only know that I love you now, as I loved you before, and will love you until I join you on the other side."

"I know, Honey, but I also know that you need more than I can give you. And it's okay, Bert."

As he turned out the light and it gave way to darkness, he sought to find solace in sleep, but it was reluctant to bring relief. He could feel Norah's presence, watching over him, keeping herself close. Tears again trickled down his cheeks with the knowledge that she was, but wasn't, there.

Missy stirred from her nap on the bathroom floor. She sensed both her companions in the darkened room. There was an overpowering sense of melancholy coming from her humans. She didn't understand it, but she could feel it permeating the room. Nuzzling Bert's hand, she sniffed his familiar scent and whined softly, letting him know she was there. Tonight, she curled up on the floor next to him, leaving her usual place by the window unguarded. She seemed to know that comfort, not security, was needed in the darkness of this Ozark motel room.

Four doors down the hallway, Becky sat on the bed in her

darkened room, having not turned on the light when she entered. She felt very mixed up with emotions that seemed to make no sense. She was happy to be working this case alongside her boss and his spirit wife. It would also be a joy to spend more time with Missy. She was happy with the hope and belief that they were going to bring closure for Billy and the rest of Annie's family. Yet, she felt a growing yearning and sadness that she hadn't felt in years. It was like looking at a beautiful full moon on a star-filled night, reveling in the glory and majesty of the lunar jewel. All the while, knowing that it is out of reach and can only be seen, not touched. Hopefully, the merciful new day would bring a fresh wind to catch her sails.

CHAPTER SIX: GATHERING INFORMATION

Thursday, August 30th, 2018, brought overcast skies and rain to Mountain View. While the temperature just before sunrise was about 66 degrees, it was predicted to get to almost 90 in the afternoon after the cold front passed. Until then, there was a tornado watch for the area.

Bert pulled up the hood of his raincoat as he checked the leash on Missy and left the motel. He knew she didn't like being on the leash, though she tolerated it well. At the edge of this small mountain town, he didn't dare let her run freely. This would be a short walk this morning. The rain was turning heavier over the past thirty minutes and was now a steady downpour. Missy didn't mind the rain. She still found some interesting places around the outer edge of the parking lot and on a vacant, overgrown lot.

Bert noticed that the light was on in Becky's room. He knew she was getting ready to contact and interview the people they'd discussed. Except for his team, the motel was almost empty. One other vehicle was in the parking lot. He started to bring Missy out of the vacant lot but stopped in the darkness to watch a dark pickup which had driven slowly into the lot and had paused behind his Dodge SUV, obviously noting the license plate. The driver hesitated for about ten seconds. Then he quickened his pace and left the motel parking and accelerated toward the downtown area. In a few seconds, the truck was out of sight.

Bert led Missy back to their room. Inside, he told Norah, "Well, Sweetheart, I think Izack Leery just made contact with us." He told her about the pickup.

"Yes, Darling," she replied. "You knew that uncle of his

would tell Izack and he'd probably want to know what you were up to. Looks like it didn't take long. What do you think he'll do next?"

"I don't think it will take long to find out," he said. "I'm glad that he went to the doghouse, first. He didn't look at Becky's truck once he saw my Wyoming plate. That means that Becky's cover is probably not yet blown, where he's concerned."

Norah nodded in agreement. "So, it might make sense to have her meet with him first about her storyline."

"I think you might be right, Norah. I'll have her contact him and see if she can set up an interview in a public place where I might be able to monitor from nearby. Until we know what's in this guy's head, we can't afford to trust him."

"That's a good idea, Bert."

He called Becky and told her about the situation and asked what she thought about arranging an interview with Izack soon. She understood and said she would try to get hold of him today, if possible.

"By the way, good morning, Boss Man," she laughed. "Tell Norah the same, also. And give my coyote buddy a hug from me."

Bert laughed at that and told her to have a good day and they would see her this evening. He added that he thought it a good idea if he monitored her talk with Izack if she'd let him know when and where. "This guy is suspected of perhaps killing and disposing of his wife, Becky. We have to be careful with him until we know otherwise. I want to keep you safe."

"Yes, Sir," she said. "I like that. It'll make it more comfortable for me knowing you're nearby. I assume you're going to be incognito?"

"Yeah, I'll wear a ball cap and mustache along with glasses. That should be enough to keep him from recognizing me later. Once you've talked with him, it doesn't matter all that much after that."

"Okay, Bert, I'll let you know soon as I set up a time with him. Good luck with what you're doing. Let's find one or both of these poor women if we can."

Bert agreed and they said so long and hung up. He decided to contact Rhonda McFadden and Daisy Long.

Daisy didn't answer her phone, but he was able to contact Rhonda. He arranged to meet her for coffee and talk at Ma's Diner. He could see that this place was probably going to become like a second office. There weren't many other options in this small town. Just five or six fast food restaurants.

Missy waited in the doghouse while Bert and Norah entered the diner, thankful that the rain has slowed to just a mist. Rhonda was already there. Bert introduced himself, took a seat across the table, and ordered a coffee. Norah stood unseen beside Bert.

Rhonda was a very warm and friendly redhead, with an average build, appearing to be in her 50's. Bert smiled at her strong Southern accent, as she said, "Good morning, sir." Her shoulder length red hair reminded him of Norah's hair just a little. Although pretty, it lacked the luster and wavy shimmer to match the beauty of Norah's locks.

Explaining that he was looking into the, as yet unsolved, disappearance of Annabel, Bert told her he wanted to know about Izack, since he was a possible suspect.

"Well, as you probably know," she said emphatically, "he's been thoroughly investigated and cleared. He had nothin' to do with her disappearin'."

Bert knew that she was a friend of the mother's family, the Samuels, so expected she would defend Izack. "I know you're a friend of his family, but why else do you believe that?"

She replied firmly, but quietly, "Izack is very misunderstood by most people. He has this rough and tough streak and is quick to fight back if pushed, but he's got a big heart and would do anything for you if he likes you."

"Did Annabel love him?"

"Oh, yes, she did. Especially at first. They were opposites and you know what they say about that. He balanced out her quiet, lovin' personality by bringing a little wi-old into her life. He's the reason she loves, loved, the woods and nature so much. Used to take her on campin' and hikin' outins all the time."

"You said at first. Did they have problems later?"

"Sometimes," she replied. "Izack could be a hothead, and he was jealous of her."

"Why?" Bert asked.

She pressed her lips together and gave a shake of her head. "It was Izack's one big fault, Bert. She was a pretty and, some would say, sexy woman. Other guys had their eyes on her most of the time when they'd go out in public. I don't think she invited it, but she always had the attention of men. He was aware of that and it bothered him. Surely ya'all can understand that."

"Yes, that's understandable, Rhonda. So, the night she vanished I heard they had a blow-up because Izack became jealous of some guy looking at her. Do you know anything about that? Or about the guy?"

"Yes, sir, Mr. Bert," she said. "That' about the size of it. No, sir, I don't know anythin' about that guy. From what I gather, he just left town right after their little spat. We've tried to find out about him, but nobody seems to know anythin' about him. Just gone."

"Would Izack be capable of doing anything to cause Annabel's disappearance, Rhonda?"

"No way, sir," she quickly answered. "Well, let me rephrase that. Capable, hell yes he was capable. Most men around here are capable of makin' someone vanish if they want to. But, no way, Mr. Bert, would Izack do anythin' evil to cause this. He was just a jealous hothead, sir, not a killer. He loved Annie Jo!"

"You've known him for a long time, then?"

"Yeah," Rhonda said. "I've pretty much known him and his family most of his life. I know him well, sir. His family is a little rough around the edges, but they're still good people. You can count on 'em in a pinch."

"So, you're certain that Izack did in fact love his wife and had nothing to do with her vanishing?" Bert asked again. He wanted to be sure of her conviction.

"Mr. Lynnes, I'm as sure about that as I am that I'm here talking with you. Believe me, sir, Izack had nothing to do with whatever happened to Annie Jo."

Bert looked her squarely in the eyes. He saw none of the obvious signs of deception. She held eye contact with him, there were no twitches around her mouth and eyes, and no hesitation or doubt in her voice. A glance at Norah told him she believed this woman. "Thank you for that honest opinion, Rhonda. We, I, really appreciate it. May I ask what you think did happen to her then, Ma'am?"

Without hesitation, she said, "Oh, someone . . .. or something . . .. took her, Mr. Bert. It just wasn't Izack."

95

"Any ideas about who may have done that?" he asked.

She shook her head with a look of seemingly genuine sadness, "I wish I did, sir, but none of us have been able to answer that question. A lot of men, women too for that matter, liked Annie. But I couldn't name one that I suspected of doing something like this to her. We might be Arkansas hillbillies, but we aren't the kind of people who do this sort of thing."

"I believe you, ma'am," Bert replied. "Rhonda, you said 'something' may have taken her. What did you mean by that?"

She hesitated for just a few seconds, as if carefully choosing her words. "Sir, there are miles of raw wilderness and Ozark Mountains around here. We have a lot of predators, big ones; big enough to grab a human, especially a petite woman like Annie."

"Any suspects?" he asked.

"She disappeared the day before gun season opened, so there were people out in the woods, scouting for deer and places to hide or stalk. That could have upset the wildlife; it usually does a little. Cougar, panther, bears, and wild hogs all could have been a threat. Hell, sir, even a squatch might have gotten her. Coyotes are a remote possibility, especially since they've been crossing with wolves and big dogs."

"Squatch?" he said. "Do you mean you'd consider a sasquatch to be a possible threat?"

She smiled a bit sheepishly. "Well, I almost didn't say that, but, yeah, there are several of us who consider even that to be an unlikely possibility. We don't talk about it much in public because there are those who think it's crazy."

"Do people have sightings around this area?" he said. "Or other reasons to consider them a potential threat?"

"Oh, yes," she replied. "There are lots of sightings across the whole state. Had one around here about a year ago. Deer hunter got a glimpse of one from his tree stand. Did you know about the Watson's incident the night Annie was abducted?"

Bert tried to remember anything about Watson's from his talks with his clients. Nothing. "No, ma'am, what happened to them?"

"Something scared the be-Jesus out of them that night. Scratching the door and on the windows, making growling sounds. Then it left after about fifteen minutes."

"Could've been a bear, maybe," Bert said.

"Not likely, that's totally not normal behavior for a bear. Or any other animal we have around here."

"Where do the Watson's live? Are they somewhat close to Annie's cabin?"

"Just about a mile away," she replied. "A five-minute stroll for an 8-foot tall creature with a 4-foot stride."

Bert leaned back in his chair and thought about this possibility. A sasquatch. Was that really something to consider? He didn't know much about this cryptid, though, like everyone, he'd heard the stories and theories. It was his methodology to consider all possibilities and try to rule them out, one by one. Do they need to try to rule out a sasquatch abduction? How would they go about that?

Norah was looking at him with a puzzled look, too. She shrugged her shoulders as if reading his mind.

He checked the time on his phone and told Rhonda they needed to be going. After thanking her profusely for sharing her thoughts, he went to pay for the coffee. However, she waved him off and said the coffee was on her. Bert followed her outside and said another quick thanks and good-bye as they got in their vehicles to avoid the rain, which was coming down increasingly heavy again.

A look at Norah told him she was sorting out her thoughts from the meeting. Finally, she turned toward him and said, "She's serious, Honey. She really believes that a squatch might have taken Annie. I still don't have the sense that Izack is responsible for whatever happened. I do still get the strong feeling of being grabbed from behind. She was definitely abducted. I'm sure of that. I just don't get any visions of what took her."

Missy was beginning to dance around in the back seat. Bert knew she needed a break to do her natural business. She whined and licked his cheek. From his map, there seemed to be a small city park near the outskirts of town, so he kicked the doghouse into gear and headed toward it.

The park was rustic, with an area away from the trails and near the forest. He donned his hooded raincoat and walked Missy out there for about ten minutes. She had a grand time checking out the various new scents, and he had to call her closer several times. Back at the vehicle, it took a good rubdown with a towel to get her somewhat clean before jumping into the doghouse.

Before driving away, he tried again to reach Daisy Long. This time she answered. After the usual introduction and explanation for his call, Bert arranged to meet her at the local Burger King. It was about 9:30 and she had to begin work there by 11:00. Bert, Norah, and Missy headed for the restaurant. The rain was again lessening to a fine drizzle.

Inside Burger King, Bert got a coffee after paying for two, fixed it the best he could with what they had, and took a seat at a corner table. The place was not busy and there was only one other person, an elderly gentleman who sat reading the newspaper. He didn't have to wait long. A petite little blonde woman entered, and he knew she must be Daisy. He introduced himself and told her he'd paid for a coffee for her. After getting her drink, she joined him and Norah at the table.

"So, you're hoping to find out what happened to Annie?" she said. "How can I help, Mr. Lynnes? She was one of my best friends."

"Just call me Bert," he said. "I'm not a formal guy. Right now, I'm hoping to find out anything about either, but right now especially Izack, which might help us know them better, and which could lead us to clues and conclusions. How well do you know Izack?"

"Us?" she said, looking around. "Do you have other partners working with you?"

Pretty sharp lady, he thought. "Yes, I do work with a psychic who likes to work in the background. I also have one other partner. We each work different aspects of a case. Were you around Annie's husband a lot?"

Daisy nodded. "I was usually just with Annie Jo, but sometimes Izack was with her. So, I knew him very well, too. He was in my grade all through school. Annie and I had regular girls'-night-out dates, once or twice a month, just to hang out and talk. Girl talk, ya know."

"Do you think Izack had anything to do with Annie's disappearance?" Bert asked, getting right to the point.

She shook her head. "No, sir. Izack could be a jerk, but he was not violent or abusive toward Annie. He didn't know how to handle her very well and she was popular with about everyone. He wasn't nearly so popular and liked. So, he was often jealous of her. But I always knew that he loved her, Bert.

99

He didn't have anything to do with whatever happened to her. I'm sure of that. She was my best friend, Bert, I'd know if she was truly threatened by him."

"Do you believe she would confide in you if she had felt threatened by him or anyone else?"

"Yes," Daisy replied. "We had no secrets between us. I knew her mistakes and she knew mine."

"Did Annie make any serious mistakes with regard to her relationship with her husband?"

Daisy sat quietly for a few seconds, sipping her coffee, and looking at the table. Finally, she looked Bert in the eyes. "Well, I promised to keep this to myself and I've never told anyone what I'm about to tell you. Please keep this in confidence. I'm only telling you in case it will somehow help y'all find what happened to my friend."

"I promise to only use your information in ways that may help me find out what happened to Annie," he assured her.

"Annie developed a close friendship with one of the guys who worked with the 4-H program. It got a little too friendly, and she had a brief fling with him."

"Brief?" asked Bert.

"Yes, sir, she stopped it after a couple of months. She'd been having some issues at home with Izack. He was going through one of his pissy periods, when nothing suited him. She saw this other guy as a sanctuary, at that time. She knew it couldn't last because he was married also."

"I see," Bert said. "Did this fling end on good terms? Any hard feelings?"

"No, Andy took it well. He was feeling guilty about it, too. He had kids and didn't want to jeopardize his marriage. They remained friends."

"Did Annie's husband know about the affair?"

"Oh my God, no!" Daisy said. "Izack would've gone berserk. She never told him, and he never knew. To this day, he doesn't know. He'd probably try to beat up Andy and would definitely make a big stink about it. But, Bert, most husbands would probably throw a fit about that, don't you think?"

Bert nodded in agreement. "You're right, Daisy. But that doesn't sound like a guy who would be harmless to his wife. If he would get that angry, don't you think he's also capable of hurting Annie? She knew she had to keep that a secret from him, apparently because she knew he'd react violently. What if Izack somehow found out about the affair?"

Daisy sat quietly for a minute, sipping her coffee. Then she slowly nodded. "Yeah, she knew he'd go nuts if he knew about it. But I'm sure he doesn't know to this day, Bert."

He persisted. "But, what if he had learned of the affair, Daisy? Would he devise a plan to do something to make her vanish? Is he capable of pulling this off?"

"No, I still don't think he'd be so devious as to make her go away. Yes, he'd throw a fit; yes, he'd probably try to beat up Andy; yes, he'd chew Annie up one side and down the other. But, Bert, I just don't believe he'd do something this permanent to her. I know his family and him pretty well. I don't think any of them would do such a thing."

"Daisy, do you have any ideas about who may have done this with Annie?"

Again, she shook her head. "No, sir. I wish I did. I and my friends and family have had brainstorming sessions trying to come up with ideas. The most logical possibility is that stranger who ticked off Izack the night before she vanished. However, he departed right after that and nobody seems to know anything about him."

"One person suggested that a large predator may have taken her by surprise while she was hiking that day. What do you think about that theory?"

"It's a remote possibility," she said. "But, very remote, Bert. Annie knew these mountains and the wildlife as well as anyone. None of us seriously think she was taken by a predator. We've even considered the possibility of a squatch grabbing her. As predators go, that seems the one we mostly agree on. However, none of us think it's very probable."

"Do many people around here believe in sasquatch being in these mountains?" he asked.

"Oh, yeah, sir. I'd say at least half the population believes in squatch. I know several who've seen them. One is Izack's uncle, Bucky. He rarely talks about it, though."

"So, Uncle Bucky is a witness to a sasquatch encounter," Bert thought. "It stands to reason, since he is an avid hunter and practically lives in the mountains much of the time. Going to have to get smart about these things and try to rule this theory in or out."

Bert noted her information. "Okay, Daisy, I know you need to be going and I thank you for sharing your thoughts with me. Can I call you again if other questions come up?"

"You bet, Bert. Call anytime if I might provide more information. I want to do anything that might bring some closure to my friend's absence. I miss her terribly." She wiped tears from both eyes and her voice faltered. "Please find her."

"Take care of yourself, and thanks again, Daisy. We'll do our absolute best to find out what happened to your friend."

"One more thing, Bert," she said. "If I really thought that Izack did something with her, I wouldn't wait for the law. I'm an Arkansas Ozarks girl, Bert. I can shoot the eye out of a squirrel at 50 yards. I can take him out if I find out that he harmed my best friend. There are a lot of places in these mountains to hide a body." She was deadly serious, and Bert knew it. He was getting the sense that people down here don't put a lot of stock in the law to do what it should do. For that matter, neither did he.

They left the restaurant and went to their respective vehicles. The rain had stopped, and patches of blue sky were showing in the west. It would likely be a hot and muggy afternoon.

After getting in the doghouse, Bert looked to Norah for her observations and inputs.

She was thoughtfully introspective for a few minutes, and he gave her time to collect her thoughts. Eventually her eyes met his. "While she was talking, I began to see a vision of a person, a man, I think, in the crosshairs of a scope. It was kind of fleeting, and I don't know if it pertains to a past event or one in the future. I feel that Daisy is being totally honest with us. I still have the feeling that Izack was not the perp to whatever happened to Annie. This squatch thing is puzzling. I don't get any sense or visions about such a creature being involved. Yet, something grabbed Annie by surprise from behind. I'm more and more sure of that. She was abducted, Sweetheart."

"Honey, I'm realizing that we need to somehow find out more about that guy who had the encounter with Izack. The signs increasingly point to his possible involvement. We must find . . .. Hello," he said to the person who just called.

"Hey, Mr. Boss Man," said Becky in her usual bubbly

manner. "Top of a muggy day to you. You ready to sit in on my interview with Izack?"

"Hi Becky, so you have an interview set with him?"

"Yes, sir, sure do. I'm doing a sit-down with a friend of Annie's, Jill Jones, at 3:00, then will meet Izack after he gets off work, around 5:30. He suggested a table on the side porch at the Wing Shack. I don't really like meeting at a bar but didn't know any better place."

"That'll work okay," Bert said. "This is a dry county, so it isn't a bar. Norah and I will wait in the car for about two minutes. That should give you enough time to be seated and we can get close. Try to take a seat, first, facing the front of the porch. That will hopefully have his back to us."

"How's your day been going?" Becky asked. "Are you drawing any conclusions so far?"

"We're more and more convinced that Annie was abducted," he said. "And, we don't think Izack was behind it, though that isn't a certainty. Your interview with him will hopefully bring more clarity to that possibility. How are you doing, Becky? Is this case working the way you envisioned, so far?"

She paused for a few seconds before answering. "Well, the case is both interesting and frustrating. I want to solve it, like yesterday, but I can see it's gonna take a lot of patience and investigative work, if we can solve it at all. As for me, I'm doing fine, just trying to get used to this muggy heat around this area. I'm getting wet just on this phone call. Sweaty, I mean," she hastily added. "Good grief," she thought to herself. "What is it about this man that makes your brain quit working, Becky?" She was glad he couldn't see her reddening face.

If Bert caught her slip of the tongue, he didn't let on. He didn't notice Norah's smile. "Boy, I agree with you on the heat and humidity. It gets hot up north but not so muggy as down this way. You're doing a great job, Becky. Just keep on point and press on. We'll see you about 5:30. Stay dry."

After completing their call, Becky sat back against her driver's seat and took a deep breath. Her face had to be bright red after his last comment. She watched the few cars and trucks passing her position along the main square of the town, where she had taken a shady spot under the canopy of a big oak tree. The sky had changed to partly cloudy after the rain passed. When the sun hit her, the heat seemed to intensify dramatically. In the shade, she sat in relative comfort as she pondered her feelings. She had just over an hour until her interview with Jill Jones. She knew there was undoubtedly something else she could do on the case, but at that moment her mind was on her boss and the emotion she felt when around him. It was despair she was dealing with. The despair of wanting more from a relationship but knowing she couldn't have it. There was no way she could compete with the spirit of a man's wife. He kept saying, "we'll see you," not "I'll see you." Somehow, she had to move beyond this infatuation, if that's what it was, and look for someone else.

She was beginning to get her thinking back on the case when her phone rang. She didn't recognize the number, but knew it was a call from the local area code, so she answered it. It was Jake Rogers.

"Howdy, Miss Becky Thompson," he said. "Jake Rogers here, from the restaurant the other day. How's your story coming along?"

"Why, Mr. Rogers, I didn't expect to hear from you." Becky knew that wasn't exactly true. "I'm still gathering information. I have a way to go before I'll have a printable product. How are you doing? Building houses today?" She remembered he had said he was a carpenter.

"Just building one house," he replied. "Taking a break and thought I'd offer you some Southern, Ozark Mountain, hospitality. See if I might have the pleasure of your company for dinner at the diner tonight? Just call me Jake, too. I'm not the Mr. Rogers type. No sweater." He laughed.

Becky thought about her interview with Izack, and the talk she'd have with Bert and Norah afterwards. She knew it would probably be a little late before they'd be done. She should say no, but there was the growing realization that she had to move on from her feelings. Maybe this was what she needed. "I appreciate your invitation, Mr. Rogers, I mean, Jake. I have a couple of things I have to do this evening, so it would be almost bedtime before I'd be free, I'm afraid."

"That's no problem, Becky, I have a bed at my place." He laughed. "Not that I'd try to get you in it, of course."

"Oh yeah," she said in a flirtatious voice. "I don't think I said that I'd want to be in it, did I?"

"No, you didn't. But those things can change, you know. If you get to know me, you probably couldn't resist." He laughed again.

"Well, we'd have to see about that," she said. "I want you to know, though, that I don't want to be pushed. I went through an extremely hard divorce not too long ago, and I'm not ready for anything until I'm ready. Okay?"

"No problem," he said. "I'll wait for a woman like you to be ready. I'm thinkin' you're worth the wait."

Definitely a lady's man, she thought, although a rather surprisingly smooth one. Maybe he was the antidote for her feelings for Bert. She was surprised at the temptation she was feeling toward this younger man, although he was only around five years younger, she guessed. Was it purely a sexual attraction, since she hadn't been with a man since her divorce? Was the temptation an admission of giving up on her feelings for her boss? Could she walk away from those feelings?

"I don't know for sure when I'll be free tonight, so how about calling me around 8:30 or 9:00 and we'll see," she answered. "Thanks for the complement. Right now, Jake, just dinner. Okay?"

She needed to focus on her two interviews, so told Jake good-bye. It took several minutes for her to get her mind on the interview with either Jill or Izack. She kept questioning herself about accepting a date with a local guy before she'd been in Mountain View a week. She concluded that it was a way of shielding herself from the growing frustration of her feelings for her boss. If she could only believe that Bert would let go of his hold on Norah. Or was it Norah who held onto him? Becky decided it didn't really matter. Either way, Bert was not, and she had to let him go from her heart. She had to just think of him as her boss.

CHAPTER SEVEN: DECISIONS AND DECISIONS

Three in the afternoon came quickly for Becky. She did not feel prepared for the interview with Jill Jones as she entered the garden store. Jill had told her about a little sandwich shop that served customers on the shaded porch. Becky was the first to arrive, and she ordered the garden sandwich special and chose a seat at a table near the end of the porch. Soon a medium built brunette, looking to be in her forties, arrived and quickly spotted Becky.

"Hi, you must be Becky. I'm Jill," the brunette said.

Becky introduced herself and explained again her interest in doing a story about Annabel. "I'm hoping you can tell me anything about Annabel which might help me understand her and her relationship with her husband, Izack."

Jill leaned forward and crossed her arms on the table. "I'm sure I can, Becky. I've known Annie's family all my life. I grew up just a half mile away from them. My Daddy and hers worked together at the lumber mill near Jonesboro for years."

"So, Annie was like a little sister to you, then?" Becky asked.

"I guess you could say that," Jill replied. "I was about twelve when Annie was born, so I did a lot of babysitting for her. She was always a cute little girl, full of life. As we became adults, we became very good friends."

"By all accounts, Annie was a loyal wife and gave no reason for her husband to have any animus toward her. Do you know of anything different from that?"

Jill looked away, as if watching the couple who had just sat down near the door. She turned back toward Becky. "No, and if I did I wouldn't want to smear her in your story. My only interest is in seeing her portrayed in the good light that she deserved and helping find out what happened to her. She was a great person and friend."

"I'm very sorry, Jill, I should have explained myself better," said Becky. "I have no desire to use anything in a negative way to embarrass Annie's memory or upset her family. What I'm trying to do is understand those things which may have impacted the way she thought, acted, or reacted prior to her disappearance. I have heard that she may have had an affair at one time and wondered if you could confirm that? From what I've heard about her husband, it seems that she may have had good reason to look elsewhere."

Jill clasped her hands on her lap and looked away for several seconds. Finally, she looked Becky in the eyes, saying nothing for several more seconds. "Becky, if I tell you what I know about that, I want your promise that you will not put it in your story."

Becky nodded. "Yes, ma'am. You have my word that it will not be in my story."

"I'm only telling you this because I trust you, Becky. You seem like a genuine and honest person. So, yes, Annie did have a brief affair. She confided in me one night when she and I went to the Wing Shake for a burger. I pretty much knew before she leveled with me."

"Thank you for that, Jill. About how long did it last and how long before she disappeared?"

"It was brief," Jill repeated. "Just a couple of months. She said she only met with the guy three or four times. I think it was about eight or nine months before she vanished."

"Do you know the guy?"

"Yeah, I know him. He's actually a pretty good guy. Like Annie, he was married, but he had a couple of kids. He was having problems at home just like Annie was. She ended the relationship after a couple months; decided it was not the right way to deal with her marriage issues and just was not worth the risks. She especially didn't want Billy Joe to know."

Becky wanted to know if the guy was angry about Annie pulling the plug on their fling.

"No," said Jill. "I get the impression that he was relieved that it was over. He didn't want to end his marriage and he had a couple of kids."

"So, he wouldn't be upset to the point of harming Annie, then?" Becky asked.

"Oh, no, Becky. I never got any impression like that from Annie when she confided in me. She talked with me because she, and apparently he, both felt guilty about it and wanted to end it."

"Did they work together? Or do you know how they hooked up?"

Jill nodded. "They volunteered together at the 4-H club."

"I know she worked there with Anderson McCreedy," Becky said. "Was there someone else?"

"No, she was involved with Andy. His nickname was Andy."

Becky thought about that for a minute. If Anderson, Andy, wanted to keep this a secret, why did he refer Becky to one of Annie's friends whom he must have known Annie might confide in? Or did he think she would confide in anyone? Did Anderson find out that Annie gave away their secret and become concerned? If so, could his anger and fear have made him do something to her?

"Did Annie have any particular habits or likes that stood out to you?" Becky asked, changing the subject.

"She was just a very nice person, mostly," said Jill. "One of a kind, really. Everybody in the area liked her if they knew her. The one thing that defined Annie above all else is her love for Billy Joe, the boy she raised, and of nature. She used to go on hikes all the time up in the mountains. If she could not take Billy Joe or find anyone to go with her, she'd go alone. Many times, she'd take a lunch and be gone all day."

Becky followed up on that. "Do you think she might have been attacked by any of the wildlife out there? I know there are some large predators around here."

"Anything's possible, isn't it," said Jill. "A lot of us have spent hours trying to come up with anything to explain Annie's sudden disappearance. We've even brought up the squatch a few times. Most of us take the supposed sightings with a grain of salt, yet there might be something to all the claims. I don't think all those people are nuts."

Becky made note of what this woman said. "Jill, the guy at the town square the night before Annie vanished; the one Izack tried to pick a fight with. What do you think about him?"

Jill wondered how this writer seemed to know so much about the case. She figured that Becky must have done some serious homework before sitting down with her. "Most of us are suspicious of that guy, Becky. I only know of one person who knows anything at all about him, though, and they've left the area over a year ago."

"Oh, really," Becky said in surprise. "Who was that, Jill?"

"The waitress that night was a black lady who moved here just a few months before whatever happened to Annie. She left shortly after that. Just did not fit in around here, I guess. Or, maybe the abduction scared her. Anyway, nobody had any idea what happened to her until just recently when my niece told me that she saw the gal working at a bar and restaurant down west of Little Rock. Her name was Bonnie, Bonnie Shackleford, I think my niece said. She served the mystery man a drink and something to eat, so she was about the only person to have any interaction with him, except for Izack's little tantrum."

Becky was making notes about everything Jill was telling her. "Do you know the name of the place where she's now working?" she asked Jill.

"It's something Roadhouse," Jill said. "Jimmy Dean and Bob's Roadhouse, or something like that. I believe the place is fairly new and is in the Bryant or Benton area."

"Okay, I'll keep her in mind if I need more information about that night," Becky said as she continued to make notes. "Jill, the primary suspect at first was Annie's husband, Izack. Even though I understand he's been cleared, do you think he may have had anything to do with this?"

Jill leaned forward and placed her elbows on the edge of the table, her hands clasped. "That jerk is only cleared because his hunting buddy, Jimbo, gives him an alibi. Yes, I think Izack is capable of doing this to Annie. But he apparently couldn't have been there that day, according to Bubba Jimbo. He was too cheap to hire someone, even if he had the money, so I guess he wasn't involved." She was reluctant to draw that conclusion. It was obvious that she did not like Izack.

"Can you think of anyone else who might be a suspect?"

Jill shook her head. "Nobody."

Becky leaned back and took a drink of her water, processing

her thoughts. "Jill, I can't think of any other questions right now. May I call you again if I need more information?"

"Absolutely," Jill answered. "Anything I can do to keep Annie Jo's memory alive."

They walked out together, through the rows of potted plants and flowers, and said good-bye in the parking lot. Becky started her truck, turned the AC on, and relished the cool air as she contemplated all she knew so far about Annabel Leery. This young woman was almost an enigma. On the one hand, she seemed to be nearly perfect. Yet, she had made one serious error in judgment. Two, if you counted her marriage to Izack Leery. Did one of them get her killed?

She jolted awake from having fallen asleep in the driver's seat, looking at her phone for the time. How long did she drift off? It was after 5:00. Less than a half hour before she was to meet with Izack. She shifted the Hemi into gear and headed for the Wing Shack.

* * *

After the interview with Daisy Long, Bert and Norah took Missy back to the undeveloped side of the city park for another 20-minute outing. Now that the rain had subsided, there was just a bit of mud to contend with. Humidity, too! As the sun pushed the clouds to the east, the sauna effect hit hard. That didn't bother the coywolf, though, at first. She ran around gleefully, happy to be out of the vehicle for a while. Bert was a different story. As he walked around the park, keeping an eye on Missy, his brow became wet with sweat, and his back and armpits dampened his short-sleeve shirt. To his delight, Missy also tired of the heat sooner than expected, so he was able to get her back in the SUV and seek sanctuary in the vehicle's air conditioning.

Since he had a few hours before the meeting with Becky and Izack, Bert decided to return to their motel and do some research on the sasquatch theory. As far-fetched as it seemed, it was apparently one he needed to take seriously and rule out. No stone unturned.

Norah rode by her husband's side, silently thinking, as they returned to the motel. Her spirit could feel the conflict raging in this man. What could she do to lessen his burden, she wondered? There was no fault to find in this situation. Neither of them wanted it to be like this nor did they do anything to bring it. It just came. So, being without fault, why was there such a feeling of guilt?

Bert led Norah and Missy into the room. He looked longingly at the beautiful apparition, the spirit of his beloved wife. Even in the spirit world, she was the original love of his life. Her beauty, personality, wit, humor, and psychic abilities remained imbedded in her spirit. She remained his wife in all ways, except one. Physical. As much as he longed to touch her, he could not.

Missy's whines brought him back to the reality of the room, and her desire for some water. She rubbed against his legs and then went to her empty bowl, looking at it as if to will it full. He filled her bowl to the brim, knowing she needed more water than usual in the southern heat. With a pat on her head and a scratch behind her ears, he turned to and opened his laptop. It was time to find out more about squatch.

* * *

The phone alarm rang at 5:00. Bert confirmed the time and

closed his laptop. He'd become thoroughly engrossed in the fascinating research into the cryptid known locally as squatch. Now, though, it was time to be backup to Becky's interview with Izack Leery at the Wing Shack. He added his military ball cap to a fake mustache and lightly tinted sunglasses. With his faded blue jeans, ankle-high hiking shoes, and short sleeve khaki shirt, he felt that he'd blend in well with the restaurant's clientele.

Outside the establishment at 5:28, Bert parked across the parking lot from Becky's pickup, masking the doghouse on the opposite side of a parked dually pickup. Izack would probably not notice it when he entered the parking area near the front door. He noticed that Becky had parked her truck between two others, backing in so that her license plate was shielded by the vehicle behind her in the next row. She was smart and didn't want Izack to notice her Wyoming plate any sooner than necessary. Two Wyoming vehicles in one day would likely make him suspicious. Bert and Norah saw that she was still in her truck, so they assumed that Izack had not yet arrived. Bert adjusted his mirrors so he could keep Becky in view as he twisted in the seat to scratch Missy's ears. He lowered the insulating sunshades on the sunny side of the vehicle, to keep it cooler inside for his tracker animal and companion. With a fresh bowl of water and the windows lowered a third of the way down, she shouldn't get too hot while waiting for his return.

They did not have to wait long. Bert felt his phone vibrate from Becky's text. She said that Izack had just arrived in the dark brown Chevy pickup, which was spattered with mud and dirt. Bert watched as she left her truck and walked over to introduce herself to Mr. Izack Leery. Leery exited his truck and closed the door, shaking Becky's hand with a smile. He was a slender guy, about 5 feet 8 inches tall. He removed his ball cap and tossed it into his truck's open window, disclosing his dark hair and eyes. Billy Joe had told Bert and team that Izack was in his mid-thirties.

Bert watched as Becky followed Izack into the Wing Shack, disappearing from view. He patted Missy and apologized for having to leave her alone in the doghouse. She licked his cheek as if to say she understood, and it was alright. After about two minutes had passed, Bert and Norah departed the doghouse and entered the restaurant. It took a few seconds for his eyes to adjust to the subdued light. He saw that Becky had done as he suggested, though inside rather than on the porch, as she sat at a far corner table facing the door. That had made Izack sit across the table with his back to the door. Bert ordered a large lemonade and took it to the table closest behind Izack, with his left side toward Izack so he could glance at their table while overhearing their conversation as he pretended to read a newspaper.

"So, Miss Becky," Izack said, "you're out this way to gather information for a story about my wife, Annabel? Why her?"

"I'm researching women who've vanished without a trace for two years or more," she replied. "I've never been to this part of the country and Annabel's plight came to my attention. So, here I am."

Izack thoughtfully sipped his iced tea. "Well, I'm guessing you want to know if I did something to make her disappear. That's what everyone wants to know, it seems."

Becky leaned forward, folded her arms on the table, and looked him squarely in the eyes. "Then let's get that question out of the way, sir. Did you do anything with your wife?"

Izack liked that Becky didn't mess around but went straight to the heart of the interview. "No, ma'am," he said with emphasis.

"I was a crappy husband sometimes, but I loved her, and no way would I do something like this to her. Whatever it was that happened to her."

Becky called upon all her powers of observation, people skills, and her empathic abilities to try to read his sincerity. "Where were you when she disappeared, sir? May I call you Izack?"

"By all means, just call me Izack. That's how everyone in the area knows me. I was huntin' with a good buddy of mine, Jimbo. I spent that night at his cabin north of town. We sat up kinda late, drinkin. I was upset about having a fight with Annie. He helped calm me down. We spent the entire next day out in the woods and valleys north of his place. He got a nice buck around 8:00 that morning. I finally got mine just before sundown, coming into the valley to feed."

"So, Jimbo can vouch for you that this is true?"

"Oh yeah, and he's had to a hundred times. I think I've been questioned at least that many times, especially the first year."

"You could have hired someone to take Annabel. Did you?" Becky went straight for the jugular.

"I suppose I could have if I had the money. I'm like Jesus, a carpenter. Except He probably made more money than I do." He laughed. "People out here don't hire someone to do their dirty work, Becky. If I wanted something done to Annie, I'd have done it myself."

"So, you can look me in the eyes and swear on your honor that you are not responsible for whatever caused her to vanish?" Becky leaned even closer to him and continued to stare into his eyes, unblinking. She wanted to put him to the test.

His reaction surprised her. Tears welled up in both his eyes and rolled down his cheeks. Lips quivering and with his facial muscles around his eyes twitching ever so slightly, he looked away and then down, ashamed of his sudden burst of emotion. Finally, he looked up at her, wiping his eyes with the back of his hand.

"Miss Becky, I loved Annie. She was the one best thing that ever happened to me. When she agreed to marry me, I was shocked. She could have done so much better than me. I'm sorrier than I can say at the shitty way I treated her sometimes. And that I couldn't give her the kids she wanted."

"Why did you treat her badly, if you loved her so much?" she asked.

"Ma'am," he said, "I'm ashamed to admit that I think I was always jealous of how popular she was. Every guy in the county wanted her. Every woman loved her. I didn't think I could compete."

Becky had the overwhelming sense that Izack was being honest with her. "Sir, I can tell you that a woman often seeks those qualities which she thinks she lacks. I'm betting that Annie loved you more than you let yourself believe."

He seemed to contemplate her words for almost a minute as he delayed his reply with a few more sips of tea. "Thanks, Becky. I guess I was afraid to think that, especially when we couldn't have kids."

"Let's shift gears," she said. "What do you think happened to Annie?"

He was quick to answer her. "Oh, there's no doubt in my mind. She was taken by someone."

"Why do you say that?"

"Several reasons," he replied. "Mainly, she had no real

reason to leave and many reasons to stay, especially her sister's boy, Billy. She's a pretty and attractive woman, Becky, with the looks that draw attention. She's a candidate for some predator. The two-legged predator. Everyone around here knew and loved her. If she had just left, somebody would have known about it. Someone took her."

"Do you have any idea who may have taken her, then?" Becky asked.

"Definitely a stranger," he said. "Nobody in this area would do that. The guy at the jam session that last night is the one I suspect."

"Why him? What do you know about him?" she said.

"That's been the problem all along. Nobody knows a damned thing about him. He was just passin' through that night, apparently. Supposedly left right after I chewed his ass that night for making a pass at my wife. The law in town didn't try to investigate him, because they all assumed that I had to be the culprit. Spent the next year trying to pin it on me."

"Do you have any idea how to find out more about him?" she asked.

"I wish I did, Becky," Izack replied. "He vanished just like my wife did. Without a trace."

She changed the subject. "So, what can you tell me about Annie? What are her qualities, interests, likes, dislikes, that kind of stuff?"

Izack went on to restate what Becky had already learned about Annabel. In particular, he also stressed her love of nature and being outdoors. He said they used to go four-wheeling all over their mountains.

"Did Annie ever get into any disagreements or have issues

with anyone around the region?" she asked him.

"No. Annie had no axe to grind with anyone that I knew about. Like I've said, she was so friendly and liked by everyone. Who would have any issues with someone like her?"

"At any time, did she ever get involved with the wrong person or crowd? People who might pull her off her normally straight and narrow path, even if briefly?"

"Not that I know of, Becky. She was so busy with being a stand-in mom to her nephew, sub teaching, working for 4-H, and taking care of our garden and animals, that she didn't have much time for anything else. Except hikes in the woods," he added.

"Was she happy with your marriage, Izack?" she said, catching him by surprise.

Izack looked away, casting a brief glance over his shoulder at Bert and the other customers at the nearby tables. His face turned solemn. She could detect tears again glistening in his eyes. After a minute, he turned back to her. "I've asked myself that a hundred times over the past two years. This has made me do a lot o' soul-searching, and I'm not proud of what I'm finding, ma'am. I was too often a jealous and pompous ass with her. There was one time about eight or ten months before she vanished when I was on her case all the time. I finally realized that she hadn't done a damned thing wrong and I was pushing her away with my accusations and jerk attitude. If she had looked for someone else during that time, I guess I couldn't blame her. The night before she vanished, I acted like a jerk with her again, even threatening to make her walk home in the dark. I know that really upset her. She loved the woods, but not in the dark."

His words hit a little close to Becky's heart. She'd been in that same position as Annabel in her former marriage. Presumed guilty by association when she had not done anything to deserve it. Her own marriage hadn't survived it. She wasn't sure sometimes if she would survive it. She did but sported two black eyes and a swollen lip on her way out the door. She shook her head slightly to get back to the reality of her interview.

"She didn't leave you, though, so you must have gotten somewhat in control of those demons."

"A little, I guess," he said. "But I still was quick to judge her and condemn her when other guys would look at her. I think that's what happened with the stranger that last night. He was probably just minding his own business when I called his attention to her."

"Maybe you're being too hard on yourself, Izack?" She sought to console him a little. "We all make mistakes which we regret later." She looked at the time on her phone. It was almost 7:30. "Sir, I probably need to wrap it up for now. Would you mind if we talk again later, if needed?"

He nodded. "Yeah, that would be fine with me, ma'am." He leaned closer to her. "You know, I think you've missed your calling."

"Why is that?"

"You should be a detective or investigator. You questioned me a hell of a lot harder than any of the law did. For someone looking to write a story, you sure know how to get to the bottom of things." He finally smiled at her. "I've never been grilled quite like this."

She laughed and smiled back. "Yeah, I'm sorry about that. When I get on a roll, I want to get to the things that matter. Thanks for taking the time to talk with me, Izack. I know this has not been easy for you and you have had to endure a lot.

121

Ultimately, I hope I might help get to the truth about what happened to your wife." She stood and offered her handshake.

Izack shook the hand of the attractive woman who had nearly reduced him to an emotional wreck. How could someone so pretty be such a barracuda of an interviewer? This time, he followed her to the door, passing an arms-length from Bert on the way. In the parking lot, he walked her to her Dodge and stood making small talk for a few minutes, before going to his own truck and departing. He didn't notice as Bert walked to the other side of the parking lot and got into his vehicle.

Becky took her time getting ready to leave until Izack had disappeared from view. Then, she called Bert's cell phone. He picked up on the first ring. "Well, boss, your place or mine?" She said, with a mischievous chuckle.

He laughed at her choice of words. "Let's meet in my, our, room in about twenty minutes. That should be enough time to get some food together. We're looking forward to discussing your grilling, I mean interview." He laughed loudly.

"I'll grab another bottle of this red Ozark wine," Becky said. "The one last night was great."

"Sounds fantastic," Bert said. "We'll see you at the room."

He, Norah, and Missy returned to their room and pulled some food from their cooler. He had barely gotten Missy fed and a couple of sandwiches made when the knock at the hallway door told him that Becky was there.

She entered in her usual bubbly manner, smiling as she kicked her sandals off at the door. She had taken the time to change into her dark green, mid-thigh-length shorts and sleeveless, camouflage, pull-over shirt. "Boy, talk about another hot, humid afternoon. Thought I might melt before we got inside that restaurant," she said as she handed over the bottle of muscadine wine. Missy arrived at Becky's bare legs and rubbed against her, licking at her toes, and yapping with excitement.

While Becky hugged her animal buddy and laughed at Missy's course tongue on her feet, Bert took the bottle and looked at Norah as she leaned against the bed headboard. Norah smiled back at him and gave a thumbs-up sign. Then she looked him in the eyes and said, "Bert, besides being a good investigator, this woman gets cuter every day. I like her, Honey."

Bert nodded but wasn't sure what to say, so he said nothing. He agreed with Norah, though. With the addition that both were cute women.

He handed Becky a sandwich and a cup of wine. Taking the same for himself, Bert said, "You did a fantastic job with Leery this afternoon. I could not believe that you even made him cry. Tough questioning. What do you think of the way he handled himself and answered you?"

"Honestly," she said. "I felt sorry for him and I believe him. I don't get the feeling that he had anything to do with his wife's situation. I think he's been genuinely heartbroken about it. Doubly so because a lot of the locals believe he was involved."

Norah added, "I also believe him, Bert. I think he's the one I've had visions of crying on the edge of a bed. He's a victim, also, of whatever happened to her. Bad enough to lose her; even worse to have so many blaming him."

"I guess it's a clean sweep, then," Bert said. "I believe him, too. I still want to have an interview with him, but at this time I think we're on solid ground to shift our focus elsewhere."

"I agree with you, Boss," said Becky. "The question is where do we focus?"

"Norah, Honey, do you have any visions which might point us in a particular direction?" Bert asked.

She moved to the end of the bed. "Yes, maybe. While Becky was interviewing Izack, I was seeing a man and woman in a heated discussion. Fighting, maybe. In the background was a shadow figure, seeming to watch them. It seems to mean that someone, or I guess something, was observing Izack and Annabel, plotting to take her. I do not think this was a random event. She was chosen."

Bert thought about that for a minute. "Becky, did anyone shed any light on the stranger at the square that night?"

Becky answered quickly. "Yes, well, maybe. Everyone seems to suspect him, but nobody knows anything about him. However, I got one possible lead. The waitress who served this guy and is apparently the only person to talk with him, left soon after Annie's disappearance. She was recently discovered working at a bar and grill down south and west of Little Rock. Her name is Bonnie Shackleford."

"That's fantastic!" said Bert. "Why don't you see if you can meet up with her and see what she remembers. I'm going to try to meet with Izack tomorrow and see if we can totally put that question to bed. Did any other things come up?"

Becky looked in the direction of Norah, knowing she was there but not seeing her. "Well, I hope you guys don't think I'm crazy for even mentioning this, but apparently some people think Annie may have been taken by a sasquatch."

Bert smiled at Norah, then looked back at Becky. "You're not alone in that regard, Becky. We've been given the same suggestion. As far fetched as it seems, I have started looking into the possibility. There's a lot on the internet about these things. How about you see what you can come up with and let's get back together later tomorrow and kick around the idea. It seems that we have to consider it and try to rule it out, if possible."

"I think that's a great idea, Bert," Becky replied. "I'm curious about these things anyway since several people have mentioned them. Never heard . . . . . excuse me. Let me take this call, quickly."

Becky's phone told her that Jake was calling, as she had suggested. What should she do, she wondered? She answered the phone, told him she couldn't talk right now, but would call back when she returned to her room. Sheepishly, she apologized to Bert for the interruption.

He could tell that Becky was uncomfortable about the call and maybe even embarrassed. His intuition told him it was probably a guy calling to ask her out. Bert knew he had no right to feel a degree of shock about that, yet he felt a little stunned to think that she might go out with someone. How could he feel so torn? Norah, after all, was with him constantly, even if as a spirit. Becky was his employee. He could not expect her to be more than that. Could he?

Regaining his composure, Bert smiled at her and said, "That's okay, Becky. We have a game plan for tomorrow, so if you need to return the call, go ahead."

She stood up, thanked both Bert and Norah, and said that she probably should be going. "I'll try to meet up with the waitress west of Little Rock tomorrow, so better get to bed early." As soon as she said that, she immediately wondered how it sounded to her employers. Maybe she was wondering how it sounded to herself.

Giving Missy a hug, and picking up her sandals without putting them on, she opened the door to leave. She took a quick look at Bert, smiled nervously, and turned to leave.

Norah waved at Bert to get his attention. "Hey, you numbskull, give her a hug and tell her good-night."

He opened the door which Becky had just closed behind her. Catching her in the hallway, he told her to hold up a second. She turned around and paused, her blue eyes trying to read him. "I wanted to say good-night," he said awkwardly, as he walked the ten feet to where she stood. "Becky, I want you to know that we, I, like you, a lot." He opened his arms and she moved against him, returning his firm hug. Her trim body felt good against his chest, and he knew he hugged her a little too long, but it felt too good to let go any sooner. "I like you, and not just as an employee. Good night, Becky."

Bert turned and entered his room, closing the door behind him. Norah was looking at him, with her own blue eyes glimmering. She smiled sweetly at him, that smile which always warmed his heart. It was like the jewel which crowned her beauty.

"Honey, there's something I want you to know."

Bert was not sure what was coming. "What's that, Sweetheart?" he said, quietly.

"When you worked the case in Cheyenne, I wasn't always gone to Minnesota with my mother," she said. "Part of the time, I was there, near you, on my own mission."

"Mission? What mission, Dear?" he asked.

She drew nearer to him, just a foot or so away. "Bert, my love, I know that I cannot be everything you need in life, not as a spirit. It breaks my heart, Honey, to know that you're often lonely for a physical relationship. As long as I'm with you, you will hold back on your feelings and needs. I know that."

"What are you saying, Norah?"

"I'm saying that I went to Cheyenne to look for someone for you. Someone that deserves you, Bert. I found Becky."

He moved to the chair and sat down, trying to comprehend what she was telling him. "You found Becky?"

"Yes, Honey. It took me a while to plant the seeds of thought into her mind, but it finally worked out to bring her to your table that first day you and the Governor went to the restaurant where she worked. I was very sure that once you met, it would grow from there. There were a few surprise twists and turns, but it's working out as I thought it would."

"You think so?" he asked.

"Yes, Honey. That woman is crazy about you, in case you haven't noticed. And I know what is in your heart, Bert. You feel the same way about her."

The realization of Norah's wisdom and love was overwhelming. Tears welled up in his eyes. This was not what he expected to hear. "I love you, Norah. I don't want to lose you."

"You haven't lost me and you won't lose me, Bert. In my spirit realm, I'm attached to you by choice. I will stay if I believe it's the right thing to do. If you can handle being loved by two women, one of whom is a spirit."

"I don't know what to say, Norah. Except I love you. I have always loved you. I will always love you."

She smiled. "And I love you, Bert Lynnes. I want you to be happy. I will be beside you, but I want you to open your heart to Becky. You are both damaged people, why not heal together. Let's all heal together. Let me share in your happiness."

* * *

Three doors down the hall, Rebecca Abigail Thompson sat on the edge of her bed, feeling confused. Just when she had made up her mind to try to let go of her feelings for her boss and accept a date with playboy Jake, Bert's hug had weakened her resolve. She had been contemplating giving in to her carnal desires and spending the night with Jake. She didn't want to, and yet she wanted to. What should she do to get a flutter back in her heart?

She dialed Jake's number.

CHAPTER EIGHT: SEEKING THE TRUTH

The red-orange glow of sunrise escorted out a fitful night for Bert, as he made his way through the outside door of their room with Missy at his side. This morning, he again kept her near him on the leash as they made the rounds of the parking area and adjacent lot. He was at the far side of the parking lot when he noticed that Becky's room was dark. His heart seemed to skip a beat as he looked for her truck. It was not there.

He had no right to want to control her actions when she was off duty. She had a life and was entitled to live it. The fact that he knew this was true did not subdue the growing angst he was feeling in the pit of his stomach. Was she slipping away? How could she slip away from where she had never really been? He only knew that she was not where he had hoped she would be. So, where was she? Did he even want to know the answer to that question? Maybe he already knew the answer.

Back in the room a few minutes later, Norah immediately sensed the turmoil in her husband. As she moved near Missy and sought to softly brush the top of her head with her hand, the animal tracker let out a barely audible whine and closed her eyes. Norah could always tell that Missy sensed her presence, even if she could not see her. While soothing Missy's soul, she wondered how to console Bert's. Perhaps only time could do that. And the truth.

Bert busied himself by calling Izack Leery. It was time to get to work and see this step through. To his surprise, Izack answered on the second ring.

He introduced himself to Izack and told him about talking with his uncle. Izack assured him that he was aware of the new investigation and asked what was prompting this go-around. Bert did not want to disclose his clients, so he told Leery that his team specialized in looking into cold cases of missing women. Annabel's disappearance had come to his attention. He said he needed to talk with Izack in order to rule him out as a suspect.

Izack was surprisingly amenable to talking. Bert had the impression that Becky's interview had softened him up, to use a military phrase. More importantly, maybe Izack felt he could trust this new team to be both thorough and fair. Whatever the reasons, they agreed to meet over breakfast at Ma's Diner in half an hour.

Bert scrambled to get ready for the interview. As he dressed, he was debating how and when to disclose his working relationship with Becky. At some point, he had to. With Norah and Missy in tow, they entered the doghouse and headed the short drive to the diner.

Leaving Missy in the car with the usual adjustments to keep the heat down, he and Norah entered the diner and located Izack Leery. Izack was sitting at a far table with his back to the wall, already starting to eat. He obviously did not have much time before being at work. Bert realized he would have to get right to the points.

After introductions and a handshake, Bert thanked Izack for his time and explained again that his interest was finding the truth about Annabel's disappearance. "I know there are people here who think you're behind whatever happened to her," he said. "Why should I believe they're wrong?"

"Because I was with my hunting buddy, Jimbo Elliot, all that night and the day she vanished. He has sworn this under oath numerous times."

"Okay," Bert said, leaning forward to look Izack squarely in the eyes. "So, tell me this. Did you, in any way, have anything to do with your wife's disappearance? Did you hire someone? Was there an accident? Anything in any way?"

Izack was getting angry but he controlled his temper. "Absolutely not, Mr. Lynnes. This is BS. I've been accused of doing something by some people around here, even though there's no evidence that I did anything."

"People witnessed you having a fight with her the night before at the town square. Also getting into a confrontation with a stranger for looking at her. How do you explain that, sir?"

Izack looked down and away for just a second, before returning his eyes to Bert's. "Sir, I was a jerk then, just as I was a jerk all too often in our marriage. I admit that freely. But I did not do anything to harm her. I loved her, Mr. Lynnes."

Bert saw Izack's eyes well up with tears. He believed this man. A glance at Norah told him that she also believed him. Softening his voice, he said, "Mr. Leery, Izack, I believe you. I had to ask these things, though. So, now, let's put your involvement to rest. What do you think happened to her?"

Izack relaxed a little. "Mr. Lynnes, she was taken by someone. I have no doubt about that. Nothing else makes any sense. She had no good reason to run away. I was a prick, but I did not abuse her and I wasn't that bad. Her nephew, Billy, was reason enough for her to stay here. She'd never leave him intentionally. No sir, someone took her."

"Any idea who, then?" asked Bert.

"I think it might have been the guy I yelled at. But he disappeared right after that. Never saw him again. So, I don't know. If it was not him, then I just don't know, Mr. Lynnes."

"I've heard some people say that a sasquatch might have grabbed her. What do you think about that?" Bert said.

Izack was a little surprised by the question. "Oh, yeah, I've heard several say that. I know they are out there and around here. I've never seen one, but my uncle did, and I think I've heard their calls a time or two when camping out deep. They're very elusive, sir, and I just don't buy that. Possible, yeah, I suppose it's possible. But I just don't think so. They're too timid and usually try to avoid us."

Bert nodded. "Yeah, I tend to agree with you. However, I must take every possibility seriously until I can rule it out. Any ideas on how to do that?"

"No, not this long after she vanished," Izack said. Unless you can find a lair and some evidence of her, I don't know how you'd rule it out. Or in. I do know that those mountains were searched hard trying to find Annie. If there was anything out there to find, they would probably have found it."

"Do you know anyone around here that you'd consider an expert on the things, the squatch?" Bert asked.

Izack thought about that for a few seconds. "There's a high school teacher, James Hawkins, who knows a lot about them. Whenever someone sees one, they usually end up talking with James. I think he's connected with some of the state level folks."

Bert made a note of Hawkins' name. "Okay, Izack, thanks for that info. I know you must get to work, so I will not tie you up any longer. If questions come up with my team, would it be okay if I call you and possibly meet again?"

"Yes, sir. That's no problem. I just can't miss too much of my job. Could meet again for breakfast like this if you wanted."

"Oh, yes. One more thing," Bert said. "Would you mind if we visit your cabin and property a time or two? I'd like for my psychic to see if she can pick up on any residual energy that might be helpful. We might even go into the woods a little way if you don't mind?"

Izack didn't hesitate. "Yes, sir. I have nothing to hide and no problem with you looking the place over any time you want. Just let me know in advance an hour or two so I can show you out there and open it for you."

Bert did not want to tell him that they had already been there with their clients. So, he asked if Izack would tell him how to get there and they would drive on out and look around the exterior.

It was not a surprise when Izack asked him to wait until noon. Then he would escort them to his home. Bert agreed and said he'd meet at the restaurant at noon.

Bert looked at Norah for confirmation that she had no additional questions for Leery. She shook her head and he stood and told Izack to take care. It seemed time to move in another direction. He took the check, paid the waitress, and returned to the doghouse. There, one overly excited hybrid canine told him that she needed a good walk.

Asking a few strangers led them to a vacant field adjacent to the local Walmart where Bert could let Missy run for a while. For thirty minutes, she had a great time sprinting from one brush pile to tree line to fence post, looking for something to chase or eat. While walking and keeping an eye on her, he received a text from Becky.

"Hey there, Boss," her text read. "I'm down west of Little Rock. Just had a very interesting interview with Bonnie Shackleford. She's the waitress who talked a little with the stranger at the square the night Annie disappeared."

He texted back. "Fantastic! Can't wait to hear about it. Will you be here this evening to discuss our findings?"

"Absolutely, Bert. I'm fixing to leave from here soon as I indulge in one of their sandwiches (diet, of course. LOL). This is a neat place!"

"What's the name of the place?" he asked.

"Jimmymac and Rob's Roadhouse," she texted in reply. "Relatively new place. We should come down here sometime while in Arkansas."

"You've got a date!"

"Oh yeah, you'd take me here on a date?"

"Yes!"

"Would that be like a boss/employee night out?" she asked.

"No! More than that."

"Hmmm! Can I hold you to that?" she said.

"Yes, ma'am. You can. I'll see you when you get back in Mountain View this afternoon."

"Yes, you will. Bye for now, Boss."

Bert holstered his phone and returned to Missy. Where was that little varmint now, he wondered? It took him a few minutes to locate her tail, waving just above a pile of brush where she had apparently found something interesting. "Coywolves," he thought aloud. "You can take 'em out of the country but you can't take the country out of them."

With Missy back in view, his thoughts returned to Becky. He was glad to hear from her. Even happier that she had had a good interview with, hopefully, a good source of needed information. No, he realized he was simply happy to hear from her.

As he lowered the lift gate of the vehicle for Missy to hop in, Norah smiled and asked how Becky was doing. His initial surprise at her question was muted as he recalled that she was, after all, psychic. Of course, she knew he had texted with Becky. He increasingly realized that she not only did not mind but encouraged him to have more of a relationship with her. During the years that she was alive, she would have been upset by this situation. However, as the spirit of his dear wife, she wanted him to have a physical and real relationship with their first and favorite employee. He was beginning to accept it, but still found it awkward. There was still a nagging sense of guilt. It would take time. But it was time he was willing to take.

However, he wondered, did he have much time for this. The case of missing Annie Leery was going to be demanding and exhausting. If they could find out what happened to her, it was likely to require considerable effort by all of them. And, Becky had shown the interest in having her own life. Last night was unsettling for him because she apparently stayed somewhere. Was she becoming interested in one of these Arkansas guys?

Bert knew he could not afford the time to dwell on these personal issues. His business had a job to do. To find out what happened to Annie. With that, he asked Norah what she thought about investigating the sasquatch theory.

She had been thinking about that. "Let's see what kind of evidence we can find that these animals, if they're real, can be dangerous," she said. "I don't know enough about the creature to have a sense of the likelihood that it might abduct anyone."

"And, in the meantime, maybe we'll find a way to track down the stranger from the square. He could be a key figure in this case, based upon our interviews. I'm anxious to see what Becky found out today," he said.

"We have about two hours until we meet Leery to go to his cabin. I'm going to continue research online about bigfoot, or sasquatch, as they call them around here. Tonight, we'll get into this with Becky, along with the information from her interview."

Norah added, "Hopefully, I'll pick up on more clues when we look around the Leery cabin at noon."

Back at their room, Bert turned on his laptop and continued his search into the cryptid known locally as sasquatch. He had much to learn before meeting up with Becky.

* * *

Izack Leery drove up to Ma's Diner just a few minutes after 12:00 noon. Bert drove next to Izack's truck, said hello through the windows, and said he would follow to the Leery cabin. As they proceeded east out of town on the familiar road, Bert and Norah paid closer attention to the thickening wilderness surrounding them. Much of it appeared to be old-growth forest of mostly oak and cedar trees, with a dense layer of vines and downed trees and branches, making it seem impenetrable at times. Farther back from the road, the forest seemed to open a little more and would be a bit easier to traverse than the 50 to 100 feet closest to the road. It seemed that once a hole is carved into the wilderness by a road, it reacts by attempting to close it with a dense layer of thickets and brush.

Twenty minutes later, after a drive that was uncomfortably fast, they arrived at Izack's home. He graciously invited Bert inside the house to look around, showing him all the rooms. From there, the tour resumed between the outside buildings, garden, and decently maintained yard. Unseen by their host, Norah followed along, pausing periodically to read the tea leaves, as her husband loved to say. Bert purposely took his time, asking questions, to give Norah ample time to commune with the spirits. Izack allowed Missy to run around the place, with Bert keeping her near with voice and hand commands.

Izack iterated how the only things missing, besides his wife, were the clothes she wore, her hiking shoes, and her light jacket. There were no other clues about what may have happened to her, he told Bert. He said that the last known person to see her at home was her nephew, Billy Joe, around 7:00 that morning when he left to go hunting. That was after a breakfast with her about 6:00.

Bert surveyed the land around the homestead. To the south of the house was the medium-size valley which ran east and west, lengthwise. All other sides of the house were surrounded by increasingly dense forest and mountain wilderness, apart from the road. It carved the route back towards town, initially to the north and then curved to the west. Izack confirmed that the nearest neighbors were two families who lived out of sight toward the western end of the valley.

Norah let Bert know that she had no questions right now, so he thanked Izack for the tour and asked if they might come back out again if they felt it necessary. Izack was completely agreeable with that, so they said good-bye and Bert, with Norah and Missy, followed the man back toward Mountain View.

"Well, Sweetheart, did you pick up on anything more out there?" Bert asked her as they bounced along on the first, rougher, part of the road.

"When we went through their bedroom, I could see that vision, more refined, of Izack, sitting on his bed by himself and crying. He was not saying anything, just expressing his grief through private tears. I'm more convinced than ever that he

137

had nothing to do with Annie's plight. He's a victim, too," she said.

"I'm feeling the same way," Bert replied. "Anything else, Honey?"

"Yes, Bert. I could sense Annie closing her door to the house and walking behind it toward their animal pens and barn. I could see the ground passing under her feet, as if I were her. I could see her hiking boots, ankle high, and her bare legs. She was wearing shorts. She was almost to the barn when my vision went dark. At that point, I again felt the intense fear of being grabbed from behind. This time I felt an overpowering force. Someone big and strong. Then the entire vision stopped. It was as if she went unconscious. Or died.

"It seems that she didn't see the assailant, then," Bert surmised. "Your vision appears to validate a complete surprise attack."

She nodded vigorously. "Yes, Dear. She did not see it coming. My vision strongly supports this."

He reflected on her inputs for a mile or two. "Well, at least we are being led in a specific direction. That of an overpowering abduction. Taken from the vicinity of her house. Based upon what you're sensing, our focus needs to be on who, or what, could and did do that."

Yes, Honey," she replied. "The bigger question surrounds the stranger. Hopefully, Becky will be able to shed some more light on that."

Shortly, as they were entering the town, Becky called.

"Hey there, number one, are you back here now?" Bert asked.

"More like number three, I think," she giggled. "Better make that number four; about to forget Missy. Yes, I just got to my room. Are you guys ready to meet up and share info?"

Bert said they were ready, and they would be in their room in ten minutes. He invited her to come over. He was anxious to see her again. He couldn't help but wonder if she'd be the same after last night. Norah could read what was on his mind.

He did not have to wait long. They had barely gotten into their room when the knock on the hallway door told them she was here. Bert opened the door and ushered her inside. Missy once again went into hyper hello mode, rubbing circles around Becky's legs and nipping at her bare toes as she kicked off her sandals. Her antidote to the Arkansas heat was to dress down to a sleeveless cotton shirt, shorts, and sandals just as soon as she got to her room. Bert really tried to be a gentleman and a businessman at such times, but it was just impossible to not glance at her trim figure, killer legs, and cute feet. Even Norah was sometimes mesmerized by Becky's looks and personality. She caught Bert's eyes and gave him that understanding smile.

Satisfied with her greeting, Missy moved back to the cooler floor in the bathroom, while Becky took the chair Bert had placed for her at the side of the bed. He sat at the only other chair at the end of the bed. Norah was at her usual place near the headboard. The team was assembled at their roundtable.

"We missed you today," he said. "But can't wait to hear about your interview with the waitress."

"I think it went well with Bonnie," she said. "Bonnie Shackleford. I met with her for about an hour before she had to start working. She did say that she waited on the stranger the night before Annie vanished."

Bert leaned forward with great interest. "Did she remember anything that might help us?"

"Maybe. I think so, anyway," said Becky. "He didn't have

139

much to say, just ordered a coke and burger, she said. She did notice something when he paid her, though. For one, he didn't talk southern; she thought he sounded like a Yankee. You know, like we do." Becky laughed. "The other thing was some kind of a hunting logo on a business card that fell out of his wallet."

Bert asked, "Did he give her a card?"

"No," Becky said. "She said he didn't notice it at first, but as soon as she reached for it, he grabbed it up as if he didn't want her to see it and put it quickly back in the wallet."

"Hmmm, that seems strange," said Bert. "Most people want you to see their business cards. So, makes you wonder what he's hiding."

"I know, right!" she replied. "She caught the word 'hunt' and a strange kind of deer head picture."

Norah had been listening intently. Her mind was tuned in to whatever thoughts or visions might come to her. She said, "Neat, or neck, or maybe nock."

"What do you mean, Dear?" asked Bert after relaying the words to Becky.

"I'm not sure, Bert," Norah answered. "I'm just now getting flashes of a word; four letters I think. So fast and fuzzy that I can't quite make it out. It came to me as Becky talked about the card, so I'm sensing that it may be residual memory that Bonnie somehow sent to Becky. I think it's another word on that business card."

Bert thought about all this for a few seconds, glancing at Becky several times. "So, it seems logical that this guy may have been a hunter who was carrying the card of a hunting service of some kind. That was just before the rifle season started for deer and other big game. Maybe he came out here to hunt. On the other hand, he might be an owner or guide for such a service. Out here to solicit business, perhaps. However, if that was the case, why hide his card? And why so reclusive? Most people with a product or service to promote are outgoing and talkative with those around them."

"Right," interjected Becky. "I was thinking that, also. My impression is that he did not want attention and preferred to remain an anonymous stranger. If not for Izack's jealousy, he probably would still be just a stranger listening to the music, barely noticed."

"Did Bonnie offer much about this guy's looks?" asked Bert, following Norah's suggestion.

Becky nodded. "Some. Bonnie is a neat black woman, cool personality. She said she tried to engage him in small talk, but he wasn't interested. Said he was a fit-looking white guy, thick sandy hair, medium height; tan, as if he worked outdoors a lot."

"How old?"

"About fifty-ish, Bonnie said."

Bert leaned toward Becky and placed his left hand on her right hand. "Good job, Becky. You just might have gotten us a break in this case. At least if that guy was somehow involved. We now have a glimmer of hope at identifying him. Going to take some research to see if we can find the business that goes with such a card." He grasped her hand and squeezed it gently, then drew his hand back.

She did not pull her hand back. Smiling at Bert, she said, "So, there might be hunting clubs, or groups, guided hunts, hunting ranches. What else have I missed?"

"I have professional hunters, guides, promoters, travel agents, coming to mind," replied Bert.

Norah added, "Or the guy who just wants to hunt and picks up a card somewhere."

"How about we divide up our search between us. Might save some time and duplication," said Becky. I could look for clubs, groups, and the like."

"Good idea," said Bert. "I'll focus on looking for hunting preserves, ranches, and guided hunts.

"I'm sensing that whatever we look for, it is probably going to be unique. Not typical. So, it may be hard to find, especially if it's a very private enterprise," said Norah.

Bert nodded in agreement. "Ladies, I think we have a plan. Now, on a different note, we have another theory to try to rule out, if it can be ruled out. A sasquatch abduction. The local squatch that several seemingly rational people have suggested."

Norah added, "If none of that seems to work out, I will try my best to channel Annie. If I'm successful, perhaps she can provide some clues for us. Other than that, maybe we could take a drive down to Bryant and meet up with Bonnie. If I can try to read her in person, I might be able to pull up some residual or buried memory from that night. Then you could have your date that way, too." She looked at Bert with her eyes flashing.

Bert smiled sheepishly and told Becky, "Well, if we go back to talk with Bonnie, maybe we could have that date?"

Becky laughed. "So, you're serious about this date, then?

"Sure, why not?"

"Is it okay for your employee to have a date with her boss?"

"Sure is, if the boss says so." He laughed, then added, "and if his wife doesn't mind."

"She doesn't mind?" asked Becky.

"No, she doesn't," said Bert. "In fact, she's encouraging me."

"Well, I would love to, Boss, I mean, Bert."

Bert looked at her blue eyes, so much like Norah's. "Done! We'll plan for it, then. Now, regarding the squatch theory, let's follow your suggestion, Becky, and divide up on it, too. How about you look for historical evidence from around the globe while Norah and I will see what we can dig up locally. I've never heard of any alleged conflicts between humans and these cryptids, so if that's the case, then we can almost rule out an abduction."

Becky was excited about that. "I like that, I know almost nothing about these things, so it should be fascinating to see what's out there in cyber-land. Or in the library."

"It's almost 5:00 and time for a bite of supper. I can put together a decent salad and sandwich from our cooler stock. What do you say to getting your laptop, having a sandwich here as a team, and we'll work on these things?"

Becky smiled broadly. This is what she wanted, to be part of the inner workings of her company. Even if it was small, it is still her company. "That's great! I'll get my laptop and be back shortly." She left without grabbing her sandals, walking barefoot back to her room. Missy looked at Bert as if asking to go with her. Bert waved his hand in their "go-ahead" gesture. She bolted out the door with Becky, turning in circles alongside her human. Once inside her room, she pulled out her phone and called Jake.

Back in his room, Bert busied himself making two salads and

a half sandwich for himself and Becky. He poured two glasses of milk, then put Missy's usual homemade meal in her bowl. He noted the approving look from Norah and smiled at her. "A supper meal fit for a queen?" he asked.

"Yes, Honey, fit for a queen. You're doing great, Sweetheart. Keep being your sweet self."

About five minutes later, Becky tapped on Bert and Norah's door. She and Missy entered following his verbal, "Come on in."

They chatted while eating. She raved about his hastily prepared salad and sandwich. "Couldn't be better," she said. "I suppose I have to pay you for food this good?"

"Yup, sure do. This stuff doesn't come cheap."

"Uh oh, well, you do know that I'm on a job that hasn't anted-up, yet."

He smiled at her. "Guess one of your hugs will be payment enough, for now."

"For now?" she said. "So, the price will be going up, then."

Bert laughed. "Free enterprise, baby. Free enterprise. Prices rise as the products improve."

They both had to laugh at their good-natured bantering. Both knowing there was a serious side to the humor. Norah looked at Bert, and nodded approvingly, giving her own killer smile. Missy raised her head from between her paws as she lay on the cool bathroom tile, as if to say, "What's all this nonsensical chatter about."

Bert leaned back in his chair, raising his knees to put his own bare feet on the end of the bed, and rested his laptop on the lapboard on his legs. He resumed his research into the cryptid known as sasquatch.

Becky had her own laptop on her legs, as well. "So," she read, "cryptid is based on the word 'cryptozoology,' and refers to a creature that is claimed to exist but has never been proven to exist. An animal whose existence is unsubstantiated."

"Yup," Bert replied. "Hard to believe that any creature can be so elusive that it can exist for centuries without proven discovery. Yet, it seems there are allegations of such creatures all over the globe. And, here in Arkansas," he added.

"Neek," Norah said.

"What, Honey," Bert asked. "What's neek?"

She shook her head. "I don't know. I just had that flash across my mind. Maybe another word to go with the others I saw. Or is it instead of them?"

"Interesting," Bert answered. "That makes me think we should alter our plans slightly."

"How so," said Becky.

He looked at her and said, "Why don't you continue to pursue the sasquatch theory for now. I'll see what I can find online that might make sense of the stranger's business card."

"I'm good with that," replied Becky. "This sasquatch thing is very interesting, if nothing else."

With the division of labor more clearly defined, they all quieted down and dug into their respective tasks. Norah, likewise, thought about everything she knew or sensed about the case and Annie, trying to channel her for anything that might come through."

Bert first searched for private hunting preserves. These included the King Llewellen Setter Hunting Resort, Legacy Ranch, Arkansas Duck Hunting Lodge, and Preserve Ranch in Arkansas. There were numerous others, often with hunting specialties, such as quail, duck, or deer. Every state had its own lists of private hunting places, it seemed. When you looked for the myriad of shooting, gun, and hunting clubs, there were just too many to have any real chance of finding a specific logo, especially one that's incomplete. After more than an hour, he backed away from his computer for a minute.

Becky started chuckling and giggling. She pushed her own laptop aside and stretched her legs. "Hey, Norah's word made me think of a joke I heard years ago. Kind of stupid, but a little funny."

Bert smiled. "What's that? Let's hear it. I could use a laugh break."

Her eyes sparkled. "What's a unique way to catch a polar bear?"

"Ummm, I guess I don't know. How?"

She laughed, "Well, you cut a hole in the ice and put a fish near it. When the bear goes to the hole to eat the fish, you neek up on him and kick him in the ice hole."

All three of them chuckled and then laughed. "Funny!" Bert said. "I like that, and it fits the word that Norah saw. I wonder if or how it may relate to our case, though?"

"Something about that is tickling my brain," said Norah. "But nothing is really changing or coming into focus. Just that aggravating flash of realization, followed by nothing."

"Tell ya what," Bert said. "Maybe we need to have that date down in Bryant soon, all three of us. If Norah gets around Bonnie up close, perhaps she can draw in more energy or vision. Maybe that would bring us some clarity about that business."

"So, this date will be chaperoned, then," Becky laughed.

Norah smiled and nodded enthusiastically.

Bert smiled and told Becky, "For your protection."

Her eyes flashed gleefully as she retorted, "Or, yours."

Bert realized that he was starting to like this new relationship situation. Still kind of awkward, but not feeling so guilty. Even better because Becky seemed to genuinely like him. Maybe Norah was right. If she chose Becky for him, then she made a good choice.

"How about a break for a glass of wine?" he said. "I think we should go to Bryant tomorrow, since it's Saturday, and see if we can talk more with Bonnie. We'll see this place you like, and Norah can try to connect with her subconscious. Hopefully, pick up on something about that card or guy."

"And my date might buy me one of their great sandwiches," Becky said.

Bert grinned, "I think that's a sure thing. Where is this place located?"

"I may have said Bryant, but it's in Benton, the next city to the west," said Becky. "I'll call Bonnie right now and see if she's available for a short meet-up tomorrow." She retrieved her phone and dialed Bonnie's number.

While Becky had a short conversation with Bonnie, Bert poured two glasses of wine, and looked longingly at Norah, wishing he could pour a third for her. Then he took a third glass and poured it partly full, also. Looking at Norah, he passed the thought that this glass was in her honor, as he set it on the desk to his right. He could see that the gesture of love touched her. Reminiscent of his military days and a table set for those missing. He wiped a tear from his eye.

"Tomorrow's good for Bonnie," Becky said. "She's working

the evening shift which starts at 4:00, so could meet us an hour before or even share a late lunch a little earlier. It's about a three-hour drive down to there."

"Let's leave here around 10:00. That will give us time to have a leisurely drive and stop once or twice if something catches our fancy," Bert replied. "And to let Missy have a run."

With the next day settled, they resumed sipping their wine and researching online.

The evening passed quickly, and it was 9:00 before they knew it. Bert told Becky good-night and hugged her as she headed out the door. Missy excitedly danced around her legs. Bert looked at first Missy, then Becky, and nodded. "Go ahead, she can stay over with you."

Without giving him time to change his mind, Becky sped off to her room with Missy close behind.

CHAPTER NINE: TRAVELING WITH SQUATCH

Saturday, September 1st, 2018, looked to be another hot day as the sun ascended the eastern horizon. Becky and Missy watched the transition from the brilliant red just before sunrise to the deepening blue sky of early morning. As they walked the nearby vacant lots, the sun became warmer by the minute. They would thankfully spend much of the day in air conditioning, which was fine with Becky. She was still finding the intense, humid heat down in the South a bit hard to get used to.

After tending to Missy's needs, Becky ate a bowl of cereal in her room as she continued the fascinating search online for information about the Squatch. During their three-hour drive to Benton, she hoped they could discuss what she'd been finding.

She arrived at Bert and Norah's hallway door at 9:50. They were all going together in the doghouse, so traveling light. Greeting Bert with her usual hug, Becky said hello to Norah. They were all anxious to get on the road.

Becky started to get in the back seat, but Norah told Bert that she would like Becky to sit in the front passenger seat near him. So, Becky entered the passenger seat, thanking Norah. Once they headed toward the south on the mountainous, two-lane highway, she asked her employers if they'd mind discussing the Sasquatch while they traveled. Both agreed.

One of the first things that came up when she searched for sightings in Arkansas, was the Fouke monster. The fictional 1972 movie, "The Legend of Boggy Creek," was loosely based upon numerous alleged sightings in that area back in the 1970's and earlier. "The incident which prompted that situation and movie sounds a lot like the event at the neighbor's house

149

the night before Annie disappeared," she said. "Something attacked the cabin and scared the daylights out of the family. They left the next day and didn't return."

She went on. "There are numerous sightings claimed all over the state of Arkansas. Stone County had three alleged sightings last year. Several websites claim to be databases for sightings. There is a Bigfoot Research Center. This cryptid, or something like it, is a national and global phenomenon. In the Northwestern U. S., it is usually called Bigfoot. In Florida, they talk about a skunk ape. Among the Native American Algonquin people, there is a legend of a terrifying creature called the Wendigo. In Russia, it is called the Yeti, Almasty, Menk, or Cau Cas Sha. Ireland has a man-ape. The list of such myths, legends, and possible fabrications seems to be endless and encompasses almost every continent and nation."

"Did you find much evidence about these things being violent or dangerous?" Bert asked.

Becky continued. "I found several stories about campers who said that something rattled around in the bushes beyond the firelight and even banged on trees or threw stones at them. In the 1950's in British Columbia, an Indian medicine man named Frank Dan, claimed that a weird-looking, hairy creature threw a rock estimated to weigh at least a ton at Dan's canoe. It nearly swamped his canoe and did block the channel. That rock can be seen on display in the Vancouver Public Museum."

"Wow," Bert said. "That's impressive. What else?"

"The Algonquin's Wendigo was believed to be evil and cannibalistic. They are in the minority and not verified, however there are accounts of mutilations, murders, and consumption of people by Bigfoot. These might be discounted, except there's the uneasy question of what happened to many of those who go missing every year, from wilderness areas."

Bert acknowledged Norah's input. "Norah brought up the famous Patterson film of an alleged Bigfoot in 1967 in California. That short film clip is perhaps the most compelling evidence of a Bigfoot, captured on film, despite the allegations of fraud and hoax. There is a cadre of researchers who believe the tape is real."

Becky turned sideways as much as her seatbelt allowed, so she could more closely face Norah in the backseat behind Bert. "There's another mystery you have got to be aware of. The Dyatlov incident in Russia, in 1959."

"Dyatlov?" Bert asked. "Is that the place where something happened?"

"No, it's the name of the leader of a two-week, camping expedition of nine students, seven men and two women. A tenth male student became sick and turned back after the first day. They were apparently all friends and very experienced at camping in the winter in the Ural Mountains of Russia. I think they were all in their twenties, fit to take on such a challenge. About halfway into their planned trip, they camped overnight about a mile above the tree line on the mountainside. It was February, so temperatures were likely sub-zero at night. They all shared one tent."

"Okay, so what's the mystery, then?" Bert asked.

"During that last night," Becky went on, "something happened to scare them terribly. Investigators discovered that the group cut slits in their tent from which to look outside, obviously looking for something they considered a threat. Then, they did a mass exodus from the tent down the mountainside to the tree line, not taking time to put on coats, gloves, or even shoes and socks in some cases. At the trees, there is evidence that one or two attempted to climb a tree and make a fire. A couple seemed to try to return to their tent. None of them made it."

"Oh my God," Norah told Bert. "What happened to them?" He relayed her question.

"They all died. Most had massive internal injuries, as if from an automobile accident. One girl had her eyes poked out and her tongue ripped completely out of her mouth. She would probably have bled to death. Freezing was the final death blow. The search party couldn't find all of them until after the spring thaw. Two bodies were lying in a creek bed. It must have been a horrific scene for the searchers to uncover."

Bert shuddered. "That's a chilling and hair-raising account of what sounds like a major crime or killing. Has it been solved?"

"No," said Becky. "There are numerous theories, but nobody has ever been able to say with absolute certainty what happened."

"What does this have to do with our Sasquatch?" Bert asked.

"There are numerous accounts in Russian lore of the Yeti, or Almasty, their version of our Bigfoot, or Sasquatch. During one of the many investigations, someone finally thought to check the students' diaries and cameras. One diary entry had a comment to the effect of 'We know they're real, they're watching us.' One picture in a camera shows what looks like a large, bipedal, hair-covered, creature standing on two legs and looking at them from maybe a hundred yards away in the trees. When I read this, Bert and Norah, I was stunned. This entire murder seems very plausibly the work of a Yeti. Nothing else makes any sense to me."

Bert looked at Norah and said nothing, taking in and digesting what Becky had just told them. He was stunned to find himself agreeing with Becky that this Sasquatch theory was taking on a more dangerous perspective. However unlikely, there did seem to be reason to consider the possibility that Annie may have been taken by one of them.

He looked at the signs as they now traveled south on highway 65. They were just a few miles north of Clinton, Arkansas. "Time for a break, I think. Let's find a coffee shop and a place to let Missy run for a few minutes."

Becky was all for that. The time had flown while they were discussing the Squatch, but now her bladder was feeling a little full. As they pulled into Clinton, she saw a small mall on the east side of the highway, and a sign for coffee. With a name like "Rock n Java," it would probably be a good place to pause.

Bert and Becky got one of the coffees from a brunette named Lake. She was cute and pretty enough to be a model, he thought. He wondered if there were a lot of girls as beautiful as her in Arkansas. While pondering that question, they all used the bathroom. Discovering a riverside park behind the shop, Bert and Becky spent about fifteen minutes walking Missy on the paved trails. Once she had relieved herself and gotten rid of a bit of pent up energy, they got back on the road toward Little Rock.

Twenty minutes south of Clinton, still on highway 65, they had proceeded through a small town of Bee Branch. While waiting at the one stop light, they noticed that this typically rural community evolved around a gas station, garage, and post office. They continued south on highway 65 to Damascus. When they passed Southside High School, Bert asked Becky to check online for information about a missile explosion, which he seemed to remember associated with the area near the school.

After about fifteen minutes and past Damascus, Becky looked up from her phone research. "You're right. In September of 1980, a Titan intercontinental ballistic missile incident occurred following the accidental dropping of a tool during a routine maintenance operation. The skin of the fuel tank was punctured and fuel began leaking out into the silo. Heroic efforts by the maintenance crews could not prevent an eventual explosion, which blew the warhead completely out of the silo and into a nearby gulley. There had been discussions among the powers-that-be at the time about how large an area should be evacuated. There was disagreement about whether the warhead might detonate or not. After about twelve hours, the explosion answered that question. The warhead did not detonate. If it had, we wouldn't be here right now," she said. "This entire region would still be a radioactive parking lot. It's a miracle that only one maintenance man was killed."

Bert let out a whistle. "Wow, I remembered some of that but hadn't realized just how potentially grave that situation was. I was overseas at the time, and it was pretty much over before the news got to us."

By the time they discussed the Titan accident, they had gotten on Interstate 40 at Conway and were proceeding the half-hour to Little Rock. Approaching Little Rock, they turned south on I-430 to cross the Arkansas River and get on I-30 going west. At the junction with Interstate 30, Bert made a mental note of the Bass Pro Shop. He loved stores like that, and you never knew when you might need some outdoor equipment in his line of work.

As they turned west on Interstate 30, Bert received a phone call from his older daughter, Sandra. She lived in northern Minnesota with her husband and eight-year-old daughter. He and Norah listened as Sandra told them she was doing fine.

"Just thinking about two years ago, when we lost Mom," she said. You know the two-year anniversary is coming soon."

"Yes, I know," he answered. "She is never far from my mind and heart."

"Do you still see her spirit, Dad?" Sandra asked.

"I do, Honey, and she's with me every day. We both think of you girls and your families all the time. She helps me all the time. This business would not be effective without her."

They talked for a few more minutes, discussing his granddaughter, before Sandra had to go back to work. Bert nodded approvingly to Norah. She may be gone, but she was not forgotten.

Twenty minutes later, they arrived at Jimmymac and Rob's Roadhouse. Bert, Becky, and Norah went inside and Becky quickly located Bonnie Shackleford. The slender, attractive, black lady, looking to be around thirty years old, joined them at a table near a side window. Norah's spirit stood near the end of the table, closest to Bert, where she could see Bonnie's face as she talked. Bonnie said she had about an hour before she went on shift. In keeping with his date promise, Bert bought the house special burgers for the three of them.

Thanking Bert for her lunch, Bonnie asked, "How can I help you guys?"

Bert nodded the question to Becky. She replied, "It's really more of the same questions that you and I discussed the other day, Bonnie. We're hoping that all of us might be able to touch something in your memories that can help identify the stranger you served the last night before Annabel Leery disappeared. He might be one of the keys to finding out what happened to her."

"Anything I can do to help," said Bonnie. "I didn't stay in Mountain View very long, but I knew about Annabel. It really scared me when she vanished without a trace. That, and conflicts with a couple of the other employees, made me decide to leave there just a few days later. I didn't feel safe there."

"Why did you move there?" asked Bert.

Bonnie looked away and shook her head before answering him. "A good friend of mine invited me to come there. However, I wasn't in town a week before he died of a massive heart attack. Who would've thought that would happen? It ended my desire to be there."

"Wow, I see why you left," said Becky. "That would take the wind out of anyone's sails. So, that strange guy probably didn't catch much of your attention that night, I suppose."

Bonnie shook her head. "No, actually he did catch my attention. He was nice to me, although he didn't say much. You know, just being gentleman-like. I did notice right off that he must be from up north by the way he talked."

"Talked like us, I bet," said Bert with a laugh.

"Sho nuff," chuckled Bonnie. "All y'all Yankees talk kind of funny, ya know."

"Yeah, I've heard that," answered Bert with a smile. "Becky said he accidentally showed you one of his business cards, or at least a card that he carried. Do you remember if it had a picture or logo?"

"I think it had a picture of some kind, or a design," she replied.

Bert then asked, "Do you remember if the design had a particular shape. A square, rectangle, circle, or such?"

Bonnie thought about that for a few seconds, before saying, "You know, I think it was sort of a circle, round."

Taking directions from Norah, Bert asked, "Bonnie, how about just sitting back, closing your eyes, take some deep breaths, and totally relax. When you feel relaxed, with eyes still closed, see that card falling and laying on the table. Don't push yourself, just let your mind see what your eyes saw that night. Let the round design on the card become clearer until you can see the middle and the edges. Do you see any writing on it? Can you make out the words?"

Bert, Becky, and Bonnie all sat quietly while Bonnie leaned back in her chair with eyes closed and her hands clasped on her lap. "There was some kind of animal head in the middle, like a deer, but not a kind of deer that I recognized. And there was writing around the circle, on the outside of the ring."

At this point, Becky said to Bonnie, "The other day, you remembered the word, 'hunt,' or something like it?"

"Yes, I said that. The card was only in front of me a couple of seconds before he grabbed it up, but I caught some part of a word with hunt in it. There were other words, too, but only that one word caught my eye. I'm sorry, but I just don't remember more about it."

"That's okay, ma'am, you're doing the best you can," Bert assured her. "On a different note, what characteristics do you remember most about that stranger? Size, build, hair, and so forth."

Bonnie looked at Becky and then looked away, staring without seeing into the parking lot. "About all I remember about him is that he had a good body, seemed to be very fit, and basically medium height and build. Also, he had thick sandy hair, a little curly. His hair was eye-catching. So were his dark eyes. I remember focusing on his eyes when I brought his order; they were so dark. Almost creepy dark if you know what I mean."

"So, eyes so dark that you couldn't distinguish the pupil from the iris," said Becky.

Yes, ma'am, that's zactly right," replied Bonnie. "Just looked like a black hole in the eye. They kinda wierded me out. Annabel's husband had swelled up like a bullfrog, but I think the guy's eyes were a main reason why the husband backed off from his accusations."

Bert looked at Norah and saw that she had her eyes closed and was in deep concentration. She was obviously taking in whatever energies that Bonnie was giving off. He patted Bonnie's hand. "Bonnie, thanks so much for meeting with us and trying to help us with Annabel's case. You've been more help than you realize. Can we get you a dessert?"

Bonnie looked at her watch. She was one of the increasingly rare people who wore a watch on her wrist. Shaking her head, she told them that it was time to get on her shift.

As was his custom and nature, Bert stood and hugged her. He could tell that she was a pretty neat woman, the kind who could become a friend if they were around her much.

With Bonnie off to take up her duties as a cashier, Bert turned his attention to Becky. "I'm sorry that this date has been a bit watered down with work. So, now that we've had these fantastic burgers, what would you like for dessert, Miss Becky?"

Becky looked Bert in the eyes, smiled her sweetest smile, and with eyes twinkling, said, "You pick something you think I'll like. I trust my date." She liked to put him on the spot and see how he handled it.

Norah gave him an equally cute smile, and just nodded. Not

going to offer him any help from the spirit realm, either.

He smiled back at them both, got up, and walked over to Bonnie. Whispering his order in her ear, he returned to the table. "I'll show you two," he said.

Shortly, a cute little red-haired, freckled, waitress named Chloe came to their table, delivering two desserts. She put both in front of Bert. The first was a piece of peach pie with a scoop of vanilla ice cream on top. The second was a square of brownie with vanilla ice cream and a strawberry on top. He thanked Chloe, then turned to Becky with a smile. "Here, my sweet date. You get your choice and I'll take the remaining one."

"Aah, good choice, Mr. Bert. Very diplomatic, as well as romantic," Becky said. "In this case, I will divulge my sweet tooth with that brownie one. Get my daily fruit with that strawberry." She laughed, as she put fork to brownie.

They continued small talk as they ate their desserts. Bert had a great time getting to know Becky better as just a woman. She was not only attractive but was also intelligent and well-informed about many things. Norah was clearly enjoying getting to know the woman she had chosen to be in their lives. They continued the pleasant visit until noticing that it was after 4:00 in the afternoon. If they did not get back on the road soon, they'd be driving those Ozark Mountain roads in the dark. This was not something Bert preferred, so they told Bonnie good-bye, let Missy out for a brief stroll around the parking lot, and retraced their route back toward Mountain View.

As they went back east on Interstate 30, to pick up Interstate 430 across to I-40, Bert asked Norah if anything came to her while Bonnie was talking.

Norah shifted forward somewhat from her place in the back

seat with Missy. For Bert to relay to Becky, she began. "I've picked up on a couple of things, maybe. For one, when she was discussing the stranger, especially his eyes, I began to get a sense of darkness. The kind of darkness that accompanies doom or evil. A sinister feeling began to take over. I think I'm sensing Bonnie's subconscious assessment of this guy. She perceived something sinister with him. I don't know what that means for Annie's case, but this guy is not someone to trust."

After Bert's repeat, Becky softly whistled. "Wow, that's why we need Norah and her abilities. Sounds like we need to continue pursuing him."

"I agree," said Bert. "There are several people who believe he might have had something to do with Annie. If he's not to be trusted, that makes him even more suspect. What was the second thing, Sweetheart?"

"As she talked about the business card, I started to hear a word. It was 'unique.' Again, I suspect that I was picking up from Bonnie's subconscious, and she felt there was something unique about the card. The question is what. I just don't have a clear picture of that."

"When I interviewed her before, I picked up on her discomfort and uncertainty," said Becky, "but not on those specifics. So, if we can figure out how his card is unique, we might have a chance of finding him."

"Yes, I think that's the case, guys," said Bert. Turning to Becky, he said, "Well, some date, huh. More work than play."

"Maybe," Becky answered. "But, when you enjoy the people you work with, it becomes more play than work."

Bert did not answer that right away but contemplated her words. So, she does like to be around us, even when working while on a date.

Becky seemed to read his thoughts. "Yes, Bert, I enjoy being with you even when we're working." She glanced in the direction of Norah, and winked, as if knowing she would understand.

They drove along in silence for a few minutes before Norah communicated with Bert. "While we're trying to figure out the stranger's business card, what do you propose we do about the Squatch question?"

Both Bert and Becky sat in silence for a few minutes, thinking about Norah's question. How do you go about confirming if Annie was grabbed by a cryptid?

Finally, Becky said, "There's no way to prove or disprove the squatch theory, is there? That is, unless we can find hard evidence, skeleton, bones, clothing, or something like that in what looks to be a lair."

"I think you're right, Becky," said Bert. "Without such evidence, it's just a possible theory. Nothing more. The searchers following Annie's abduction had the best chance of coming up with evidence, and they did not. What's the chance that we can find what they didn't, two years later?"

Becky thought for a second. "Guys, I think that Norah's psychic gift is probably the only way to try to rule such an attack in or out. I don't know if that's possible, but I don't see any other way."

Norah looked at Bert and nodded. "She's right, Honey. Maybe I can spend more time at their cabin and pick up on something else. Unless Annie's spirit has left additional clues for me, I can't do much more than I've already done, I'm afraid.

He pushed back on the steering wheel and stretched his arms. Highway 65, north of Greenbrier, faded away behind them as Bert drove the doghouse up the increasingly hilly road to the turnoff at Clinton for Highway 16 toward Mountain View. Norah was in the backseat, softly stroking Missy's head as she slept. Becky was giving way to sleep as she reclined on the front passenger seat. In the approaching darkness and on the forested, mountain road, Bert kept wondering if something unknown could be watching them pass by, unseen. Something like a Sasquatch. Or, like a stranger from somewhere to the north.

Norah was watching the rugged terrain go by, too, sharing some of the same thoughts. She wondered if she could go by the Leery's cabin and pick up any lingering sensory or psychic perceptions from the abduction that she didn't catch earlier. She was certain that Annie was grabbed from behind and abducted, or killed, but the frustrating and nagging question was by what, or whom?

Bert cast occasional glances at Becky as she snoozed on the passenger seat, curled up as much as the seat belt would allow. She was such an attractive woman and a good investigator and partner. She seemed to like him and their working relationship. He couldn't help but wonder, though, if she was getting involved with one of the local men. She apparently stayed out all night a couple nights ago. That did not bode well for a relationship with him.

"Oh wow; that was close!" he exclaimed. The female deer, apparently a young doe, had seemed to come out of nowhere to run across the road in front of them. Between hitting the brakes hard and swerving the couple feet to the right edge of the road, he'd missed her. It was a close call, though. The sudden lurch of the vehicle had awakened everyone. Both Missy and Becky were a bit wild-eyed for a few seconds as they settled back into their places.

"Maybe what they say in Wyoming is also true of Arkansas," she said. "There are two kinds of drivers. Those who've hit deer, and those who are going to hit deer."

Bert chucked and nodded his agreement. "Well, we just about joined the first group."

"Sometimes you can't help it, no matter how good a driver you are," said Becky. "They just don't give you any option. At least it wasn't a Squatch. Might be harder to miss one of them." She laughed.

"Well, I'll take it a little slower for the last thirty minutes. Don't want to press my luck." He couldn't help but wonder if he was pressing his luck with Becky. He liked her a lot but did not want to seem pushy or presumptive. After such a nice trip, he wondered why his thoughts had turned this direction now that they were almost back to Mountain View. Maybe it was best for now if he went back to being businesslike. Like a boss.

"Tomorrow, let's see if we can find out anything more online about whatever gives a unique quality to that guy's business card. I'll also arrange with Izack Leery to visit his cabin again for an hour or two, if necessary. Hopefully, that'll give Norah enough time to read the psychic winds and maybe come up with something more."

"I think it may be wise for me to interview Anderson McCreedy," said Becky. "If I tell him that I know he was having an affair with Annie, maybe it'll shock him to the point that I can rule him in or out as a suspect. Then we can hopefully eliminate that as a possibility."

Bert nodded in acknowledgement. "You're right about that. We do need to consider if he was aware of her disclosing their secret and angry about it. Angry enough to do something to silence her."

Norah sensed the mixed emotions in her husband. She knew it had to do with Becky, but she wasn't certain how. What she did know, or at least what she felt, was that it would work out okay. At least that's what she hoped.

It was just fully dark when Bert parked the doghouse in their motel parking lot. He asked Becky if she'd like to stop in and have a glass of wine, but she graciously declined, saying she was very tired and wanted to get an early start next morning so she could go with them to the Leery cabin. However, she stepped up to her boss and wrapped her arms warmly and snugly around his waist, giving him an inviting hug as she rested her head on his shoulder for a second. Bert returned her hug with the strong arms of a military man who had been active all his life. She didn't wear perfume, yet he could not help but notice how good her hair smelled.

Norah stood near Missy, smiling at the obvious affection between these two people she cared about. Her psychic soul told her that she made the right choice with Becky.

Bert stepped back and smiled as he thanked Becky, and Norah, for the date. Then he watched as she walked to her room and entered. He turned toward Norah and thanked her for being so understanding. Grabbing Missy's leash, he carried it for insurance as he walked her around the outer perimeter of the parking area. As usual, she was thrilled to be out of the vehicle and back on her turf, where the vermin and small prey lived.

Back in his room, Bert watched the news for a few minutes to see if anything of interest was going on, and then he turned on his computer. Somehow, they had to decipher that business card. The stranger seemed to be an increasingly key suspect in the disappearance of Annabel Leery. Before he went to bed, himself, he would call Izack about going to his cabin sometime tomorrow.

* * *

Back in her room, Becky busied herself getting ready for bed. Hair brushed, teeth brushed, putting on her pajama shorts and short-sleeve top in a matching floral pattern, getting herself a drink of water. She was basking in the glow of a good day. Bert was growing closer to her and Norah seemed to genuinely approve of it. As strange as she found this set of relationships, they also felt like some of the more genuine ones that she had had. Even her growing role as an alpha female to Missy had a good feeling about it.

She was pulling the covers back on her bed when her phone rang.

"Hi, Miss Becky," said Jake. "How about we try this again?"

CHAPTER TEN: SEEKING ANSWERS

Sunday morning came with the glory of a blood red sunrise. It stretched the length of the clear, eastern horizon as Bert led Missy from the outside door of the room and toward the back of the parking area. The Eastern Star was a brilliant white spot a short way above the eastern horizon. He could still easily make out the seven stars of the Big Dipper, with its two end cup stars pointing the way to the North Star at the end of the Little Dipper handle. Also known as Ursa Major, the Great Bear, and Ursa Minor, the Little Bear, they are among the most recognized constellations.

As he walked Missy, he noticed that Becky's truck was still parked where it was last night, but that there was no light in her room window. He found the latter a bit unusual, since she was normally an early riser, like him. However, she did seem tired last night. She was probably just sleeping a bit longer. It was Sunday, so a good reason to sleep a bit longer. He continued to stroll along the perimeter of the lot while Missy sniffed around the various points of interest and marked her territory. After about ten minutes, she trotted over to him as if to say she was done out here and wanted something to eat. With a good rubbing of her coat and a scratch behind the ears, he trotted to their room door and led her inside.

Back in the room, Bert conversed with Norah as he fed Missy and refreshed her water. He decided to walk down the hall to the motel dining area and have a coffee. With a pat on Missy's head and another ear scratch, he opened the door and proceeded to the lobby. As he was walking that direction, Becky walked into view from the lobby. She was wearing a light green sleeveless shirt, tan shorts, and open-toe sandals. She looked very pretty with her sandy blonde hair slightly tousled.

Her cheeks were lightly blushed.

"Hey there, good morning, Becky," he said. "I didn't know if you were up yet."

"Hi, Boss Man. Yeah, I've been up for a little while. Wanted to have a coffee there myself."

"Care to join me? I'd love to have your company."

She smiled. "Yes, I'd love to sit with you. Not sure if I want another coffee or not. How are Norah and my puppy?"

"They're good. Missy had a good walk but didn't find anything to chase or eat. A mixed bag for her. Had to come back to the room for a can of Alpo." He laughed at his untrue reference. Becky knew that he made Missy's food and didn't feed her anything processed.

"So," she said, "I guess this is like a second date; this time for coffee?"

Bert laughed out loud. "I think you could say that. At this rate, we'll be dating before long."

She laughed at that. "Yeah, well, just so you know. I'm not the kind of girl who sleeps her way to the top."

He roared at that, nearly spitting his sip of coffee. "Oh, boy. Unfortunately, there isn't a lot further to go to reach the top in this outfit."

She just smiled. There was another rung on the ladder, and she knew it.

"You know," he said, "I thoroughly enjoyed the trip yesterday and sitting here with you this morning. You're quite a woman, Becky, as well as a big asset to this company."

She smiled, a little red-faced from the compliments. "Thank you, Bert. I am so lucky to be in your company with you, Norah, and Missy. I love you guys and I love what we're doing."

"I, we, love you, too, Becky." He hastened to add "we." He was not sure how far he should go with his deepening feelings for her.

"So, what're we going to do today, since it's Sunday," she asked.

"I've heard that there is a non-denominational, outdoor, service at 10:00 near a local stream and waterfall. Would you like to go with me, us, to that? After that, I'll try to get on Izack Leery's calendar to spend an hour or two at his cabin this afternoon. Maybe you can line up an interview with that Anderson guy for Monday. In between, I'd love to share a glass of wine and lunch with you and brainstorm about the unique business card. I know that makes a sorta day off into a sorta workday."

"I came here with you to work, Bert, and to find Annie. I don't mind working with you. I don't have anything else to do. The service should be interesting and probably beautiful."

He had finished his coffee and offered to walk her to her room. She was happy to accept his gentlemanly gesture. As they approached her door, she looped her arm inside his, a precursor to another increasingly customary hug. She resisted the temptation to throw her arms around his neck and hang a kiss on him. Wanting to didn't mean that she should. She entered her door, agreeing to come to his room in a few minutes after she dressed for the service. They would discuss the business card until time to leave.

With spirits running high, Bert entered his room and knelt to hug Missy and wrestle her playfully for a couple minutes, while chatting with his spirit wife.

Norah easily picked up on his good mood, and she knew why.

168

She smiled as she talked with him, her blue eyes flashing, and her red hair shimmering. She was stunning, as always, trapped in a permanent state of middle-aged beauty.

"Honey," she said, "I keep having a premonition about that business card of the stranger. I see the rectangular outline of a typical card, the fuzzy circular emblem or design within it, and keep hearing the word, 'unique.' What on earth is unique about it? What did Bonnie see and bury deeply in her subconscious?"

"I guess that's one of the questions we have to try to answer, Sweetheart." He looked out the window for a few seconds, looking for answers in the few billowy clouds floating high in the sky. Realizing the time, and knowing Becky would be there soon, he quickly changed into a pair of tan slacks, a short-sleeve, white, pullover, cotton shirt, and a pair of laced, brown, leather shoes.

Norah looked him over and nodded approvingly. "You look very handsome, Honey. No classy woman will be able to overlook you. By the way, Bert, Becky is a very classy woman."

He just cast somewhat nervous glances at her and nodded.

Pulling out his laptop, he began to look for a business card site. Maybe if he could begin to create a card with known features or similarities, he could search for those with the same characteristics. As he was starting to design such a card on one of the seemingly better sites, Becky knocked on their door.

Bert let her into the room, letting out a low whistle. She wore the same black skirt, silver belt, and green silk blouse that she had on the first time he met her at the restaurant in Cheyenne. She was stunning then and she was stunning now. "Wow," he said, "you look gorgeous, Becky. Eye catching to say the least."

She smiled, did a bow, and turned slowly around, as if

modeling the outfit. "Why, thank you, sir. You look pretty handsome, yourself."

He looked at Norah, who just nodded and mouthed, "Wow!"

"I think you'll be my cover this morning," he said. "Nobody is going to notice me with you there. I'll remain anonymous."

They all laughed. Becky gave one of those "Oh, my," kind of looks. "Well, we'll just see about that. Are we going out to the Leery cabin afterwards?" She wanted to get the conversation off herself.

"Yeah, I got hold of Izack last evening," Bert replied. "He'll be ready for us at 1:00 this afternoon. Said we can stay as long as we want and look around all we want."

With that discussion out of the way, they proceeded to discuss the business card question. They all brainstormed to help Bert get the card he was building online as accurate as possible. After fifteen minutes, they stepped back to survey what they had so far. The composite they all agreed upon was a typical rectangular card with a slightly oval circular pattern in the middle and the word "hunt" in the perimeter of the circle. A small antlered deer head was centered inside the circle. It was an African deer, with long curved antlers, to represent exotic prey animals in general. Bert did a Google search for the image, and numerous similar cards came up. However, none of them shed any real light on the actual business they were looking for.

No further along with the business card, they left in the doghouse with Missy in the back seat near Becky. It was just a fifteen-minute drive on this mostly sunny morning to the outdoor service. The natural amphitheater faced the fifteen-foot-wide waterfall and a stone platform. Rows of seats made of native stone formed a semicircle facing both. Sunlight played on the scene, dancing in splashes between the tree leaves as they slowly swayed in the almost undetectable breeze. The seats were almost half full when the team arrived. Bert and Becky took seats on opposite sides of Missy. There were several other dogs and even one cat in attendance, so she was in good company. With her recently brushed coat, Missy drew a lot of attention as looks and quiet whispers flitted from the audience. A man in the row ahead of them turned and chatted with Bert about her. Norah floated around the amphitheater, taking it in and enjoying the beauty.

While he was telling this pleasant and well-dressed fellow about how Missy came to them, another man worked his way over to Becky.

"Well, hello again," Jake Rogers said to her. "I see you've found our little best-kept secret here. You look gorgeous today."

Becky glanced quickly at Bert before answering Jake. "Fancy seeing you here, Jake. How are you this morning?"

It was not lost on Bert that this nice-looking man with black hair, mustache, and black felt hat was talking to Becky. He had a neat appearance with his western cut blue jeans and a short sleeve blue shirt. He was a handsome guy and he obviously knew Becky. Was this the guy she was seeing?

"Bert," Becky said, "This is Jake Rogers. I met him the first day I was here when I was asking for information about Annie."

"So, that's how she met him," thought Bert to himself as he shook Jake's hand.

"Mind if I join you?" asked Jake of Becky.

She nodded okay and he sat down next to her. Missy was showing keen interest in him, and Bert could feel a low growl in her chest. She did not seem to like him. He knew that Missy had good instincts when it came to judging people.

Becky was uncomfortable with Jake sitting beside her, a little too closely. She also could feel the silent rumbling in Missy's chest and sense the subtle change in Bert's demeanor. Her anxiety was thankfully interrupted by the start of the service. For the next hour, they took in the well-done and beautiful service. Afterwards, Becky quickly told Jake good-bye and walked with Bert, Norah, and Missy to the parking lot and the doghouse.

"He seems to be a nice and good-looking fella," said Bert as they walked.

"Yeah, he's okay and very friendly," Becky answered. "Seems to be a nice guy. Anyway, I am hoping that Norah will pick up on more leftover vibes out at the Leery cabin. We can head out there now, I guess?" She wanted to change the subject from Jake.

"Yes, we'll head that way now. We're a little bit early but that'll let us have a relaxing and slow drive and enjoy the scenery." Bert knew that Becky was nervous about Jake's showing up. He let her change the subject, but it didn't stop him from wondering just how involved she was with Jake.

They all made casual small talk about the Ozarks and what they thought of the area as they drove to the Leery's cabin. Extending from Interstate 40 across central Arkansas and north to Interstate 70 in central Missouri, the Ozark Mountains covered the northern half of Arkansas, the southern half of Missouri, western Oklahoma, and extreme southeastern Kansas. The Boston Mountains of Arkansas and the St. Francois Mountains of Missouri are the two major ranges within the Ozarks. The highest point is Buffalo Lookout in

Arkansas' Boston Mountains. There are approximately 47,000 square miles in the Ozarks. Plenty of room for a cryptid to hide and thrive. Springfield, Missouri bears the nickname, "Queen City of the Ozarks," and shares the tourism traffic along with such cities as Branson, Missouri; Fayetteville, Arkansas; and St. Louis. Smaller communities also capture and promote the Ozark Mountain hill, craft, and music culture. These are mountain towns, such as Mountain Home, Eureka Springs, Marshall, Clinton, Greers Ferry, Heber Springs, and Mountain View. Besides mountains, wilderness, and agricultural lands, the region is known for its water resources, which include Bull Shoals Lake, Norfolk Lake, Greers Ferry Lake, and the Buffalo River.

They had about exhausted their collective knowledge of the region when the Leery cabin came into view. Izack met them near the front gate of the decently maintained yard. His greeting was warm and friendly, though he was surprised to see Becky.

"Well, Miss Becky Thompson, what are you doing here?"

Bert and Becky both realized that he was not aware that they worked together.

"We owe you an explanation, Izack," said Bert. Becky is a member of our team, but we decided that, for a short while, we would keep her separate to give ourselves another option in dealing with people here."

Izack let out a low chuckle and nodded. "So, that explains why you grilled my ass when you interviewed me a couple days ago. You really are an investigator. Guess you got one over on me." He laughed a seemingly good-natured laugh.

Becky gave him a big smile, the kind that would melt the coldest heart. "Yeah, I was a little hard on you. I'm sorry about that." She extended her hand in greeting.

"Ah, well, no harm done. So, now that y'all are here, let me give ya the run of the place. I'm almost afraid to hope that you guys might find out what happened to Annie. By the way, what kind of animal is this?" He pointed his thumb at Missy.

Bert waved that question off to Becky, figuring it was time for her to show off her knowledge of their coywolf companion. She smiled broadly at him, then proceeded to give Izack the thorough run-down about both the coywolf hybrid and Missy, in particular. When she had finished, he was obviously impressed. Norah was close to Bert, and she was smiling at how well Becky knew their canine tracker.

"Amazing!" Izack exclaimed. "I didn't know a thing about those critters. Well, let 'er run around as much as she wants. My chickens are all cooped up so not a problem. Y'all are welcome to walk and look around as much as you need."

Bert watched as Norah was already doing just that. She was slowly moving along the back of the house and toward the barn, about two-hundred feet from the rear of the house. He knew she was reading the tea leaves, trying to channel the residual energy left by a woman who was last there two years ago. He wanted to give her the freedom to move at her own pace, so he asked Izack if they could look inside the house. With a wave of his hand, Izack invited Bert and Becky inside.

Bert noted that Izack was a reasonably decent housekeeper. The place was clean, dishes were washed, and his bed was roughly made. There were no obvious signs of Annie other than several pictures of either her or them together. The impression given was that of a man who hadn't forgotten his wife.

Becky looked around the house, not particularly expecting to find anything significant. Mostly, she was listening to Izack, allowing her own empathic gift to once again size him up. She quietly absorbed his dialect, tone, and emotion, striving to read his sincerity. She was also a clairsentient, having the ability to sense the presence of other entities, such as ghosts. If Annie was dead and her ghost was hanging around the cabin, Becky wanted to perceive the presence. After almost 45 minutes of drifting room to room and discussing anything that might pertain to Annie, Becky came to the same conclusion she had reached earlier with Izack. He was being honest with them. And, Annie's ghost was not at home.

She looked at Bert, made eye contact and shook her head. He caught her meaning. There was nothing new here. Annie was still gone, and there was no trace in her house about what happened to her.

Bert told Izack that they would like to see the outbuildings next. He and Becky followed their host outside and around back toward the small barn and attached chicken coop. Both structures were well made and maintained for their usual purpose. That was to be expected of a carpenter, Bert knew. He did make note of a large oak tree along the path and about twenty feet from the barn. It was big enough to conceal a large man from anyone walking toward the barn. The rose bush next to it would add additional cover for a would-be assailant.

The chicken coop had an enclosed yard, roughly twenty by twenty feet, and an entry gate which was lockable from both outside and inside by a large hook and eyebolt on both sides. He saw that it was just barely possible to latch and unlatch the hook on the outside from inside the yard. Someone could enter the yard, latch the outside hook, and hide inside the coop itself, waiting for a victim to enter. There were at least two logical places for an attack to occur.

The remaining tour was uneventful. Neither Bert nor Becky

perceived any additional clues or revelations which might shed light on Annie's plight. Bert noticed that Norah was done with her investigation and was back near their vehicle. He thanked Izack and told him that they would do their best to find out what happened to his wife. As he was saying good-bye, Izack held onto Becky's hand for almost a minute. He had the look of a man who was beaten and alone as he told her that he believed if anyone could find Annie, she and her team could.

Bert could see that his pretty investigator had made an impression, obviously a favorable one, on this man. Not just with her looks, but with her aura of confidence and competence. Izack trusted her and believed she had a good chance of solving the case. As they walked back to their vehicle, Bert reached out, took Becky's hand for just a couple of seconds, and squeezed it gently. "You're doing fantastic, Miss Becky Thompson," he said.

The drive back to Mountain View was enlightening and cathartic. Bert told his ladies about his assessment of the couple of places where an assailant might have assaulted Annie. He described how he thought someone could have used the cover of the big oak to get behind Annie and launch a surprise attack as she walked to the barn or coop.

Becky enthusiastically described her empathic evaluation of Izack and how she felt that he was being honest and sincere with them. She repeated her belief that he was also a victim and had nothing to do with his wife's disappearance.

Bert knew that Norah was patiently waiting to share her insights. "I think you picked up on some more leftover energy there, didn't you?" he asked.

"I believe so, Honey," she answered. "I continue to see her feet, walking toward their barn, I think. But during the sensation

176

of being grabbed from behind, I saw what seemed to be a black hand slamming over her face, over my face. It seems to be a dark glove, I think, possibly one soaked in something designed to make her go unconscious. I just feel grabbed and then have a split-second glimpse of this hand going over her face, it feels like it's my face. Then the vision went blank. It was all so fast and then it was gone, Bert." Norah began to sob quietly.

Bert sat quietly absorbing Norah's visions. After a minute, he said, "So, it seems that we can rule out the Sasquatch theory, at least for now. What you've described sounds very much human."

Norah replied a bit hesitantly, "Yes, Honey, I think it was a human hand, but since it was a dark, almost blurry, hand and happened so fast, I can't say for absolute certainty, guys."

"A hand over her face, covering her eyes, and a choke hold could account for her seeming to go unconscious so quickly," said Becky. "A Squatch still could be a remote possibility, though a human seems more likely."

"What do you two see as the probability that a human took Annie? Seventy per cent, eighty per cent?" asked Bert.

Norah didn't hesitate. "Ninety per cent likely a human."

"Eighty to ninety per cent that a human was involved," said Becky.

"I agree with you ladies," Bert said. "So, for now, unless additional information comes along, let's put the Squatch theory on the back burner and consider the abductor to be human, probably a man. Let's focus on that."

"And, if we happen upon a Squatch somewhere along the way, let's neek up on him and get a picture," laughed Becky. "Maybe we can prove the existence and become famous."

They all had a good laugh about that reference to Becky's earlier joke. As they drove along the curving road back toward town, Norah suddenly turned sideways in the passenger seat. "I'm feeling the sensation of moving, but in the dark. Totally dark. I feel movement, as if I'm in a vehicle, but in total darkness. It's as if she was in the trunk of a vehicle along this road. Or, maybe she was bound and blindfolded."

"All the more reason to figure out who that strange guy was that night. More and more clues seem to point his direction. We've got to figure out that card," said Bert. "It could be the key to determining what happened to Annie."

Norah faced forward and seemed to be looking into empty space. Something had been said which was beginning to tickle her sensibilities. What was it?

They arrived back at their motel. It was about 4:00 in the afternoon. The partly cloudy day was turning hot, with the local bank showing a temperature of 96 degrees.

"Give me a few minutes to change into some shorts and I'll be right over," said Becky. Her dress from the service was nice but not ideal for hot weather. She popped out of the doghouse and walked briskly to her room. Bert, Norah, and Missy went into their room, where Bert dressed down into a pair of shorts and a cotton T-shirt. He gave Missy her evening feeding, a little early.

As she was changing in her room, Becky's phone rang. It was Jake Rogers calling again.

"Hey, there. I told you I was persistent," he said. "It was good seeing you this morning. Thought I'd try you again if you're willing."

Becky talked with Jake for about ten minutes, then told him she needed to talk with her boss. She hung up and went down the hall to Bert and Norah's room.

She spent the rest of the evening with Bert, Norah, and Missy in their room. They discussed her youth to some extent, and Bert was highly interested in knowing how she grew up. Missy was also, apparently, since she kept coming to Becky and laying her head on Becky's legs, looking at her with her big brown eyes. Four or five minutes of petting and ear and tummy scratching would satisfy her coywolf needs and she would go back to the cool bathroom floor.

The talk kept coming back to the stranger and his business card. What was it going to take to find out who he was? They felt so close to cracking the mystery of his card, and yet the undefined wording continued to elude them.

When 7:30 rolled around, Becky said she was going to go back to her room. She thought she might try to relax with a movie. Possibly, there might be a movie at the one theater in town. That could be a worthwhile way to relax, she told Bert. They arranged to meet in the morning around 7:00 for coffee in the motel dining room. After that, they would try to figure out anything else they could about that stranger. Perhaps Monday would be the day when his identity became clearer.

Missy rubbed against Becky's legs and around her, nipping and licking at her toes. Becky laughed and giggled as she tried to save her feet from the coarse wet tongue. Bert gave Becky his customary warm hug before she left his room. It felt good to hold her close for just those couple of seconds, and yet he felt compelled to let go and step back. A stumbling block was between them and he just could not quite understand it. Was it something? Or someone? He watched her walk down the hall to her room before closing his door and returning to Norah and Missy.

In her room, Becky picked up her purse, slipped on her sandals, and left her room by the outside door. She just needed to get out for a little while. What she really wanted still felt like it was in the distance, not close. Maybe she was destined to have only her second choices. She picked up her phone and looked at the time.

CHAPTER ELEVEN: A UNIQUE DAY

Bert had found a walking trail on the outskirts of town during an online search for parks and paths. The sun was just peering over the eastern mountains as he and Missy departed the doghouse and chose one of three available trails. She excitedly raced circles around his legs, yapping and whining with anticipation. Her summer coat was sleek from his earlier brushing and it shone in the first rays of the morning. As they started up the most secluded-appearing trail, one listed as a two-mile hike, the happy canine sprinted ahead about a hundred yards, then came racing back to bump against his legs while excitedly yapping. She dropped her chest to the ground, with her rear end up and tail swinging low to the ground, eyes flashing and tongue panting. She was overdue a good walk and letting her alpha male know it. The second he started toward her, she jumped up on all fours and sprinted off again. This exercise was repeated and again over the next five minutes of the brisk walk. It was not interrupted until a fox squirrel began chattering at her from a tall oak tree, its red hue flashing in the occasional ray of sunshine that sneaked below the canopy of leaves.

Missy circled the tree, searching above for her irritated spectator. The squirrel circled the trunk of the big tree, about fifteen feet above Missy, keeping almost out of her sight, but not quite. It proved to be a grand standoff for about five minutes before Missy tired of the game and followed Bert on down the trail. There must be bigger fish to fry on down the trail.

The half-hour hike ended back at the doghouse as the sun was fully above the horizon. Missy jumped immediately into the doghouse and drank feverishly from her bowl of water, happy to relieve the thirst from the already-warm morning.

Bert drove the ten minutes back to the motel, with his mind on the attractive blonde woman just down the hall. He was already looking forward to meeting her for coffee. And looking forward to figuring out who that stranger was.

In the room, he chatted with his spirit wife for several minutes while feeding and brushing the seeds and twigs from Missy's coat. Norah remained as before, the apparition of a cute and bubbly redhead, linked to him by a bond of love and devotion.

"You better go meet up with Becky for coffee," she said. "She's probably waiting down there for you." Norah, of course, knew that Becky was there, having a coffee while anticipating Bert's arrival.

"I really love and adore you, Norah," he said. "What would I do and be without you. I hate to think about that." He smiled and waved at her as he exited the room and walked toward the dining area.

"Without me," thought Norah, "you'd be free to follow your heart. With me here, I'm not sure you ever will, my Love."

Becky looked up from sipping her coffee as Bert came into view from the hallway. She had been waiting nearly fifteen or twenty minutes for him and was talking with a tall, slender fellow who was driving the big rig parked in the back of the motel lot. He had been hitting on her and was not overjoyed to have Bert show up. When she stood up and gave Bert a tight hug, the driver realized he was never competition to this strongly build and handsome guy. He soon left after meeting Bert.

Bert sat down and proceeded to fix his coffee. "I'm really sorry to keep you waiting," he said. "Missy needed a good walk and I found a great place for a short hike."

"I know, I missed you," she said. "Been waiting here for hours."

"I've been looking forward to having coffee with you this morning," he replied. "Can I tell you something?"

She nodded.

"Do you remember when we met at the diner in Cheyenne?" he asked. "Was there anything unusual about our chance meeting?"

"Not that I can think of," she said. "I was going to take that day off, but at the last second decided to work when one of the other waitresses called in sick. If not for that, I might not have met you. I've thought a lot about that, but it didn't seem unusual, just one of those twists of fate that happen. Why do you ask?"

"I don't know how to tell you this, so here goes. It may not have been such a twist of fate. Norah said that she chose you."

Becky sat quietly, somewhat stunned. "She chose me. For what? To work with your business?"

"No, she was match-making. She wanted you for our business, or for me. Somehow, she helped fate bring us together."

Becky just sat silently, taking in his words. So, Norah really did accept her being in their business and having feelings for her husband. She must have known those feelings would be there, eventually. Not only did she accept it, this is what Norah wanted, for Bert. A wave of emotion came over her and tears trickled down her cheeks. How awful it must be, she thought, for Norah's spirit to so love her husband but not be able to have a physical relationship with him. How could she take away a man so loved by his wife's spirit?

"I'm not sure why I felt compelled to tell you this, but I did. I guess I want you to know that Norah totally accepts you, and I want you to know that you're free to follow your own feelings.

Those that aren't related to the business."

"What do you mean?" she asked.

"Well, I know other guys are interested in you. I mean, who wouldn't be? I just want you to know the situation and know that you can date other men or whatever you want. You're not obligated to me for your private life."

"It doesn't matter if other men are interested in me, Bert, unless I'm interested in them. I'm not."

"I thought you were kind of seeing that fellow from the service, Jake."

She smiled. "Well, he'd like to be seeing me. He's made that pretty plain."

"Anyway," he said, "you make your own decisions. Just know that I like you, and not just as an investigator."

Becky looked down at her coffee for a minute, before looking her boss in the eye. "Thank you, Bert, for telling me this. Give me some time to think about everything. For now, I guess I need to help figure out that business card and set up the interview with Anderson."

They walked back down the hall, with Bert stopping at her door to hug her. She went inside her room and sat down on the bed. Why hadn't she thrown her arms around him and kissed him? That's what she wanted to do. What was holding her back? She reached for her phone.

Bert went back into his room and talked with Norah after a brief play and ear scratch with Missy. He did not talk about his coffee with Becky, but Norah could tell that he was conflicted. She knew why.

He studied his wife's spirit as he communicated with her. In death as in life, she was so stunningly charming and pretty, locked in a permanent state of beauty. Her red hair always seemed to shimmer and her blue eyes sparkled. It was impossible to not remain attracted to her and her spirit. Impossible to not feel a sense of loyalty to her. Impossible to not feel guilt for being attracted to another woman.

"Okay, bud," she said. "Enough of this goofing off. Time to get to work and find that mystery man."

He pulled out his laptop. Together they reviewed what they knew so far. And brainstormed about what they still needed to know. What was the business name on that card?

Norah frequently leaned back and closed her eyes. There was something that she was missing. Somehow, she had the feeling that the answer was just out of reach, yet right in front of her.

* * *

Becky got lucky. She managed to contact Anderson McCreedy on the first attempt. He was planning to go by the 4-H building at 11:00, but said he could come in early and have a 10:00 coffee with her. They arranged to meet in a back corner of Ma's Diner.

She checked the time. It was 9:30. Enough time to dress a bit more professionally, with slacks and a short-sleeve shirt. She loved the shorts for dealing with the Arkansas heat, but knew they were a little too casual. The stares from guys did not really bother her, because she knew she had nice legs. Too nice not to look at, she surmised with a smile. She was used to the looks. She took them as compliments, nothing more.

Anderson arrived at the diner about ten minutes late, and Becky was already sipping a cup of java when he strolled in and ordered a coffee. She stood up to greet him and thank him for meeting with her on such short notice.

They made small talk for a few minutes about the hot weather and 4-H. He told her it was almost always hot this time of year, and frequently big storms could spawn severe weather. The 4-H program was common in most of the rural communities, such as Mountain View. Standing for head, heart, health, and hands, the 4-H program was one of the most popular and effective youth training and development programs in the nation. It was geared primarily toward rural youth, and offered a combination of education and hands-on learning.

Then Becky decided it was time to get to the point of her meeting. "Anderson, I know we discussed the Annabel Leery case last week, but I've learned some new information that I want to ask you about." She noticed the slight look of panic which crossed his face before he answered her.

"Umm, okay. I'll do my best," he said with an uneasy smile.

Becky hesitated for just a few seconds. "Sir, I've learned that you were having an affair at one time with Annie, not too long before she disappeared. What do you have to say about that?"

Anderson sat in stunned silence. Her question was reverberating from one side of his mind to the other. Finally, he replied almost under his breath in a near stammer. "Where'd you hear that, Miss Thompson?"

She leaned forward with both arms crossed on the table in front of her. "Mr. McCreedy, you know that I can't tell you my sources. Just trust that they're credible and I believe them. Are you denying it?"

He looked down for a second and then out the window at the passing vehicles on the nearby street. He turned back to Becky.

"No, ma'am, I'm not denying it. It was one of those things that just happened and ended quickly. We both ended it."

"How angry were you at Annie? Did you know that she must have confided in a friend or two?"

"No, I didn't know anyone else knew until right now," he replied.

"Nobody, none of your friends or family, ever brought it up to you?"

"No!" he said emphatically. "I thought she and I were being very discreet about an obvious mistake. I didn't know she told anyone."

"You would have been pretty mad at her if you knew she talked about it with someone, wouldn't you?" Becky asked.

Anderson leaned forward. "Yeah, I would've been upset if I'd known she was talking about it. I didn't want it getting back to my wife. I still don't want it getting back to my wife, Miss Thompson," he said with a rather cold glare.

Becky perceived the veiled threat; however subtle it was made. "Don't worry, Anderson, we have no intention of disclosing your secret as long as it has no bearing on finding out what happened to Annie. So, tell me. Does your secret have anything to do with her disappearance?"

He made a point of looking her squarely in the eyes. "Absolutely not! I did not know she told anyone, so had no reason to be angry with her. That is, until now. Yeah, it upsets and disappoints me, but I did not and would not do anything to her if that's what you're asking."

"That's exactly what I'm asking, Sir," Becky replied in a quiet but firm voice. "This would be a motive that most would accept. So, I'm asking again. Did you do anything to harm

Annabel Leery?"

Again, Anderson was adamant and kept eye contact. "No, ma'am. I did not do anything to hurt Annabel Leery. I'm sorry about whatever happened to her and I have wished her no harm. I hope you find her because she'd erase any doubts that you have about that."

Becky leaned back, took another sip of her coffee, and said nothing for a few seconds. She quietly allowed her empathic personality to read Anderson McCreedy and assess his credibility. After nearly a minute, she concluded that he was being honest with her. There was a hidden dark side to this man, and he might be capable of harm if he'd known about the violation of trust. However, she believed him that he did not know and wasn't involved in Annie's dilemma.

"Anderson, I'm going to believe you. I don't get the sense that you had anything to do with what harm befell Annie. I'm sorry to put you on the spot, but I know you appreciate that I had to ask you. If you remember anything that might help, please let me know."

He was quick to answer. "I will, and thanks for keeping this matter private. I'm sure you know the effect on my marriage if it gets out."

"As long as nothing else comes up, your secret will remain in confidence with me and my team. Just know, though, if we find reason to think you're being dishonest, we'll do whatever is necessary."

"Fair enough," he said. "I'm telling you the truth."

They talked for a few more minutes before he had to go to the 4-H building for a meeting. Becky also wanted to report back to Bert and Norah and see how she might help with finding the stranger's identity. She returned to her truck and drove back to the motel.

* * *

Bert sat in the room's typical swivel, desk chair, one hand scratching Missy's ears, while he talked with Norah. He steadied his laptop on his outstretched legs, still trying to make sense of the mystery man's business card.

"I wonder if there's any connection between Annie's and Debra Trayner's disappearances," Norah said. "Debra's been missing now for four years, apparently without a trace. How sad that two women from this area have vanished like that."

"Yeah, I'm with you there," he replied. "I've been wondering if we should make an effort to look into Debra's case, but Annie has to remain our focus as long as we have any leads at all to follow."

"I know you're right, Sweetheart. I just feel for the Trayner family. How terrible to have no idea what happened to her."

"Honey, I've been studying the list of missing people on the namUS website. The one thing that surprises me is the fairly significant number of young men who've gone missing. You know that women and kids are often abducted into sex or child trafficking. But men aren't normally taken for either, so why are some of them being abducted? For what purpose?"

"Good question," she replied. "We know that some number of people are taken by a parent or other family member, some run away, there are those who want to vanish and change their lives. There are the others, though, who are taken against their will for an unknown reason."

"You're right," he said. "The one best lead we have so far with Annie's disappearance is this strange . . . ." He paused with the knock on their door. Missy jumped up from her nap on the bathroom floor and raced to the door. She knew before Bert opened the door that her other favorite person was outside.

Becky entered and gave her boss a hug and a smile. Then she knelt to hug Missy and try to pet her as the coywolf did the customary circles around her legs and nips at her toes. The rough wet tongue on her toes always made her laugh and giggle.

Bert and Norah listened intently as Becky discussed her interview with Anderson. They agreed that he could go on the back burner unless other information pointed to him. They all felt that the best lead was the stranger and his card. He had to somehow be ruled in or out.

Norah told Bert that she needed their help in resolving a nagging question. She said that something kept tugging at her, something that seemed to involve her partners.

"Was it something that one of us said or did?" asked Becky.

"I think so," said Norah to Bert. "Ask Becky about that joke she told a couple days ago."

"Joke?" he asked. "Do you mean the one about kicking the bear into the hole in the ice?"

He relayed Norah's request and Becky repeated the joke. They all chuckled again. This time, though, there was more focus on the mechanics and words of the joke.

Norah thoughtfully said, "We are looking for a unique business card it seems, and your joke says the word twice. Could there be a subconscious connection going on?"

Bert considered that for a minute, then asked Becky, "In the joke, is the word 'unique' used or spelled the same way both times?"

"I don't think so," said Becky. "I've never seen it written

out, but in my mind I see the second one as something like 'u-neek.' It means you sneak up on the bear."

Norah then interjected, "Maybe that explains why I saw that strange word, neek, recently and had no explanation for it."

"What if the unique that we're looking for is a different spelling of the word, and not the card itself," said Bert. "What if Bonnie's subconscious picked up the word in the split-second glance she had of the card."

"Let's try a search online for it," said Becky, excitedly. "We may be onto something, guys."

Her enthusiasm was catching. Bert went back to his laptop, with Becky hanging on his shoulder, and began a search for "You-neek hunts." Nothing. He entered "U-neek Hunts." He scrolled through several similar sites but found nothing. Norah suggested that he enter that around his business card model and see if a similar image might come up. He did that, and after a few adjustments, a logo came up. It was the logo at the top of a business page in a listing for "Unique and Guided Hunts."

That page did not say much. It boasted of unique hunts for the high-end, qualifying, and discerning hunter. The address was a post office box in Crane, Texas, which Bert saw was southeast of Big Spring. The bottom line said, "Referrals by clients only."

All three of them sat back for a minute, trying to make sense of the page. Finally, Becky was the first to say something.

"What kind of business operates entirely on referrals from previous clients?" she asked.

Norah made a suggestion. "It must be a hunt so unique that they figure the past clients are most likely to know a few others who might be interested. Do not have to advertise or spend money on marketing that way. Once you get started, you let the clients promote your business."

Bert nodded but said nothing for a while, thinking about it all. Eventually, he said, "They deal with 'high-end, qualified' clients. That tells me that they are expensive hunts, probably tens-of-thousands of dollars. They don't need a lot of business. Wealthy hunters are likely to know other wealthy hunters with similar interests. When another is referred, they apparently 'qualify' them in some way."

"Should I text a copy of that logo to Bonnie Shackleford and see if she thinks that's what she saw?" said Becky.

"Great idea," said Bert. "If she believes that's it, then we know we're really onto something." He copied and emailed the logo to Becky so she could pull it into a text for Bonnie.

While his star investigator was doing that, Bert moved onto the middle of the bed, leaned against the headboard with Norah to his left, and continued looking online for any other information on U-Neek Hunts.

After a couple minutes, Becky said she had sent the text and she sat on the bed next to Bert. She intentionally sat lightly against him. An obvious sign of affection, which was not lost on him. It wasn't lost on Norah, either.

"Finding anything, Boss?" Becky asked.

He nodded. "I just found a phone number associated with that business."

"Sweet!" said Becky. "I'm anxious to hear what they say."

Norah said the same thing.

Bert dialed the number.

A recording answered. "You have reached U-Neek Hunts, 12,000 acres of the most exotic and unique hunting opportunities on the planet. Send your serious inquiries to Post Office Box 329, Crane, Texas 79733. Thank you for calling."

Bert hung up his cell phone. "Well, isn't this interesting. Nobody answers and you can't leave a message. Looks like the only way to contact them is to write them. Rather unusual in this electronic age."

"Almost seems like they don't want . . . excuse me, that's Bonnie calling me back." She answered her phone, putting Bonnie on speaker.

Bonnie said hello and then excitedly told them that this was the logo she saw on the card. As soon as she saw it, she knew that was it. They continued to talk for another ten minutes, discussing any other memories she might have about the stranger as well as finding out how she was doing. She was a very pleasant lady to talk with. Bert thought to himself that she was a fantastic representative of her black heritage; pretty, intelligent, and charming. He asked her to please stay in touch with them. She happily accepted the invitation.

After hanging up from the call, Bert asked, "Well, my ladies, it looks like we've finally identified the card and business. We still don't know the stranger, though, and how he's related to it. What do you think? Do we focus on this lead now?" He wanted to know their opinions.

Norah spoke to him first. "Yes, Honey, I have the growing sense that we're on the right track with this."

"Yes, I think so," said Becky. "There are other possibilities, I know, but this feels like the most likely. I vote for pursuing U-Neek Hunts and see where it leads us."

He was not surprised by their unanimous conviction. It was his own opinion, as well. It was the most promising lead they had for finding out what happened to Annie. They needed to update their clients before taking the next move. He dialed Billy's number.

After arranging to meet with both Billy and Bobby in two hours, at 6:00 P.M., he turned back to his two girls. "Are you ready to go to Texas?" he asked.

Becky's eyes lit up like diamonds. "Oh my, yes, Boss, yes. I've never been to the Lone Star state and I am ready to go. When do we leave?"

Missy raised her head from the bathroom floor with an inquisitive look, while cocking her head from side to side. She could tell from Becky's voice that something exciting was in the works.

Norah was also enthusiastic about a change of scenery. "I'm with you guys all the way. I have a positive feeling about this, though also a bit of apprehension. I'm feeling a sense of danger and fear, too."

Bert knew immediately that when Norah sensed danger there was reason to heed her concern. He also knew that if she sensed danger then this was probably the right way to go. "Let's plan to leave in the morning around 8:00, assuming our clients are okay with it." Becky got up to go to her room before their meeting with Billy and Bobby. Bert walked with her down to her door.

"Becky," he said softly, "If you'd prefer to stay here and be our Arkansas point woman for our clients, you may. I just want you to know that."

She looked at him, puzzled. "Why would I want to stay behind, Bert?"

He took a low breath, hoping he would not sound stupid. "I know you might want to stay around here for a while, to see how things go here." Yeah, he thought, that does sound a bit stupid.

She was not sure what to say so just managed an, "Okay, I'll think about it." She went into her room, feeling a little confused. 'What's going on with him?" she wondered aloud.

Sitting on her bed, Becky tried to understand the sudden offer from her boss. "Does he want me to stay behind, and not go?" Then she began to realize that he must think she has a thing going with Jake. "Why would he think that? Does he think I've been seeing Jake?" Slowly, she began to realize something.

About ten minutes after walking Becky to her room, there was a knock at Bert's door. Opening it, he was surprised to see Becky so soon.

"Bert, can I talk with you for just a second out here?" she asked.

"Sure," he replied. Walking out and closing his door.

She stood in front of him, looking him in the eyes. "I want you to know two things, because I think you might misunderstand. Last Thursday night, I went to my room and spent the night there, trying to figure out this case until I got tired. I left early Friday morning to go to Benton and interview Bonnie. It was well before sunrise; before you walked Missy, I suspect. You would not have seen my truck parked outside. The second thing is this. Jake has been trying to get me to go out with him for several days, but I've declined every time. He's a nice guy, I think, though a bit of a playboy. However, I'm not interested in him, Bert."

"Okay, I guess maybe I did misunderstand that," he said, somewhat sheepishly.

"You should know, though, that I'm interested in someone

else, Bert," she said.

"Oh, ah, okay."

"And I want to go on this trip to Texas with him, Bert. Okay?"

He realized what she was saying. "Okay, Becky, great! I'm glad." He knew he might be a bit red-faced, with a touch of the school-boy love-bug tempered by adult reality. He wrapped his arms around her and hugged her tightly for several seconds. She felt and smelled so good that he hated to let go, back away, and go back toward his room. Right now, though, they needed to get ready to meet with their clients.

As he opened his door, he knew that, somehow, he had to find his way past the guilt he felt with Norah. The guilt from knowing he was falling in love with Becky.

He closed his door and walked over to the bed to look at the beautiful spirit of his wife, stunning and charming as always. He would forever be in love with her; with her memory.

Norah smiled at him. "It's all going to work out okay, Honey," she said, as if she read his mind. He knew it should not surprise him. She was psychic, after all. And, she chose Becky for a reason.

* * *

Bert, Becky, and Norah were in Ma's Diner when Billy and Bobby entered and joined them. The diner owners were okay with Missy accompanying them on a leash. So, she dozed contentedly between Bert and Becky, occasionally raising her head or flicking her ears to let them know she was aware of all going on around her. Over the next two hours of supper and talk, Bert and team brought the clients up to speed on the progress of their investigation. They encountered a little resistance at first when Izack came up for discussion. Billy did not want to let go of his belief and hatred for the man he thought had done something to his surrogate mother and aunt. However, in the face of strong arguments from both Bert and Becky, he had to finally acknowledge that maybe he was wrong about Izack. In any case, both men said they wanted the truth and whatever chance it might bring of finding Annie.

The clients were especially interested in the Texas hunting business and the sleuth work that led to it. They were totally supportive of further investigation down there and wanted to be kept abreast of any developments. If possible, they both wanted justice for Annie. Billy made it clear to Bert that revenge was okay, too. Bert told them the team was leaving in the morning and he would report back every evening about their findings.

After departing, Bert drove his team back to the motel. All three walked with Missy around the parking area and adjoining lot, while she marked her territory about a dozen times and searched a couple of brush piles. Norah remained nearby while Bert hugged Becky and told her they would be ready to go by 8:00.

Bert and Norah went to their room, while Becky took Missy with her for the night. Both were excited about sharing the room.

Becky put on her pajamas and readied for bed while alternatively playing with her coywolf companion. As she brushed her teeth, climbed into bed, and stroked Missy's head where she lay beside the bed, Becky was trying to grasp why she had a nagging discomfort with her feelings for her boss. What was it that kept holding her back?

CHAPTER TWELVE: TEXAS

The team of B & N Investigations left Mountain View at 8:10 on Tuesday morning, September 4th, with Becky and Missy following Bert and Norah. It would be about an eleven-hour drive to Big Spring, Texas, where they planned to get rooms for the night. All agreed that it was still wise to have both vehicles along for the additional options that afforded.

Passing through Clinton, they once again stopped at the Rock N Java coffee shop. Becky smiled as she noticed that Bert had a difficult time keeping his eyes off the same girl, with the unusual name of Lake, who had waited on them earlier. She was certainly pretty, thought Becky. When she ordered her drink, she was compelled to compliment Lake, who smiled and thanked her. Becky noticed her sweet and genuine personality as they chatted while the coffees were being made. If Lake was typical, then The Natural State had some beautiful women, both inside and outside. Becky noticed a couple of very nice- and good-looking young guys working there, also. She found out that their names were Dana and Harrison. Okay, there are some nice-looking young men here, too, she thought.

Back on the road, Becky decided to find a radio station and relax her mind with some music. She continued to be tormented by whatever was standing in her way with Bert. The fourth song to be played was one by Bette Midler, "The Rose." Headset on, Becky listened intently to the words. She turned the radio off after the song ended. For several minutes, she followed the words as they played between the synapses of her brain. Finally, she glanced at Missy on the back seat of her truck and turned back to the road. "Bert Lynnes," she said out loud, "I believe that you're my endless aching need. I just have to find a way to deal with the sense of guilt I feel at taking you from Norah's spirit. Losing her physical connection with you must be devastating for her as well as for you. I can't bear the thought of bringing any more pain to her wonderful spirit and memories." She wiped away the tears that began to cloud her eyes and obscure her vision of the long ribbon of highway that stretched out toward an undulating, curving, and unknown future.

Up ahead a couple hundred yards, Bert and Norah cruised toward Little Rock on Interstate 40. He asked Norah if she would mind if he listened to some country music for a little while. She told him that was fine. He found a station out of Little Rock. As he tuned it in, a Travis Tritt song began to play. They listened to the heartfelt strains of lovesickness as "Anymore" played to the end. When it ended, Bert turned off the radio and kept glancing out his driver's side window, hoping Norah wouldn't notice the tears welling up in his eyes. He realized that he could not pretend that he didn't love Becky anymore. Norah knew it, and yet he couldn't bear the thought of loving anyone but her.

He quietly drove in silence until they were nearing the turn onto Interstate 30. At that point, he took the exit for Bass Pro Shop. If he was right about the journey they were embarking upon, he needed a few things.

After giving Missy a quick walk, Becky joined Bert and Norah inside Bass Pro. Following Bert's lead, they bought ghillie suits for him and Becky, and a tactical, camouflaged vest for her. He already had one in the doghouse. At a hardware store a little down the road, he added a 16-inch bolt cutter, large zip ties, and two dozen strips of cloth, about three feet long. He added these to his box of surveillance gear and they headed back down the highway, toward Texarkana and on to Texas. It would be a long drive.

* * *

After a ten-hour drive which took them through Dallas, Fort Worth, and Abilene, the B & N team finally arrived about 7 P.M. in Big Spring. The original home of Webb Air Force Base, those facilities have since been turned into a federal prison. According to some of the pilots that Bert knew who had their training there, the prison was a much more appropriate use of the place. They settled quickly into the Super 8 motel for the night. Becky had a room right next to Bert and Norah's. A quick snack from the cooler would fend off the hunger until morning. After the long drive, they all, including Missy, were ready to stretch out and get some sleep. Tomorrow they'd hit the ground running.

After a good night's sleep, tomorrow showed up at 5:00 A.M., welcomed by a brilliant red sunrise in the dry air of west Texas. Norah accompanied Bert as he took Missy outside for a walk. Becky was also up, and she joined them as they were leaving the motel. She was a morning person just as were Bert and Norah, so they had a lively conversation as they strode around the truck parking area of a nearby gas station. The grandeur of the spectacular sunrise and the cool morning air lifted all their spirits. There was a combined feeling of optimism about making real progress in finding out what happened to Annie.

The optimism was dampened somewhat when Norah confided that she had a dark sense of fear about where the investigation was taking them. "I'm sensing gunshots," she said. "Also, there's something else that I have no explanation for."

"What's that, Honey," Bert asked.

She hesitated for a few seconds before answering him, as if trying to figure it out first. "Well, it's just plain confusing," she said. "I'm seeing pigs, a bunch of pigs, milling around and squealing. It makes no sense, Bert. The vision comes and goes, here for a few seconds and then gone."

"Good grief," he exclaimed. "That's a strange one. Any idea what that might mean?"

"Haven't got a clue, Darling."

Becky was a bit wierded out when Bert told her of Norah's visions. She did not like pigs. One knocked her down when she was little and stepped on her leg. The bruise lasted for weeks. Ever since then, she'd had a phobia about them. "Well, let's just stay away from them, okay."

Bert could see that it bothered her. So, he reassured her that they would do everything possible to avoid pigs. They finished the walk, taking turns playing with Missy. She loved to run around just out of reach, yapping and dodging them as they tried to catch her. It was grand fun for about five minutes, but they had to get serious and get back to the motel, get some breakfast, and get started on some serious investigation. Besides that, the sun had climbed above the horizon and the cool of morning was giving way to the heat of high and dry west Texas. The weatherman reported a high of 102 by afternoon.

Daughters, Sandra and Summer, arranged a conference call as Bert's group arrived back at the motel. They wanted to talk with Bert on the two-year anniversary of Norah's death. It was important to them to remember the day, and have their own children talk with their grandpa. Norah could hear them and despite her tears she felt good about her children remembering her. It was a moving phone call and touched Bert's heart. Becky, likewise, was moved to tears. After hanging up, everyone went inside and got ready for breakfast.

They had breakfast at the motel's dining room and made plans. All agreed that the first order of business was to learn as much as they could about U-Neek Hunts. That assumed there would be information an hour-and-a-half from the place.

"Becky, how about you ask around at the post office, game and fish office, and anywhere else you think. I'll see what a couple of sports and gun stores might tell us. Let's meet back up at the motel at 11:00. After that, we'll drive to Crane."

"You bet, boss man. What's our pretext going to be?"

"Let's tell them that you have a banker friend in Billings who may be interested in going on a hunt there and asked you to find out a little about them before he contacts them. He knew you were going to be down here for a couple days."

"Aye, aye, Captain Kangarooski," she said with a smile.

Norah smiled. She had done well in choosing Becky. She even had some of the same little mannerisms as herself. She looked at Bert. "Honey, I'm feeling a lot of fear about this. I believe we're on the trail of what happened to Annie, and if I'm right, this will be a dangerous mission. We have to be careful with Becky and not endanger her unnecessarily."

He grew somber. When Norah sensed fear or danger, he knew to believe her. She had always been right, so far. His guidance to Becky had to be measured to not bring suspicions to her.

"Becky, if anyone asks more questions, tell them your Banker friend is both wanting a phone number for the business to maybe line up a hunt, but he's also looking to invest if the property seems to his liking. He wants to remain anonymous for now."

"Aye, aye, boss," she replied. Pretexts were a legal white lie with the intent of investigating while deflecting attention from the investigator. She knew that and knew that Bert wanted to make sure she was protected.

Becky hopped in her truck with Missy while Bert and Norah headed out in the doghouse.

* * *

By 10:30 they were all back in the motel lobby. Bert was unsure if they would have much success getting information in this different county, and they did not. Becky had found one fellow at the local fish and wildlife office who was aware of the hunting business, but he had no useable intelligence about it, other than the place was very "secretive."

A gun store owner told Bert that he knew of the hunting club, but that it was very "high end" and "tight lipped." He told Bert that two hunters who entered his store the past couple of years had arrived in private jets. They both mentioned that they were going to U-Neek Hunts.

"It's about an hour-and-a-half drive on to Crane," Bert said to the ladies. "Let's grab a sandwich at the Sonic and eat while we drive down there. I'll give Missy a snack of jerky."

Soon, lunch in hand, the team and both vehicles were headed westerly on Interstate 20 toward Odessa. There, they turned south on US Highway 385 toward Crane and oil country. Crane was the only town in and the county seat of Crane County and had been at the center of the oil boom since about 1920. The population density of the county was less than two people per square mile. Combined with the rugged landscape, it seemed like an almost perfect place for a remote and discreet hunting property.

It was almost 2:00 when they arrived in Crane that Wednesday afternoon, September 5th. Bert and team had already discussed their game plan. He parked in the shade on a side street so it would be more comfortable for Missy. Following her brief walk on a vacant lot, Bert went to the County Courthouse. Becky headed for the Post Office.

At the Courthouse, Bert asked for the public records and plat related to the Hunt business. While the clerk was a bit reluctant at first, the pretext explanation of a possible investor relaxed her caution. She gave him a copy of the plats which showed the almost nine square miles, also called sections, of the ranch. On them, he was able to locate the ranch headquarters, which sat about two miles south of the northern-most property section. This looked to be almost fifteen miles southeast of the town.

He left and drove to the Crane County Airport. There, he purchased a visual flight rules aeronautical chart. It showed topographical features and, in combination with the plats, gave him a decent picture of the geographical area of the ranch. Leaving the airport, he called Becky and arranged to meet her at the Crane County Park near the swimming pool.

She arrived about ten minutes after Bert and Norah and parked next to the doghouse. They all exited and gave Missy a walk around the park. She was not a fan of her leash, though she obeyed it, but in town it was a necessity for a coyote-looking animal. While they walked, they discussed the case.

Becky brought them up to speed on her trip to the post office. "There was one woman I bumped into who drove the mail route that served the U-Neek Hunts ranch," she said. "This lady confided that a James, or Jamison, McDougal owned the property. She said she had only met him one time and he was not very pleasant. Said very few people in the area know him or anything about his business. She said she'd love to see anyone else buy the ranch."

"Good job, girl," said Bert. "My impression at this point is that trying to arrange a visit would be fruitless, even if we can find out how to contact him. Seems like we're going to have to get creative if we're to figure this out."

Norah had been listening quietly. Finally, she moved close to Bert. "Honey, since we've arrived here, my feelings have grown stronger. I'm not sure what they're telling me yet, but it feels like this is where we need to be if we're to find out what happened to Annie. I have this overpowering sense that the ranch here is somehow connected to her disappearance."

After Bert shared those feelings with Becky, she walked along quietly for a minute. Then, she told them, "Guys, I've learned that Norah's visions and sensations are a key part of our investigation strategy. I believe in her and if she thinks there's a connection here, then we need to pursue it. Besides that, I also have the feeling that there's something here. Whatever it takes to find Annie, or find out what happened to her, count me in."

Bert thought about what they had said. He also had sensed a pull to this place and was thinking about what it might take to investigate that theory. That's what induced him to buy the things he did before they left Little Rock. As a former Army Ranger, he was used to making hard decisions and doing creative things to further the mission. The clients were the same kind of people. They wanted answers about Annabel.

"Becky, can we pile in your truck and drive out by the ranch entrance and check out the area?" he asked. "A pickup will be less noticed than my SUV might be. The lay of the land will dictate how we may have to proceed."

Becky smiled and nodded. "Yeah, for sure, boss. Hop in and we can head out." She loved this man, but when it came to business, she knew he was all business and he was the boss.

Bert climbed in the front passenger seat while Norah entered the back seat with Missy. He studied both sets of charts for a few minutes so they could find the main road to the ranch. Satisfied that he knew the way, they headed out of town on a two-lane road. The sun was sinking in the western sky, so they did not have a lot of time before darkness.

After five miles, the road became a one-lane oil road and then soon turned into packed dirt and gravel for the final several miles as it wound through the hills, bluffs, and arroyos. The cactus plants, yucca, mesquite trees, and sparse brown vegetation were stark reminders of the dry, arid, and harsh land through which they traveled. A few oil or gas wells loomed nearby. Nothing hinted at a high-end hunting property.

Finally, after nearly 30 minutes of driving from the town, they came to a traditional but well-built barbed wire fence attached to both ends of a chained and padlocked gate made of welded 3-inch pipe and painted dark green. Next to the gate was a nondescript black mailbox with the white numbers 329 on both sides. On both sides of the gate was a "No Trespassing" sign.

"Well, they certainly are skilled at looking like just another ranch, except for the impassable gate," Becky said.

"Uh-huh," Bert replied. "Just like any ranch except for the locked gate that could stop a small armored vehicle. This place has something to hide. I can feel it."

Norah had not said much for the last ten miles. She just remained in the back seat, occasionally glancing at the hairbrush which Billy Joe had given them. Annabel Leery's hairbrush, now laying on the console in a plastic sandwich bag. Bert knew that she was reading the psychic tea leaves. He also knew that was the time to let her be and not interrupt her thoughts.

After they passed the ranch entrance and proceeded to the

west and then a ninety-degree turn south in half a mile, she finally spoke up. "Annie was, or is, here, guys. I can sense her."

Bert was not surprised by Norah's revelation. Becky nodded and mouthed a "wow." She was still learning about Norah's gift and the certainty of perception did amaze and surprise her a little. "So," Becky continued, "Now that we have reason to believe that Annie could be here, how do we do this? The only way we have to contact the owner is by email, and the place is locked up tighter than Fort Knox with 'No Trespassing' signs on display. Do we see if the local sheriff can get us access?"

Bert shook his head. "That seems like a good idea, except that he, or she, is not likely to believe us. We have virtually no hard evidence to present, and only psychic premonition to base our conclusion or suspicion upon. Almost zero chance of any lawman, especially a west Texas, small-town, sheriff, giving us any credibility. Most would tell us to get lost."

He looked at Norah. She gave a half-hearted smile and nodded reluctantly. She knew the situation they almost always faced during an investigation. For every blessing there is an associated curse. Her gift could provide insight that no amount of legwork could obtain, but the curse was in rarely receiving credible consideration from the law.

"I know you have a plan, Bert," said Becky. "So, how do we do this?"

He frowned slightly with lips somewhat clenched. "I don't see any way to legally go any further."

She looked at him with bewilderment showing in her face. "So, are you saying that we give up and go home?"

He shook his head and looked into her inquiring blue eyes, briefly getting sidetracked by her attractiveness. Getting back on point, he said, "I don't see a way to legally do this. I may see a way to put ourselves and our company on the line and do it illegally."

"Oh, I see what you're saying," Becky answered. "So, you want to know if I'm still in? The answer is Yes, I'm with you all the way. I'm dedicated to finding out what happened to Annie."

Bert expected her answer. "We have the interests of our clients to hold us," he said. "They want us to find out what happened to this young woman, mother, and aunt. On the other hand, if we do this we can't tell them until it's over. We do not want to pass liability on to them, so we cannot tell them what we're about to do. It's going to be on us if it goes to hell in a hand-basket."

Norah nodded in unison with Becky. They did not yet know the plan, but they knew it would be risky. Bert was not a talker; he was a doer. Give him a job to do and he would find a way to do it.

They continued down the dirt road, looking for ideas. The road was desolate and they were the only vehicle in sight. Bert asked Becky to stop along the road. He asked her to accompany him and let Missy out. Norah would remain next to them. They walked briskly to the top of a small hill on the right side of the road. He had brought his binoculars and stood surveying the area to the east, toward the ranch. After a minute, he handed the binoculars to Becky and directed her gaze toward a dip in the distant ridge. Just above it you could make out the tips of treetops.

"There's the ranch headquarters," he said. "I think I'd be able to get a good look at it from somewhere on that ridge."

Becky studied it for a minute. "Yes, I bet you could. You'd be trespassing to get there, though, wouldn't you?"

He nodded. "Yup, like I said, there's no way to legally do

this. So, we have to look at plan B."

"That's why you bought the ghillie suits, isn't it?" she said. "Plan B."

Bert smiled at her and nodded. "Military and Ranger mentality," he said. "Let's see where we could park this vehicle so it's not too conspicuous."

They made a mental note of this spot on the road, which could be easily identified by an odd stack of rocks near the top of the hill they had looked from. Glassing on ahead, Becky was first to spot what looked like a side dirt road off the right side, away from the road they were on. Everyone returned to her Ram truck and they eased on south until reaching the side road. It was about a half mile from the hill they had stood upon, and it seemed to be an old trail which was not used much. It curved around a small rocky hill, which took it out of sight of the more traveled road they were on. For a short time, they might be able to keep the Ram out of sight of any passers-by. It would be a bit of a walk to get back to the first observation point, though. However, if they stayed on the west side of the hills, the walk would be mostly out of the sight of anyone driving the main dirt road.

Bert asked if the ladies saw any place nearer the truck where Becky could be undetected and yet see the ridge to the west of the ranch headquarters. After checking out a couple of possible hides, they settled on a large boulder which stood mostly upright and about seven or eight feet tall. There were several large cacti and a few yucca plants between there and the road, which was roughly 200 feet down the shallow hillside. It could offer some degree of shade, depending upon which side of the boulder she stood or sat beside. By moving slightly, Becky would have several clear views of the ridge where Bert was hoping to be.

The cool of darkness was soon to replace the heat of daylight, so the team returned to the truck and retraced their steps toward Crane. Missy stayed in Becky's truck while Bert and Norah got in the doghouse. They had already discussed going to Odessa for the night. There was a motel in Crane, but Bert didn't think it was a good idea to be more noticeable in this small town. There could be local support for the ranch, and he did not want to tip them off to the investigation. It was only a half-hour drive to the anonymity of the larger city.

The drive to Odessa passed quickly, with everyone thinking about the next day. At the motel, the discussion ensued over supper in Bert's room. He began by reviewing his plan for checking out the ranch. Becky would drop Bert and Missy off at sunrise by the first point they had picked. While he and Missy began their stalk toward the ridge above the ranch headquarters, Becky and Norah would take the truck to the side road hiding spot, and then they would take up a vantage point by the second point with the tall stone. Becky would be in her ghillie suit, the same as Bert, and should be hidden from any traffic on the dirt road. Bert suggested that she wear lightweight workout clothing to help stay more comfortable in the heat of the Texas day, made the worse by the ghillie suit. Her main job was to watch for anyone who might see or threaten Bert and notify him by the walkie talkies they would each carry. Both would be as discreet as possible by using an earpiece and a small boom microphone which would allow them to whisper, if necessary. They both would need to carry several quarts of water and some jerky, since they would probably be there all day. Becky would carry binoculars and her concealed handgun with one extra magazine. Bert would carry a small bowl in his camouflaged pack to give water to Missy. Her training would be put to the test because he needed to control her every movement so they would not be detected.

Bert packed his bag as they were talking and offered advice to Becky for doing her pack. He checked out his pistol and packed two extra magazine clips of ten rounds each, along with his military combat and survival knife. After considerable thought, he finally decided to carry his AR-15 rifle, inside a lightweight, camouflage, tear-resistant gun bag, along with two 25-round magazines. The rifle was chambered for the .243 cartridge and had an adjustable sniper scope and a silencer. This operation would be risky and he needed to be prepared for anything. A small pair of hunting binoculars, the bolt cutters, zip ties, and a dozen pieces of cloth strips rounded out his gear. He didn't expect to need most of the equipment for this initial surveillance but decided to take it in part to refine his plan for the next phase.

Norah had the ability to be near both Bert and Becky, in her spirit realm. Bert asked her to spend most of her time near Becky so that she could tell him the details if anything happened to Becky. If he needed her, he would summon her.

With the plan worked out, it was time to get some rest. They would need to leave the motel an hour before sunrise. Bert gave Becky his usual hug, though with a firmer embrace.

"This will be a big day tomorrow in the search for Annie," he said to her. "I'll be counting on you to keep me out of trouble. While staying out of trouble, yourself."

"I won't let you down, Bert," she replied. "I'm nervous and a little scared, but I'm also anxious to learn what happened to Annie." She gave Missy one last hug and ear scratch and went to her room.

Bert turned back to Norah. "Well, my Love, our pursuit of the truth about Annabel Leery has brought us from Wyoming to Arkansas and now to Texas. Now, the real investigation begins."

She nodded. "Yes, my Darling. And I'm afraid for you, Bert. I sense danger all over this. You must be incredibly careful. You're the Captain of my ship and I do not want anything bad to happen to you. I love you, Bert."

He nodded and smiled at her with tears welling up in his eyes. "I love you, too, Norah. Always have; always will. I'm nothing without you."

In her room next door, Becky readied herself for bed. Just as she pulled the covers back and turned out the light, she knelt beside the bed, bowed her head, and prayed for Annie. Then she prayed for the man she was falling in love with, and for the spirit of his deceased wife.

CHAPTER THIRTEEN:
A SHOCKING SURVEILLANCE

It was going to be a clear, sunny, and hot Thursday, September 6th, as the team of B & N Investigations left their motel at 5:00 for the half hour drive to Crane. They were with Becky in her Ram truck. If not for the adrenaline of facing a challenging and risky case, they would have been fighting sleep. As it was, Missy was the only one who slept on the drive.

When they reached Crane, they proceeded southeast toward the U-Neek Hunts ranch. It was not long before the rough dirt road reminded them how close they were to both sunrise and to the surveillance of the ranch. Bert was in the backseat and had put on his ghillie suit. His pack and rifle were at the ready. Missy was on the leash and whined in anticipation of something out of the ordinary. Darkness was giving way to the dawn of the sun, still hiding below the eastern horizon.

Bert had pinned the location of his drop-off point on his phone map, and soon spotted the rock formation which marked the spot. There were no other lights to be seen, so Becky stopped to allow him and Missy to disembark.

Bert looked at Norah and mouthed an "I love you, Sweetheart." Then he looked at Becky. The interior light of her truck subdued her blonde hair and blue eyes, but her soft, unsmiling, face left no doubt of her concern and fear. He reached for her hand, held it firmly for several seconds, gently massaging her fingers. Releasing her hand, he put his first and second fingers together, touched his lips, and reached back through the window to touch her lips. With this first kiss, he motioned to Missy and removed her leash, turned, and walked toward the barbed wire fence.

Missy went under the wires while Bert carefully pushed the

third one from the ground far enough down that he could carefully climb through. There was an art to climbing through a barbed wire fence, under the best of circumstances. One skilled in the art could be on the other side within a couple of seconds. That was with typical country clothing of denim pants, boots, shirt, and hat. This skill was mastered by most farm and ranch kids from an early age. Bert was reasonably competent at the art, also. However, his earlier mastery did not include a full ghillie suit. He was acutely aware that one or two wrong or fast moves could have him almost hopelessly stuck in the fence for several minutes, dancing perilously on one leg as he sought to unstick the sharp barbs from arms, legs, and crotch. In the worst case, a careless or impatient person might be caught up like a bug in a spider web. The only thing which might make matters worse would be the approach of a giant arachnid. On this morning, the arachnid would go hungry, as Bert's caution was rewarded with a safe but slow access to the east side of the fence.

On the other side, and now comfortably trespassing, he turned to wave as the Ram truck rolled on down the road. Then, with a deep breath and exhale, he began the slow and methodical walk toward the ridge, about a half-mile away. The orange glow of the rising sun gave an eerie and almost surreal quality to the rough ground.

Using low voice or hand commands, he kept Missy near his left side as he picked his way through cactus, yucca, and scattered rocks. About once a minute, he stopped and surveyed the area in all directions, looking for any signs of human activity. Seeing none, man and animal moved as one toward the uncertainty awaiting them over the approaching ridge.

Back inside the Dodge Ram, Becky had turned off the headlights and drove by the light of dawn, looking for the side road. While she could not see Norah, she could sense her presence, and she knew Norah would be aware of Bert's romantic gesture. Becky couldn't help but feel a sense of betrayal. Could this lovely and loving spirit really accept the taking of her husband. But then again, Bert had said that she chose her.

"Well, here's the road, Norah," Becky said, knowing she would not hear a reply as she turned right onto the old, rough, trail. The Ram truck lurched from side to side as it was eased up the road and out of sight of the main road. Becky parked it when she was sure it was not in sight from that road. She pulled a sheet of paper from her bag onto which she had written a note in large letters. Placing it on her dash in front of the drivers' seat, she stepped outside to make sure she could read it. "Bob, we've gone a little way into the hills to see if the big ones are there. Be back soon, Beck."

"I think that should make any visitors think twice about messing with the truck. What do you think, Norah?" No discernable answer, but Becky thought she could sense approval. As she pulled on her ghillie suit, camouflaged lightweight hat and face netting, and picked up her bag, she said, "I appreciate your looking after me. I feel much better knowing that you'll keep Bert apprised of how I'm doing. So, what do you say, let's get to our hiding spot?" With that, Becky locked her truck, hiked her bag onto her shoulder, and began the careful walk in the rocky terrain to the tall rocks.

Once she and Norah arrived at the discreet observation place, Becky settled down on an aluminum 3-legged stool and began glassing the far side of the valley with her binoculars, looking for Bert. Even though she knew about where he would be, it took several minutes to finally spot Missy's slight movement as she walked carefully beside her master. They were nearing the top of the distant ridge, presumed to be above the ranch headquarters. Becky scanned the surrounding area, looking for anything or anyone who could pose a danger to her boss.

"Radio check," she said as she keyed her mike.

"Loud and clear," came his reply.

"All clear, nothing in sight."

"Roger. Thanks. Good job."

She knew her boss was now all business. There was no time for extraneous chatter. Adjusting the focus, she continued to scan the countryside, getting familiar with the lay of the land as well as watching for danger. It was time to get as comfortable as discretion would allow and watch the six of the man she was falling in love with.

* * *

Bert crouched and crawled as he slowly crossed the crest of the ridge with Missy at his side. Her training was paying off as she obediently stayed next to him and crawled when he crawled, staying low and as invisible as possible to any eyes at the ranch, which had come into view before them. He surveyed the rough ground around him, looking for a hide. Soon, he caught sight of a small outcropping of rock above a slight depression, and with several scrubby bushes near it. A small, gnarly, mesquite tree grew from the rocks just to one side. If they could crawl the one-hundred-plus feet to it, there was a decent chance of having a discreet position that afforded some degree of movement. There might even be a little shade at times from the intense Texas sun, which was now just above the horizon. Staying in a low crouch or crawl, he led his companion slowly toward the anticipated observation point.

It took nearly ten minutes, but man and animal finally made it to within six feet of their chosen spot, when Missy let out a low growl. Bert froze and told her to stay. He looked down the hill and across the slope, at first. Seeing nothing, he moved slightly to his right. The rattle told him the source of Missy's warning. A diamondback rattlesnake had taken up squatter's rights under the overhang.

Maneuvering until he was behind a patch of prickly pear cactus which sat just to the left of the depression, he began to reach for loose rocks. It took about a dozen throws and several hits to convince the snake there were better digs elsewhere. Still rattling, it slithered around the right, back side of the overhang and disappeared.

With crisis averted and co-habitation ruled out, Bert resumed his crouching crawl into the depression. He moved Missy beside him and told her to lay down and stay. There was activity at the ranch. He took his binoculars from his bag and began to make mental and later written notes.

There were two men outside the one-level ranch house with a wrap-around porch. They wore denim jeans, boots, and western hats. The first seemed to be carrying what looked like a food tray around the house to Bert's right. He walked about eighty feet to what looked like a small dormitory or guest house to the left rear of the main house. Placing the tray on a table near the door, he appeared to unlock the door to the dorm, picked up the tray, and entered. The door closed behind him.

The second man had walked to and entered the large barn which was about a hundred yards to the north of the main house. Four saddle horses were in an attached corral at the far end of the barn. In a couple minutes, the man reappeared with a pitchfork full of hay, which he tossed into the corral for the horses. He went back into the barn.

By then, the first fellow had left the dormitory, locking the door behind him. He carried the tray, which appeared to be empty. Bert found it odd that this building had no windows, at least on the sides he could see. This guy returned to the main house and disappeared inside.

A commotion caught Bert's attention back near the barn. He could see the edge of a pen which was apparently attached to the rear of the barn. The man there must have thrown some feed out because there was considerable squealing. Bert recognized it as that of pigs, though they were hidden from view. He remembered that Norah had seen a vision of pigs. Was this what she was seeing, he wondered.

It was not long before the barn hand returned to the main house. There was no more visible activity for over an hour. During that time, Bert studied the rest of the several outbuildings which made up the ranch. One reminded him of a small guest cabin. It sat across the paved driveway from the main house, closer to Bert and more to his left. The driveway appeared to be paved almost to the top of the low hill to the north, in the direction of the gated entrance. He remembered that a dirt road entered the ranch through the gate, so the paved area looked to be purposefully incomplete. To someone arriving at the gate, it looked like just another dirt road, but once over the hill it was paved the last quarter-mile to the turn-around in front of the ranch house.

About a half-mile south of the ranch headquarters, Bert noticed through the binoculars a tall and well-built fence going east and west across the ridges until out of sight. It appeared to be a high-tensile-strength fence, probably about ten-feet tall. That would be in keeping with a hunting operation containing exotic animals. A large, presumably locking, gate interrupted the fence in the low part of the valley. A well-worn dirt trail led from the ranch driveway to and through the gate.

Bert returned to observing for activity around the buildings. He noticed a young man walking from the pen behind the barn toward the back of the house, where he disappeared from view. Missy was getting restless, so Bert gave her some water and a piece of jerky. That was followed by some subdued ear and stomach scratching.

It was close to noon before there was any other activity at the ranch. At that time, a man and a dark-haired woman walked to the guest cabin carrying what looked to be a pail and cleaning supplies. Bert had the impression that the guy was there to watch the woman. He sat on a chair on the cabin's porch while she went inside with the pail. She did not exit the cabin for about twenty minutes. At that time, the man escorted her back to the main house.

"That's unusual behavior for an employee to be escorted like that," Bert said under his breath.

He had no more than expressed that opinion when one of the other men left the main house and walked to what appeared to be a large garage which was tucked under the hill below Bert and next to the circular driveway. After a few minutes, the sound of a recreational vehicle wafted up the ridge to Bert's ears. Shortly after that RV was turned off, another started up. It seemed that the guy was checking them out. The same occurred with a third vehicle. Then the fellow walked toward the barn, where Bert observed him catching one of the saddle horses and leading it into the barn.

While that was going on, a new man emerged from the main house, wearing a black western hat and smartly dressed in blue jeans, boots, and a long-sleeve western shirt. He stood on the front porch, sipping a drink, and appearing to wait for someone. This was a well-built, trim but stocky man, with light colored hair, sandy blonde looking. Bert had the impression that he was a big shot at the ranch, possibly even the owner.

He studied this owner-guy through the binoculars for several minutes. While doing so, he noticed the horseman riding a big sorrel gelding from the barn and loping up the driveway in the direction of the locked main gate. Bert watched as this rider and horse disappeared over the low hill which shielded the ranch buildings from the gate.

With a constant crosscheck of the goings-on at the ranch below, Bert offered another bowl of water to Missy and drank some, himself. They each had another piece of jerky, mostly out of restlessness. She was doing quite well for being confined in the small depression on the shady side of the rock overhang for over six hours. It was now almost 2:00 in the afternoon, and the sun had become intense. Despite still being mostly in the shade of the rocks, rivulets of sweat ran down his back. He knew that Missy was also hot. It reminded him of many days on patrol or on watch in Afghanistan.

The owner-guy had gone back into the house about fifteen minutes earlier but had now returned to the front deck. He stood looking up the road.

Bert shifted slowly and fixed his gaze in that direction. In a few seconds, a black limousine with very dark-tinted windows came into view, driving carefully toward the ranch house. He watched as the car stopped in front of the house and a well-dressed passenger, a man, got out and shook hands with the owner guy. They stood talking while the limo driver unloaded several bags, including two rifle cases, and took them into the guest house. Once the bags were in the cabin, the passenger said a few words to the driver. Then the limo departed toward the hill and the locked entry gate.

As the limo disappeared over the hill, Bert was curious if the gate was operated remotely from somewhere in the house. The rider had gone in that direction about an hour earlier and might have waited at the gate for the limo. If so, he could have unlocked the gate for the vehicle. Speaking of the rider, where was he?

He was still pondering that question when Becky's voice came over his earpiece. "Rider on horse at your nine-o-clock, 300 yards. Don't think he's seen you but coming your direction."

Bert shifted very slowly to look north along the ridge toward the main entrance gate. The rider must have operated the gate for the limo, and he was now surveilling the area to the west of the headquarters as he rode south along the crest of the ridge. Missy was watching him, too, and he could feel the low growl in her chest as he laid his arm over her and told her to stay. He hunkered down into the depression as tightly as he could, pulling her next to him. Keying his mike, he quietly answered Becky, "Copy that, in sight."

Horse and rider picked their way along the ridgeline, easing between yucca, cactus, mesquite, and rocks as he seemed to be mostly focused on the area to the fence line near the dirt road. Several times he looked in Bert and Missy's direction. The rider passed slowly about twenty yards to the west of Bert's position, not seeing them. It was an agonizing fifteen minutes until the rider was out of view to the south and west of their hide. Bert felt Missy begin to relax and her deep growl subside.

He returned to his focus on the ranch headquarters below. There was no more visible activity, and everyone apparently had gone into the ranch house. For the next half hour, Bert kept a watchful eye out for any activity while he scratched Missy's ears and tummy and shared another piece of jerky and a drink of water with her. He paused in that activity when he saw the rider come back into view from the south, near the fenced area. The man had apparently been checking out the fence along that side of the hunting containment area. The rider urged his big sorrel into a lope for the half mile remaining to the barn.

While the rider unsaddled and took care of his horse, Bert changed position with Missy in order to get her more into the shade of the overhanging rocks of their hide. The sun was getting lower in the western sky and the brutal rays were coming into their space. They were a little more exposed to anyone at the ranch who might be looking through binoculars, but he did not see much risk of that. So far, they seemed to have no idea that he was watching them. His ghillie suit, and the natural vegetation, would make him extremely hard to notice.

He watched another hour tick by as the sun dropped to just a short distance above the western hills. It was about time to head back to Norah and Becky. Just as he was readying to leave the hide, he saw the guest and owner-guy walk out of the main house and stand talking for a minute. Then the owner called one of his men from the house and appeared to give him a task. The worker nodded and walked toward the right and behind the main house, unlocked the door of the dormitory, and entered. After about ten minutes, he reappeared with a dark-haired woman, locked the door, and began to escort her to the main house. Bert studied her through his binoculars. She appeared to be an attractive woman perhaps in her upper twenties or early thirties. She was wearing a short skirt, western boots, and a form-fitting, short-sleeve shirt. Bert had the impression that she was not happy; she seemed subdued and submissive. She was introduced to the guest, who took her hand. He said something to her, and then to the owner. After that, still holding the woman's hand, he led her to the guest cabin.

Bert and Missy stayed in their hide until the sun was almost out of sight behind the far hills, waiting to see if the woman might reappear. She did not. From all appearances, she was one of the benefits for the high-roller guest. Apparently, an all-night benefit.

"Returning to the pickup point," he said over his mike.

"Roger that," came Becky's reply. "Will get the truck when you're closer."

Bert and Missy crawled back toward the road, until he knew they were out of sight of the ranch. Then he stood and walked deliberately down the long shallow slope toward the barbed wire fence and dirt road. Halfway down, he asked Becky to call for Missy, so she would get a good run going to her.

He saw Becky stand and wave and could barely hear her call. However, Missy heard her loud and clear. She looked at her alpha male for guidance. When he said okay and waved her forward, she went tearing down the hill, across the dirt trail, and up the far slope to her pretty blonde alpha female. And to the red-haired alpha female that she could not see but could sense.

By the time Bert had reached the dirt road, Becky, Norah, and Missy were nearly there in Becky's truck. She paused long enough for him to place his pack and rifle bag in the box of the truck, and then hastened up the trail past the ranch entrance and toward Crane. In the passenger seat, Bert undid his ghillie suit as much as he could to bask in the cool air of the AC. He was drenched in sweat and knew he probably smelled like it.

Becky just gave him her pretty smile as she mischievously rolled her window halfway down and pretended to gag.

In the back seat, Norah smiled at him as she crunched up her nose, too.

"Can't win with either of you gals, I guess," he laughed.

"Oh, I think you've already won with both of these gals," Becky retorted. "Neither of us are going to run from a little B.O."

Norah nodded and smiled her own sweet smile. "She's right, you know."

As they drove the 45 minutes to Odessa, Bert proceeded to tell them about his observations and assumptions from the day's surveillance.

"I think there are a minimum of three, maybe four, permanent people at the ranch. The guy I call the owner, and at least two ranch hands, all men. There is another guy I think, but only saw him once. Then there's at least one woman. I think she's there against her will. Cannot be sure, but she was escorted both times I saw her. She seemed to be like a cleaning lady and a sex slave unless she's a hooker. But I don't think so. I didn't get the impression that she was happy being there. She seemed to be one of the benefits of doing business at the ranch."

"So, there was a business guest there?" asked Becky.

"Yes," Bert said. "You probably couldn't see it from where you were, but a limo dropped off some apparently well-heeled guy this afternoon. He was in the main lodge or house for quite a while, then went to his cabin with the woman."

"Any chance that the woman could be Annie?" asked Becky.

Norah's eyes told Bert that she had the same question.

"Maybe," he answered. "To save weight, I didn't bring my

224

long-range camera gear, but she seemed to be the right age, had dark hair, and was attractive. Just like Annie."

Norah listened intently to his discussion. Finally, she said, "Honey, I have a strong feeling that Annie is or was here. I'm feeling a sense of fear, longing, and loneliness; and hopelessness. Everything that a captive would feel. Especially fear and hopelessness."

"We need to be sure, Sweetheart," he said. "How would you feel about going in there tomorrow and trying to find out more?"

Norah sat quietly, thinking, for a moment. Finally, she gave a nod. "I'll do that for us, Honey. Just remember, though, that I'm attached to you. Once I leave your side, or Becky's, then I become susceptible to the influence of other spirits. There are some very dark places and spirits in this world that are risky to be around. They could be able to trap me."

Bert was aware of that potential risk. It was not a risk that he took lightly. At this point, he had no reason to suspect that other, perhaps dangerous, spirits might be roaming the ranch, so felt that she would be okay. However, he wanted to surveil the place one more day and see what else they might learn, first. She could stay with him at the hide and provide her psychic insight

They discussed doing the same surveillance plan the next day, except that Bert preferred to have Missy remain with Becky while Norah went with him. They needed to start early, though, and hopefully see what happens to the woman. Maybe at some point he would send Norah inside to provide some needed answers.

The same motel still had rooms, so they checked in and reassembled in Bert and Norah's room. Bert suggested that

Missy stay in Becky's room, for added security. It was going to be a short night, so they said their good nights quickly. Bert took Becky's hands in his own as she was about to leave his room.

"You did a great job today," he said to her. "You have a natural instinct for this kind of work and you're a great member of this team. I . . . ." He still could not bring himself to say what he wanted to say. "I hope you have a good rest and I'll see you at zero-dark-thirty."

She smiled at him and squeezed his hands firmly. Then when he released her, she stepped forward and kissed him quickly on the cheek. "Thanks, Boss." With Missy following behind, she went next door to her room.

Norah turned from her position at the window. Her blue eyes sparkled and her shimmering red hair seemed to wave as in a gentle breeze. "You'd best not get too used to her calling you boss, my love. She feels the same way as I do about you. You aren't going to be boss to her for much longer."

Bert looked away as he hung up the ghillie suit to air dry. Then, he turned to her. "Norah, nobody can ever take your place with me, not in my heart. Loving you has been the best thing of my life. As much as I like her, you have always had my heart."

She moved closer to him. "I know, Honey, but I also know that you need physical love as well as spiritual. You are my world and my heart, too. For that reason, Bert, I want you to be happy. Don't fight your feelings. My love is big enough to share you. Especially with a good woman like Becky."

"I love, adore, and miss your touch, Norah," he said as he turned out the lights and crawled into bed. "Nobody can ever take your place with me."

"Honey, nobody has to take my place. They can have their own place beside mine. She's welcome beside me. There's no law against a ship captain having two first mates."

In the darkness, a tear rolled down his cheek as he tried to push away his inner turmoil and breathe in the much-needed sleep.

Next door, Becky took care of Missy's needs. Then she knelt and wrapped her arms around her animal buddy, feeling the soft warmth of her coat. Nestling her face against Missy's neck, Becky closed her eyes, and with deeply controlled breathing, allowed the canine's soul to comfort her own. Scooting back against the bed, she pulled her legs up and held Missy close. The coywolf's head rested on her lap as she stroked the reddish-grey hair and felt the heartbeat of this wild, but gentle, animal. It reminded her of the paradox between the love she was increasingly feeling and the sense of guilt which was beneath the surface and threatening to drown it.

She got into bed and turned out the light. Resting her hand on Missy's shoulders, where the animal lay beside her on the floor, Becky felt safe in the knowledge that Missy's keen nose and instincts were on duty. Missy's proximity also made it feel like Bert was next to her. It spoke volumes to her that he would share his beloved animal with her. She smiled at that, even as a tear welled up in her eyes. Sleep would be an all-too brief but welcome respite from her emotional wrangling.

* * *

The team arrived back at the first surveillance point about twenty minutes before sunrise, tired, but emotionally fired up. Bert had driven Becky's truck at her request, so she could catch a few more winks.

He loved her Ram pickup. His Durango was a great vehicle, too, but he still loved a good truck. As he stopped near the getting off point, he placed his hand on Becky's shoulder as he turned to tell Missy good-bye and to take care of her second alpha female. He squeezed Becky's shoulder gently and told her how much he appreciated her radio discipline and good work yesterday.

Carrying his gear and with Norah near his side, he walked to the fence and climbed through. He continued another two-hundred feet toward the ridge before stopping to pull on his ghillie suit. This was to make sure he was far away from the road in case another vehicle came along. With his AR-15 slung over his right shoulder and the bag of gear in his left hand, he resumed the hike up the shallow hill. Fifteen minutes later, he and Norah were in the same hide he used the previous day. The red glow just below the eastern horizon was a visual reveille for the coming day.

He hunkered down, with Norah nearby, and began his vigil. For about twenty minutes, there was no activity to be seen, except for the sun rising in the east. Then he saw the guest and the dark-haired woman leaving the cabin and walking to the main house. She wore the same short skirt, snug shirt, and boots. Again, she seemed subdued and just walked seemingly without talking. They entered the house. For about five minutes there was no observable activity. Then one of the men led the woman, who carried a large tray of presumably food, back to the dormitory, let her in, and locked the door behind her. It seemed obvious that she was being held against her will. Was this Annabel Leery? From nearly a quarter mile away, Bert could not be sure. "What the hell is going on here," he wondered.

Suddenly, he was surprised to see a man running from the

barn and across the driveway toward the ridge. This fellow seemed to be frightened and running from something. He ducked around and often jumped over the rocks and vegetation that interrupted his sprint toward Bert's position. Bert began to shift his position and consider the options if this guy continued to run in his direction. Norah watched with interest as the event unfolded, also.

The scared runner had gone almost halfway up the ridge, when he suddenly pitched forward and disappeared behind a large patch of cactus. Bert kept his binoculars focused on this spot for several minutes, but he saw nothing more. There were no other people in sight, either. Baffled, he lowered the binoculars.

"That man was shot," said Norah.

"Shot?" he asked.

"Yes, Honey, I could sense the pain and I felt the bullet. He's mortally wounded."

He watched in stunned silence for a minute. "Who shot him, then? I didn't see anyone else. I didn't hear a shot, either."

She replied, "I don't know, Sweetheart. But I know he was severely injured by a bullet. It was an undeniable sensation."

Bert knew that when Norah had such a strong vision or perception he was wise to take it seriously, no matter how puzzling it was. However, this was indeed puzzling. Nobody had even left the house to retrieve the victim's body. Were they just going to leave him there to rot in the Texas sun?

As he was pondering these questions, he was pulled back to the surveillance task. The owner, guest, and two of the other men had all left the house. The owner and guest were dressed down into hunting or work clothing. Both the other men wore faded denim jeans, boots, and long-sleeve, tan shirts. One man wore a black felt hat, while the other guy had a grey hat. The two workers were either very tanned Caucasians or were maybe Mexican.

The owner and guest walked toward the guest cabin, while the worker guy with the black hat went to the barn. The black hat guy at the barn caught one of the horses and took it inside, presumably to saddle up. Grey hat walked to the garage and in a few minutes drove out on a recreational vehicle, an all-terrain vehicle or ATV. He drove to the dormitory, unlocked it, and went inside.

Bert keyed his mike. "We're still here and observing. A little confusing."

"Copy that," Becky replied, reassuring him that she was doing okay.

Bert and Norah remained vigilant, observing while making mental notes. When he was able, Bert made brief notes in his small notebook and took video or still photos with his HD camcorder. It had decent zoom capability although he chose it because it was light weight. It would document the activity but was not strong enough for identification shots from his position.

Five minutes passed before black hat departed the barn on a bay horse, heading south. A couple minutes later, grey hat came out of the dormitory holding a younger looking, red-headed, Caucasian man by the arm. This man looked to be in his twenties, fit, and he was wearing a camouflage jumpsuit. Bert noticed that grey hat was wearing a sidearm. He had not noticed it before. He led the younger man onto the ATV as black hat arrived next to them on his horse. Quickly, ATV, horse, and rider all traveled south.

The investigators watched from their hiding and vantage point near the top of the west ridge as the group of three men made their way at the speed of the trotting horse to the large, locked gate of the apparent animal enclosure. Once there, black hat dismounted, unlocked, and opened the gate just enough to allow the younger man to pass through. Black hat and grey hat seemed to be shouting instructions to the young man, who stood inside the enclosure. After relocking the gate, black hat returned to his saddle and waited for the ATV to be turned back toward the ranch headquarters. Both vehicle and rider headed up the dirt trail to the main house.

Bert studied the younger, red-headed man. The guy seemed confused and unsure of himself at first, as he looked in all directions. After a couple of minutes, he began to walk at first and then began running to the south. That end of the valley merged in a quarter-mile into a rugged pass, which also faded into the adjoining rocky hills. The young fellow worked his way through the pass and across the top of the first hill, before he disappeared.

It was nearly fifteen minutes before Bert lost sight of the young man. Several glances told them there was no other activity taking place down below them. Lowering his binoculars, he looked at Norah and shook his head.

"I don't like the looks of this," he said. "Suspicious, to say the least."

"I agree," Norah said. "As I watched him go, I kept getting this unsettling vision of him as a skeleton. A walking and running skeleton. Right before he went over that hill, I felt like he turned for just a second and looked back at me. It felt like he wanted to tell me something."

"Honey, there's something very sinister going on at this place," he said. "It's almost lunch time, or as they say out here, dinner time. I'm guessing that the guest and company are getting ready to eat soon." He turned his binoculars back to the ranch buildings below.

He was right. Within twenty minutes, the guest appeared walking from the cabin to the main house, carrying a long gun. To Bert, it looked to be a hunting rifle. The man entered the house. Remembering the man, they had evidently seen shot below them, Bert scanned the hillside below for any sign of movement. There was nothing. He lowered the binoculars.

No sooner had he put them down, than grey hat emerged from the house. Watching again, Bert followed the man as he walked toward the garage. Out of sight in the building, the sound of an ATV could be heard starting up. Within a couple of minutes, grey hat drove the vehicle in front of the main house, turned it off, and entered the house.

It was not long before the four men came out of the house. Black hat and grey hat went to the barn to get their horses, while the owner and the guest climbed onto the vehicle. The guest was carrying a pistol as well as his rifle. When the two riders came alongside the ATV, the owner, who was driving, gunned the vehicle and sped down the trail toward the locked enclosure. Ten minutes later, vehicle and riders had passed through the gate and relocked it. Bert watched as the group moved on south through the pass and onto the far hill. From there, they appeared to fan out as they disappeared over the hill.

Bert felt a cold chill moving up his back despite the heat of the day, which was in the low nineties on this Friday, September 7th. Was this really what it was beginning to look like? He shook his head as he looked at Norah. She gave him a similar look back.

A movement down below caught his eye. A man had just jumped off the fence behind the barn and was walking toward the back of the house. Bert wondered if this was the same guy that he saw yesterday in that area. Once again, this guy went out of sight behind the house.

"So, there are at least three men here, besides the owner and guest," he said to Norah.

"It seems that way," she answered. "Well, there were four before the man this morning was shot."

They remained in their hiding spot for another two hours, watching for any signs of activity, and mulling over the entire situation. He checked in with Becky another two times, mostly to make sure she was doing okay out there with Missy. As they quietly discussed the case, a distant sound caught Bert's ear. He listened intently, realizing it was a gunshot well to the south of them. About thirty seconds later, another shot, followed quickly by a third. Then silence.

"Those were gunshots, Honey," he said.

"Yes, I know," she replied. "The hunters have found their big game."

They sat quietly for a few more minutes, listening. Then, Norah said, "I'm having that vision about pigs again. Weird. I wonder where that's coming from?"

"They have a bunch of pigs in a pen behind the barn, Babe. We can only see them when they're near the fence on this side. I'd guess there are about a dozen or more. You can hear them squealing when about to be fed."

She watched the short segment of fence that was visible on their side behind the barn. "Oh yes, I'm hearing them now, faintly. And I catch a glimpse of them occasionally."

"You must have sensed that there were pigs at this place," he said.

"I guess so. It just seemed like a strange vision to be having. Makes me wonder if it really had anything to do with the case. Except, there are pigs here."

Before he could say anything more about that, a rider came into view coming over the far south hill, riding at a gallop. Bert watched him through the glasses as he reached the big gate, unlocked it and left it open, and galloped on to the barn. Black hat seemed to be hurrying as he unsaddled his horse. Then he went out past the barn on the back side to a large, round container of some kind. He seemed to do something there, then went into the house. A few minutes later, he returned carrying two bags of what apparently was trash. Bert realized that the container was a type of incinerator and the guy was preparing to burn the trash.

The ATV and the other rider, grey hat, were now coming up the valley from the south. They passed through the gate, where grey hat dismounted and closed and locked it. Then he hurried to catch up to the all-terrain vehicle as it rambled on to the guest cabin. There, the guest got out of the vehicle and went into the cabin, carrying his firearms. Grey hat caught up to them as the owner began to drive over to the side of the barn. The owner stopped the vehicle and departed for the house.

Bert and Norah watched as this second rider also unsaddled and put his horse in the far corral and pen. Both men then walked back to the ATV. They appeared to be inspecting a large plastic bag on the rear cargo rack. Each man positioned himself on opposite sides of the rack, picked up the bag, and carried it to the rear of the barn, placing it next to the pen.

Watching through the binoculars, Bert sat in stunned horror

as the two men unwrapped the bag, picked up the lifeless and bloody body of the red-headed man, and heaved him over the fence into the squealing mass of hogs, waiting to be fed.

CHAPTER FOURTEEN: PREDATOR
AND PREY

In shocked silence, Bert and Norah listened to the squealing hogs as they jostled and fought over the body of the red-headed man. The two men who had thrown him in the pen placed the trash in the incinerator, left the door open and the fire unlit, and went to the house. For several minutes, with no activity to be observed, the investigator and his spirit wife began to talk quietly.

"I've served in war in both Iraq and Afghanistan and I've seen some things I've tried to forget," he said. "But I never thought I'd see anything like those in this country. These people are barbaric and purely evil, Norah."

With tears glistening in her soft blue eyes, she nodded. "I know, Honey. This must be stopped. To think that Annie might be caught in their web of scorn for human life. It's beyond heartbreaking. We have to stop this, Bert."

"We're going to stop it, Honey," he replied with conviction. "Just have to find the way to do it without us going to jail. You know the drill. How did you see this, Mr. Lynnes? Well, sir, I trespassed. Oh, and what was your basis for trespassing? Oh, that was psychic premonition, sir. Bailiff, take this man into custody. Throw away the key when he's locked up."

"Yes, I know, Honey. And I know you. You'll find a way. An Army Ranger always finds a way."

"Well, we have to find a way, Norah. I cannot let this place continue. Let's watch this operation for a while longer. We have about another hour or two before dark. I think we're going to need you to go in there and find out more about them."

She said without hesitation, "Whatever you need, I'm willing to do, Bert."

"I know you are and I appreciate you for that," he replied. He looked away toward the ranch buildings as movement caught his eye.

The hunter guest walked from the cabin toward the house. As he knocked and entered, the two hired men, black and grey hat, walked from the rear of the house toward the barn. Bert and Norah watched as the men took a wheelbarrow from the far side of the pen, entered it through a small back gate, and threw some pellets out of view toward the far side of the pen. They apparently did that to distract the pigs while they pulled on surgical gloves and began the grisly task of picking up the skeletal remains of the victim and putting them in the wheelbarrow. With that task completed, the men left the pen through the same gate and went to the incinerator. They threw all the remains into the container, lit the trash on fire, and closed the door. Smoke billowed from the smokestack as the trash and evidence burned. Black hat went back to the barn and disappeared.

"I'm guessing that tomorrow they'll empty the cooled ashes and take them out a ways to be buried. When that's done, the red-headed man will truly remain among the permanent missing." Bert looked away and shook his head in disgust. Norah could see the anger building inside him, even though his military training had taught him to control it. Her retired Ranger was not going to let this go on much longer. She knew he was going to do something. But, after they found out if Annie was there.

The guest and owner walked out onto the driveway and talked as they appeared to be waiting for something or someone. Soon, the investigators saw what the wait was about, as a black limousine came into view from the main gate. Black hat was riding back over the hill from the gate. He had apparently left the far end of the barn, unseen, and had gone to unlock the gate. He remained sitting on his horse at the top of the hill. The limo coasted to a stop in front of the guest cabin. A lone driver exited and began to load the guest's bags from the cabin.

After a few more minutes of talk, the owner escorted his guest to the limo and said so long as the limo circled the driveway and departed. Black hat and horse went before the vehicle, presumably to close and lock the gate.

"One more unique hunt completed," Bert said partly to himself and partly to Norah. The disgust and scorn in his voice wasn't hard for her to notice.

The owner and grey hat went back inside the main house. In a few minutes, grey hat went to the dormitory. He was inside only a few minutes before he exited with a blonde woman, looking to be in her early twenties. After locking the door, he escorted her to the main house.

"That's not the same woman," Norah said. "There are at least two of them there."

He nodded. "You're right, Sweetheart. Whatever we do, we have to make sure they stay alive. Their testimony will be the final nail in the coffin that buries this place. And keeps us out of prison."

Keying his mike, Bert updated Becky. "Still here in position. Much to tell later."

Her reply came to his earpiece, "Copy that, Boss. We're fine." She was extremely glad to hear from him. She'd been worrying since she hadn't heard anything for hours. It was obvious to her that there had been considerable activity. She stroked Missy's head and scratched her ears, before sharing some water and jerky with her companion. All the while, Becky maintained her vigil, watching for any threat to her man. "My man," she said aloud to Missy. "Our man."

Near the top of the ridge, Bert and Norah continued their surveillance. Another vehicle, this one a white SUV, was coming over the hill from the main gate. It parked in front of the house. The driver, who appeared to be alone, got out of the vehicle.

"Oh my God," he whispered to Norah. "He's wearing a law uniform. I think he's a Sheriff. Maybe this place is about to be busted."

She whispered back to him, "Why is he alone, though? Shouldn't he have some backup?"

"Boss, you've got company coming. From the main gate. A rider." Becky's voice almost startled him before he could respond to Norah.

He and Norah turned to their left and saw black hat riding along the crest of the ridge toward them. He was still about 250 yards from their position but was right at their level. He was armed with a pistol.

Bert grabbed his AR-15 and drew his pistol as he wriggled on his belly as far under the overhanging rock ledge as he could get. He hoped there were no rattlesnakes tucked up there out of sight. At least it was somewhat reassuring that the only sound he heard was the horse's hooves as it picked its way along the rocky ridgetop. He rolled onto his side enough to bring his pistol into a firing position, if needed. In the mildly darkened area under the overhang, he would be visible if the rider looked at him from close range. If the rider saw him, the rider would surrender or die, but Bert did not want to alert the rest of the ranch residents if he could avoid it.

Across the road and up the far slope, Becky watched with growing apprehension and fear as the rider approached closer and closer to where she knew her boss was hiding. She unholstered her own pistol, even though she knew she couldn't do any good with it from nearly a quarter mile away. All she could do was watch and hope.

Black hat and horse picked their way carefully along the ridge, stepping over and around rocks, cactus, and yucca. The sparse and gnarly mesquite trees caused only minor diversions to their travel. They continued to approach Bert's position. When only about twenty yards away, the rider halted his horse. He seemed distracted as he looked to his right, in Becky's direction. Then he nudged the horse forward, continuing to glance frequently to his right as he passed Bert's hide and slowly went out of sight.

Bert relaxed as he very slowly inched out from under the overhang, listening for the horse's hooves. He realized that Norah was just reappearing near the front of his surveillance position.

"That was too close for comfort," he told her.

She smiled at him. "Yeah, he needed a nudge to get on by us."

"A nudge?"

"Yeah, I whispered in his ear that a coyote was near the road. That, and blowing on his cheek."

Bert gave a low chuckle. "That's twice that you've been able to influence someone that way. Thank you, Honey."

Norah just smiled; that smile that always melted his heart. "If love is boundless and cuts across time, space, and distance, then my love for her will live forever," he thought.

For a few seconds, he almost forgot about the surveillance they were doing. But reality took over and his eyes went back to the ranch below. The white SUV was still parked, but there were no people in view. He came back to Norah's question. Why was the Sheriff there alone and without backup? Was this just a social call?

Norah read his mind and knew his thoughts. "I'm going in there, Honey. We need to know what's going on."

Almost before he could say anything, she was gone. He intensely watched the scene below, looking for any sign of movement. Suddenly, he saw movement behind the barn. Four men, all seeming to be young, maybe in their twenties, were walking from the hog pen fence toward the back of the house. Suddenly, the chilling realization hit him. His gift was playing tricks on him. These were dead men's souls and he was seeing the manifestation of their spirits. Just as suddenly, he knew that the guy they saw being shot yesterday was also a spirit, living the reenactment of his death while trying to escape. Bert had nearly forgotten that his ability as a medium, able to see the dead, was still trying to evolve. A chill started at his neck and crept down his back. More spirits were walking out of the barn and just wandering aimlessly. Several others manifested outside the dormitory, and slowly moved toward the southern enclosure.

The place was full of the spirits of the dead victims, and Norah was down there with them. Was there an evil or angry one there which might try to keep her? A fear began to take root.

He waited in nervous anticipation, watching and listening, trying to count the spirits of the dead. He lost count after thirty-nine. Then the house door opened and the Sheriff and owner walked out. They talked for a few minutes as the owner motioned for grey hat to go to the dormitory. Five minutes later, grey hat returned with the blonde woman beside him. After a brief introduction to the Sheriff, she followed him to the cabin. Grey hat took a bag and a rifle case from the Sheriff's car and took them to the cabin. Then he left the Sheriff and the blonde inside the cabin.

"Good grief, he's on the take here," said Bert under his breathe.

"Yes, he is," said Norah. She had just returned to Bert's side.

Bert let out a sigh of relief. "Thank goodness you're back, Honey," he said. "I saw nearly four-dozen spirits around there and was worried sick about you."

"I know, Bert. I talked with several of them while I was there. The Sheriff is not merely on the take, he's a shareholder in the company. He comes out here several times a year for an overnight with one of the girls and a hunt the next day. Says it keeps him sharp and ready to perform his job. He likes to give his prey just a 30-minute head start. Thinks it makes the chase more exciting."

"Who's the owner?" Bert asked.

"He's named Jamison McDougal. They call him Jimmy. He's very mean, Bert, a killer. Everyone sucks up to him. Even Sheriff Angle. The other spirits say he's vicious and cruel. A former Army guy, Bert. But he was kicked out for killing a prisoner. He was not charged because they couldn't prove it. You either play his game or you become the next prey. Same for the women. Two girls refused to be sex slaves and they became prey."

"Speaking of sex slaves, Norah. Is Annie one of them?"

"Yes, Honey. We've found Annabel Leery. She's the brunette that you've seen. I went to her room in the prison, what you call a dormitory. Each room is like an efficiency apartment. Ridiculously small. She is there and she's a survivor, just trying to stay alive. But she is so depressed. I think she's considering suicide."

"You can't blame her for that. We must get her out of there. Soon. Is Angle doing a hunt tomorrow?"

She nodded. "Yes, the intended prey victim is a nineteen-year-old from Alabama. His name is Tommy. They are turning him loose about 10:00 in the morning."

"Are there others there?"

"Just the two girls, the blonde is called Kathy, and the boy. Oh yeah, the two hired hands are Hank, the one who wears a black hat, and Freddie, who wears a grey hat."

"They're about out of prey victims, then," Bert said.

She nodded. "Yeah, they talked about that. McDougal and his partner do the harvesting, as he calls it. He's leaving in the morning, early, before the Sheriff's hunt. The partner is already out in Colorado, looking for another girl. Guess where McDougal's going?"

"Don't tell me it's Arkansas, or Wyoming?"

"Mountain View, Arkansas," she said softly.

"Why there? How does he choose a location?"

"The spirits were very anxious to tell me what they know. They said McDougal likes small rural towns or communities. Says the guys are fit, fast, know the outdoors, and dumb. Makes them good prey. The girls are the same and very pretty. Makes them great benefits for the guests. Besides that, he thinks all the small-town lawmen are idiots. And the feds don't care about them so stay out of it. It also helps to have the local Sheriff on the board of directors."

"What did anyone have to say about the money in this?" Bert asked.

She gave him a solemn look. "Stay sitting down, Honey. McDougal gets $200 G's for each hunt. Another $25,000 if they want a girl every night they're at the ranch."

Bert had a look of amazement. "These guests must be very wealthy to pay that kind of money."

"They are among the well-connected, both politically and financially. The guy who just left owns at least a dozen banks and a half-dozen car dealerships."

"I'd make a wild guess that they have at least 25 or 30 hunts a year," Bert surmised. He did a few calculations in his head. "That means this place takes in almost five-and-a-half-million a year. Just for abducting about 25 young men and another half-dozen young women, all from rural communities where the people are generally trusting and unsuspecting."

"That's a disgusting way to become wealthy," Norah said with contempt. "And for what?"

"Apparently, there are enough wealthy playboys out there who want the thrill of killing another human being, without the reality of making it personal. I've known one or two like that in the military. Thankfully, there aren't many. McDougal is the rare exception, not the . . ." A movement down below captured his attention. A dark blue pickup truck was backing out of the garage and stopped in front of the main house. McDougal brought two bags from there and placed them in the back seat. "He's getting ready to leave in the morning."

"Yes," said Norah. "They said he spends a lot of time on

Facebook and other media, picking his potential victims. Before he leaves, he knows at least two people in each area who meet his criteria. Our desire to be someone on social media does his work for him."

"I need to know the details about that truck, Norah. Would you jump down there and get the particulars, including license plate, please."

"You bet, Honey." She disappeared.

He waited for about three or four minutes, watching McDougal finish loading his gear. All the men went into the main house. The two hired guys evidently had rooms in this main house. None of them appeared to be married. Why get married when they had at least two women available for their amusement. Bert's contempt for these men was growing steadily.

The spirits of the victims had disappeared as suddenly as they had shown up. Were they just coming out because they knew that Norah was going down there? An outsider to tell their stories to.

Norah returned suddenly beside him. Her eyes sparkled as she relayed the truck information. It was a dark blue, Ford F-250 with extended cab; with Texas license: (UNH3006).

"How clever," thought Bert. "UNH for U-Neek Hunts, and the number was obvious to any hunter. A 30-06 rifle cartridge."

The last edge of the sun was just above the horizon. They needed to get back to Becky and Missy. Bert began his crawl to get out of sight of those below before it was safe to walk. Then he almost trotted down the hill toward the road, calling Becky to say they were on the way.

Becky was overjoyed at Bert's call. She and Missy were getting very antsy after being in their own hide all day. She had only seen about three vehicles on the dirt road below throughout the day. Missy had stayed by her side the entire time, sharing some water and jerky several times.

Trotting around the hill, they retrieved her truck and drove back to the dirt road to pick up Bert and Norah. By the time they arrived at the pickup point, Bert was nearly to the fence. The sun was behind the hills, and darkness was setting in. Becky parked, and ran to the fence to take his rifle and pack across the fence so he could crawl between the wires more handily. She threw her arms around him and hugged him tightly.

"We missed you guys."

"Missed you and Missy, also," Bert replied. "We have a lot to tell you on the way to the motel. I'll start by telling you what you may already know. We have to be back out here tomorrow to rescue Annie."

"She's here, then! I'm elated that you've found her. Hop in and let's get going. I want to hear all about it while I'm driving." She literally skipped around her truck and slipped into the driver's seat.

While the team drove back to Odessa for another night in the motel, Bert brought Becky up to speed on everything they had seen and learned. She was mortified to hear about the hunt and disposal methodology. While it increased her fear about what they were doing, it also increased her resolve to see it through and get Annie out of there.

Becky glanced at Bert after hearing his recap of the day. "Bert, please make sure that Norah knows how much I care about her and respect her for what she did to find Annie. We'd be nothing without her. She's the reason we've found this poor girl."

Norah heard her. She smiled and looked at Bert with the

look of someone who knew they had done well. It was not the trip to the ranch that she was thinking of, though. "Tell her I appreciate that, and I appreciate her being with us. She's a keeper in my book."

It would be another short night with a quick snack in the room while they refined their plans for the next day. There were no delays in going to bed.

* * *

The sun was creeping over the eastern hills as the team of B & N Investigations drove along the dirt road outside the ranch. Bert had Becky drive another mile-and-a-half farther south before he found a place to exit the vehicle. From his study of the maps last night, he knew he could stay on the military crest of an east-west hill until reaching the area south of the hunting enclosure gate. He expected to encounter high fencing, so added half the zip ties and the bolt cutter to his pack. Leaving Missy with Becky for her added protection, Bert climbed through the barbed wire fence and began a fast walk to the east, rifle in hand and pack on his back. He again asked Norah to stay with Becky so she could tell him if anything threatening happened. There were no guarantees that the radios would have any reception.

Becky was not able to find any comparable place to park her truck out of view of the road, so she pulled it as far off to the west side as she could and left it with her note. Then she and Missy, along with Norah, headed up the increasingly steep slope until she could find a place to be mostly out of sight, yet high enough for her to have some view toward the ranch. She hoped there might be decent radio reception, too. Her first radio check with Bert was reassuring, but he wasn't as far in as he would be going.

Shortly after their radio check, Bert passed over the first hill. Part way down the eastern side, he encountered the fence. This ten-foot high, welded-wire, enclosure was topped with a barbed-wire lean-in. It was designed to keep animals, or people, inside. As he suspected, the fence seemed to enclose a vast area of the ranch to the south and east. He noted exotic antelope in the valley below. With the likelihood of dangerous animals, he knew he had to be very vigilant, once inside. He opened his bag and removed the bolt cutter.

The wire looked to be about an eighth-inch thick. Strong enough with its 4-inch square mesh to repel almost anything trying to breach it. Bert could see that it had a lone insulated, electrified wire running the length of the fence about two feet from the top. It was buried an unknown depth into the rough ground. It was a formidable barrier to any man or woman trying to escape. However, it was no match for the bolt cutter as Bert cut a hole along the ground level and up both sides, large enough for him to crawl through after bending the section upwards. Once through with his gear, he bent the section back into place and used a lone zip tie to hold it down. It would not be so noticeable to a passing rider, but one slice of his knife would allow him back through.

Safely inside the hunting ground, he cautiously but rapidly advanced toward the peak of the hill which he knew was about two miles south of the enclosure gate. It was now almost 8:00 in the morning. Two hours from the release time of the prey, Tommy. He tried to contact Becky, to no avail. No reception. He took up an observation hide just below the north side of the hilltop, where he should be able to see Tommy approaching. This assumed that Tommy fled up the valley and gulley over the first hill, which seemed a logical escape route.

Becky was increasingly perplexed and worried. She was unable to contact her boss. As she pondered his situation, she knew it was critical that he knew what Tommy was doing once released. Would she have reception from his former hide above the ranch? From there, she might be able to report what the prey and predators were doing, if he could hear her. She picked up her bag and told Missy, knowing that Norah was listening, that she needed to get above the ranch so she could report to Bert. She hurried to her truck with Missy and drove back to the former position. With her ghillie suit on, she crawled the fence and half walked, half ran, to the outcropping above the ranch. It was 9:00.

As she started to crawl into the depression below the outcropping, Missy growled. Freezing, Becky looked for a threat. The sound of the rattle told her that a snake was there first. She tried to move it along using Bert's method of pelting it with rocks, but her aim wasn't as good as his. The snake stayed put. She decided to move around the formation of rocks to the right side. From there, she had a good view of the ranch below, but she was also more exposed. She would have to move very carefully and stay low. She told Missy to lay down beside her as she did a quick check through the binoculars. She saw the grey hat guy, Freddie, lead the blonde girl, Kathy, from the main house to the dorm, or prison. Apparently the Sheriff had all the fun with her that he intended for the day. She was locked back inside. The man just sat down outside the door, apparently waiting for his cue to bring out Tommy.

Another call to Bert was without reply. She could hear static as if his mike were keying but heard nothing from him. Was there a problem with his radio? Did he hear her call? Very slowly, she stood up and leaned back against the rocks, holding the radio as high as possible while still transmitting. This time, she could hear his barely audible voice, but it was garbled. She could not understand him. Was he able to hear and understand her?

It was closing in on 10:00. The Sheriff and the black hat, Hank, walked to the cabin. A few minutes later, they came back to the white SUV and Sheriff Angle laid out his rifle on the hood. Hank went to the garage and returned shortly with a covered recreational vehicle.

Becky decided to report to Bert as if he was hearing her. Better to assume that he heard her. While pondering this, she suddenly sensed Norah's presence. Norah could hear her even if Becky couldn't hear Norah. They could work together to make sure that their man had current information.

"Norah, I know you can hear me. Let's work together to keep Bert aware of the situation. Would you return to him when Tommy is released and let him know? Then come back here so we can get the next step reported. I'll wait until I sense you."

Ten-o-clock arrived and there was no movement below. Hank had gone back inside. He soon came back out with his own rifle. He and the Sheriff leaned against the ATV, talking and laughing. Hank turned toward the dorm and motioned with his hand. Freddie nodded, stood and entered the building. In a couple of minutes, he returned, grasping Tommy by the arm. Like the previous victim, the young man wore a camouflage jumpsuit.

After giving Tommy several minutes of instruction, Freddie led him to the ATV and drove him to the big gate of the enclosure. Within minutes, young Tommy was on his own inside the locked killing field. He surveyed the area quickly, then began running toward the end of the valley.

"Norah, we need to tell Bert that Tommy is heading his way

as expected and running fast." Becky paused for a few seconds. "Also, tell him that two armed predators are soon to follow."

She keyed her mike and relayed the same message, as an instinctive backup, not knowing if her boss would hear it or not. In her anxiety, she didn't notice Missy slowly standing and moving to the east to peer around the rocks and overhang.

Someone else heard the call. Freddie had ridden his horse up the driveway past the barn and then cut to the west onto the ridge. It was always his job to check the area on horseback for anyone who might be suspicious. He was riding the crest and as he approached the large overhanging rocks, he heard a woman's voice somewhere on the other side.

Dismounting, Freddie drew his pistol, held the reins in his other hand, and slowly led the horse around the rock. As he inched forward, he saw the ghillie suit. He took another step to get more into view. Suddenly, his horse bolted backwards, jerking the reins from his hand and turning him halfway around. The big bay gelding stumbled over a pile of rocks and lost his balance completely as he fell over a patch of prickly pear cactus. He fell over and rolled. Before Freddie could catch his balance, he stumbled as Missy's teeth ripped into his gun arm, taking him to the ground. The pistol went spinning fifteen feet down the slope. His hands went up instinctively to protect his throat, which the now wild animal was going for. She tore at his arms as she fought to get to his neck.

Becky's startled command to stop, caught Missy's attention. She kept hold of Freddie's arm but stopped her attack and just held him until he stopped struggling. Becky realized she had to subdue this man.

"Move and I'll order her to kill you," she told Freddie. He lay quietly, his arm in the powerful jaws of a forty-pound coywolf, jaws capable of crushing his wrist. The pain he felt was nothing like the pain he could feel if he struggled. He saw his horse struggling to get up, cactus plastered all over its legs and butt. The animal finally got up but was limping badly.

Becky opened her pack and found the zip ties which Bert had given her. She took three of them and tied Freddie's arms behind his back. Using three more, she bound his ankles together. Then, the strips of cloth were used to make a gag and to bandage his bleeding arm.

Finally, satisfied that her assailant was under control, Becky returned to her surveillance position. By now, the predators below had started their all-terrain-vehicle and were gunning the engine. They would be gone long before the injured horse made it back to the barn, and long before Freddie could be freed.

CHAPTER FIFTEEN: PREDATOR OR PREY

Nineteen-year-old Tommy Ahrens jumped rocks and cactus, dodging the few mesquite trees, as he sprinted to the far end of the valley and the possible safety of the hills. A star runner in high school, he was still very fit and had only been held by his abductors for two weeks. It only took him ten minutes to reach the rough gulley leading into the hills. Ten more minutes in the rugged terrain and he arrived at the crest of the first hill. He paused for just a few seconds to survey the area.

Behind him, he could hear the revving of a recreational vehicle engine, telling him that his pursuers would soon be leaving the ranch. In front to the south was another shallow valley followed by a steeper hill. While there were rocks and arid vegetation all over, he could not see any decent hiding places. As he ran toward the steep hill, he began pulling handfuls of grass from the few clumps he passed. He pushed them inside his shirt collar as he ran. They might help him hide if it came to that. He had to slow to a walk for a few minutes to catch his breathe. He had been running for nearly 45 minutes. The predators would be on the way and not far behind.

Tommy saw a small depression, a wash caused by water during some past heavy rain. It was about fifty yards to his left. He could not outrun the ATV, so he had to rely on stealth. He dove into the depression, reaching out to pull small rocks and any grass onto his feet and head. His only chance now was for the pursuit to pass by without seeing him. He breathed deeply to catch up his aching lungs. Once the vehicle was closer, he would have to control his rate of breathing.

Just over the crest of the hill, Bert was lying on his stomach, watching through the scope of his AR-15. He had gotten the message from Norah. He saw the boy sprinting toward him and then taking up a hide. It was about two-hundred yards away. Even if the boy heard him clearly, Bert was not sure if the lad would know he was his friend. He could not risk calling to him. Besides, the ATV was just coming into view from the first hill. He couldn't let them get to the boy. He was a witness and had to be alive to testify.

The pursuers stopped as they reached the slope below Bert. Soon they turned off the engine and both men got out. They stood, looking in all directions. The boy had taken them by surprise when he hid rather than run. For several minutes, they searched the area. Then they returned to the vehicle and began to drive slowly up the slope, weaving as they drove to survey the area.

Bert knew they had not seen the boy, yet, but they would probably go close to him if they continued along their present path. He knew they were coming closer to his own position, too, and to his rifle. It was just a matter of time and distance before he had to act. They were about 250 yards away. He couldn't afford to miss. That boy was the best witness to this place, besides himself.

Norah joined him. She had just returned from Becky and told Bert about the encounter with Freddie. He could not take his eyes off the scene below, but he felt a slight chill as he thought about what might have happened. It was the right move to leave Missy with her.

The situation with the boy was becoming critical. The hunters were getting closer to him as they weaved across the slope. They seemed to know he didn't have time to get over the hill. They were now within about twenty yards of Tommy's position. Bert placed the cross hair on the driver's chest, flicked off the safety, and moved his finger carefully to the trigger. They made a slow right turn back up the hill, toward Tommy, and stopped. They saw the boy. Sheriff Angle moved forward in his seat and raised his rifle. They were also facing Bert. Now!

Bert took a clearing breath, exhaled, and squeezed the trigger. The muffled shot and slight recoil accompanied the lurch of the driver and the sudden acceleration of the vehicle as he apparently hit the accelerator. The ATV did a wild swing to the left as Hank fell out, rolled, and lay motionless. Sheriff Angle tried to step out of the moving vehicle, lost his balance, and nearly fell. He pulled up his rifle and began to look up the hill. Tommy lost his nerve and began to flee from his hiding place. The .243 round hit Angle directly on the sternum, second button from the top. He dropped like a rock and didn't move.

Bert stood up quickly, holding the rifle to the side, and began to wave and yell, "Tommy, Tommy, we're here to rescue you." He continued to repeat this as he walked down the hill. The young man was poised to flee but held his position. He was almost afraid to believe that he was saved from the hell he had been brought into.

Bert removed the cover from his head and continued to the young man. Once he reached him, emotion took over and the lad burst into tears. He threw his arms around Bert and sobbed. Bert patted his back and told him the ordeal was nearly over. They still had work to do, though, because two women were still captive back at the ranch headquarters. He led Tommy to the ATV, which was still running, though bumped up against a rock. With Bert driving and Tommy as passenger, he backed away from the rock and started to drive toward the ranch. Then he stopped the vehicle, got out, retrieved the keys from Hank's lifeless body, and resumed the trek.

As they were crossing the hill closest to the gate and ranch,

Bert was able to reach Becky. She was eager to get down from the ridge and meet them at the driveway. She and Missy stood at the top of the steep slope and watched down the valley to the south, looking for the vehicle. They didn't know that they were being watched.

After several minutes, the men came out of the gulley and were heading for the enclosure gate. Becky led Missy down the slope from the ridge as Bert and Tommy drove up the dirt trail to the house. Norah was with Bert. They rendezvoused at the circular driveway.

Bert asked Tommy to accompany Becky and him to the prison dormitory. He found the right key on Hank's key ring and opened the door. They went inside and looked for Annie and Kathy but didn't find them. As they were about to leave the building, Norah noticed a discreet back door which had light around the edges. Bert checked the door and it was unlocked. Someone had taken the two women out the back. Who?

They went out the door. There was nobody in sight. He called Missy. Reaching into his bag, he removed Annie's hairbrush which he had been carrying all through the search for her. Kneeling, he offered it to Missy and gave the command, "Missy, find."

At first she ran through the prison, stopping at the room which was obviously Annie's cell. Then, she ran out the back door, sniffed at the ground, and began running toward the barn.

Bert, Becky, and Tommy ran after her. She hesitated near the pig pen but continued running with her nose to the ground around the back of the pen. Near the far end of the pen, she veered in a northeasterly direction, down a small draw which curved around a low hill. Tommy outran Bert and Becky as he raced after Missy. He yelled "stop" to someone. When Bert caught up to them, Missy was in an aggressive stance three feet from an older looking man. He was holding a pistol but seemed afraid to use it. Bert approached him with his sidearm drawn and ready to fire. Beyond the man were the two women. Beyond them was what looked like a root cellar. Another fifty feet and they would have been hidden underground. This was apparently a contingency plan in case a visit went sour. Somehow, they had missed seeing this third member of the staff.

Bert held his gun at the ready as he approached the man and took his gun. Then, Becky ran to the brunette and took her hands.

"Annabel Leery," she said. We are the team of B & N Investigations, hired to find you. I'm Becky. Our owner is Mr. Bert Lynnes, there. Our coywolf tracker is Missy, and the fourth member of our team is a psychic, named Norah. We are so happy to have found you!"

Bert introduced himself to Annie and then to Kathy. Both women had tears of joy and relief as they all walked back to the ranch. Annie sobbed uncontrollably as she clung to Becky. Over two years of capture and degradation were over. The suddenness of it left her in a state of emotional overload. At the ranch, Bert had some calls to make. The first was to the state police. He could not trust the local lawmen.

After the police, he called his clients, Billy and Bobby, bringing them up to date and letting them talk with Annie. That very emotional call lasted ten minutes. Becky let Kathy borrow her cell phone to call her family. She then allowed Annie to call her husband, Izack, if she wanted. Annie was hesitant at first, but with some encouragement from Becky, she called him. It was apparently a good call, as it seemed to brighten Annie's spirit even more. Becky smiled. She saw more to Izack than he was credited with.

With those calls completed, Bert walked out of hearing range and made one more call.

* * *

The afternoon passed slowly, with the taking of statements by the State Police, especially from Annie, Kathy, and Tommy. Five cars had eventually arrived and were starting their own investigation, including that of Bert's team. Bert took them to the bodies of Hank and the Sheriff. He had shown them where Freddie remained constrained up on the ridge. The third hired man was arrested. In between all of that, he and Becky caught up with Freddie's bay gelding and led him to the barn, where they spent over an hour removing cactus spines and caring for the animal. The individual cops had frequent questions and considerable interest in Missy. One of them said he wished they could get a dozen like her for their force.

They had gotten permission to have speedster, Tommy, run to retrieve Becky's truck. He was happy to do anything to help while waiting for his father to arrive the next day.

Tommy told Bert, "Everyone dies, Mr. Lynnes, but not everyone really lives. This experience has made me realize that I'm going to live every remaining day of my life. Really live. Thanks to you and your team, Mr. Lynnes."

Bert was moved by this young man. He gave him a hug as if the lad was his own son.

Finally, an hour after darkness had set in, the police allowed Bert's team to leave. A police car followed with Annie, Kathy, and Tommy. They would stay at the same motel while waiting for family to arrive. B & N Investigations were directed to remain in the Odessa motel for a day or two until released by the police. At that time, their weapons would likely be returned, too, depending upon further investigation.

They alternated between silence and chatter on the drive to the motel. Becky kept looking at the man in her passenger seat. She felt so much respect for him that she felt like she might bust. He was all she thought he was, and more. Tommy's words to Bert were playing on her mind. After this, she knew that she wanted to really live.

Norah raised a question. "What's going to happen to McDougal, the guy behind all of this evil?"

Bert was thoughtful for a minute before replying. "My concern is that, with all of the connections he has to influential and wealthy people. Many of them clients with a vested interest in his innocence, he'll get off. McDougal wasn't here today when this all happened. He'll claim he didn't know what the others were doing when he was gone. He'll try to blame it all on his partner."

"I'm curious, Boss," said Becky. "You called someone else back at the ranch. May I ask who you called?"

"You may ask," replied Bert. "But, that was a personal call that remains with me."

Norah nodded slightly. She knew the unspoken code between military men.

At the motel, they were all keyed up but also very tired. A delivered pizza and a beer helped them relax and Becky said good night to her teammates. She went to her room, realizing that she did not want to go to a separate room much longer. She had to resolve her feelings. Soon.

Bert took Missy out for one last evening walk around a nearby park. Then with her fed, watered, and a good scratching, he told his lovely spirit, Norah, that he needed to get some sleep. "But first, my Love, I want to say again how much I love you and miss your touch. You were my first true love and will always be my first true love. I will love you for the rest of my life, and beyond the grave."

"I know, Honey," she said. "I have loved you always, too. You're my first and only love and the reason I remain in this dimension."

"I need you, Norah, we need you," he replied.

"And I'm here and I'll stay here as long as I'm wanted, Bert."

"You'll always be wanted, Norah." He turned out the light and lay back on his pillow. Sleep was waging a battle against the ache in his heart. Sleep finally won the round.

The rest of the weekend looked to be a boring exercise in being available for any further police questions, making any more statements, outings for Missy, and looking after each other. They were stuck in Odessa until cleared to leave by the State Police.

* * *

Sunday morning, September 9th, was off to a warm and partly cloudy start in Mountain View, Arkansas. It was expected to clear as the day went on. The small town was moving at its typically easy-going pace as the residents went about their routines. The breakfast crowd at Ma's Diner, sixteen people, was buzzing with the usual chat about church, college football, and the upcoming hunting season.

Nineteen-year-old Robbie Long sat with his girlfriend,

Rebecca, having biscuits and gravy before she went to her job at another restaurant. He would normally be going to church. However, he had taken the day off so he could scout for the big bucks reported to be in the mountains west of town. This was the year that he intended to win the big buck contest, which he and a dozen friends participated in. He had a secret place and was sure it would make the difference. An uncle had 400 acres of pure wilderness at the end of a Forest Service road. The place was teeming with wildlife.

Rebecca put down her phone for a minute. She and Robbie had been going through their Facebook pages, leaving posts, chatting with friends, and uploading pictures.

"Excuse me, sir," he asked of the man at the table behind them. "Would y'all mind handing me the hot sauce, please, if you're not using it?"

The guy looked up briefly from leaning over his plate and the newspaper next to it. "No problem, happy to." The well-built, sandy-haired, middle-aged man handed the bottle to them. Then, he turned back to his food and tugged his dark brown Stetson hat farther down on his forehead. He also had his phone out and was looking at Facebook.

"Robbie, please tell me where y'all are going," Rebecca asked him. "I won't tell anyone, but I'll worry if nobody knows where ya went."

He made a face at her. "Okay, sweetie, but I'll break up with ya if y'all tell anyone. You know that Forest Service road that goes past Samuels' place and dead-ends in about five miles?"

She nodded slowly. "Yes, I think so. I think I was down that road two years ago. It's way back up yonder, Robbie, so be careful."

"I'll be careful," he said. "I'm going in about an hour, so

I'll be back before dark. Let's meet when I get back. We can watch some TV."

The waitress showed up. "Are y'all kids done now? Need anything more or are y'all ready for the check?"

Robbie asked her to bring the check. They continued to talk and laugh as they discussed hunting and his Facebook chats. Meanwhile, the man behind them dropped a $20 bill on the table, told the waitress to keep the change, and walked outside. He entered his dark blue Ford pickup and left the parking lot. Parking again, nearby, he debated calling his business but decided it was not necessary on a Sunday. Besides, he was on the job, himself.

It was about forty minutes later, before Rebecca had to get to her job. She and Robbie left the little mom-and-pop diner and went to his muddy, Dodge pickup. Standing next to it, he gave her a kiss and said he would see her later this evening. She went to her small car in the next row while Robbie climbed in his pickup, tapped his horn, and blew her a kiss. They both drove away.

While Robbie drove the nearly one-hour drive to his friend's property, he daydreamed about meeting up with his girl that evening. All his friends talked about how hot she was and when was he going to get lucky. He would laugh and joke with them, but to himself he knew that he really liked this girl and wanted to treat her right. This was a local and rural gravel road with a few country families, so he was not surprised to see a vehicle or two.

He parked at the small clearing at road's end. There was enough room to maneuver and turn around when he was ready to leave. Gathering his backpack, strapping on his hunting knife, and putting his spotting scope in its case over his shoulder, he stepped onto a visible game trail and began his twenty-minute walk into the forested hills and mountains. His objective was a mountain meadow, about four acres in size, which he knew was a primary feeding ground for deer.

* * *

The pickup coasted quietly to a stop at the edge of the gravel road, the engine turned off, and a man stepped out. He put a backpack on. The gear inside was essential to his business, and his prize represented a quarter-million dollars. He was a hunter and his prey was out there in the woods, just a short distance from him. He cut across the short distance until he picked up the well-worn game trail. As he started up the trail, he noted the set of fresh boot tracks in a muddy spot along the same path. The hunter quickened his step.

Ten minutes passed, then fifteen. The terrain was getting increasingly rugged as he neared the top of this low mountain. The meadow and his prey were just a short distance ahead, maybe less than a quarter mile. Slowing down, and then stopping to listen, the hunter stood motionless, trying to identify the faint sound he had heard. He slowly turned, straining to make out the sounds of the wilderness.

It was not the muffled sound, but the punch in his mid-section, which took his complete attention. He doubled over in pain, dropped to his knees, and fell backwards, gasping for breath. Blood began to trickle down his abdomen. It was on his back, too, where the full-metal-jacket .243 round had passed cleanly through. He tried in vain to roll over and get to his feet. Then he just laid back, trying to understand what happened.

For several minutes there was only the sound of the birds as they returned to singing. Then, he heard the footsteps as two people arrived and stopped beside him. Through cloudy vision, the hunter saw two people, one large and one much smaller, move to his feet. A rugged male voice said, "Good shot. Got what he deserved."

The hunter felt ropes tied to his ankles. They tightened and he began to drag, lying on his back with arms and hands dragging behind his head. Rocks, sticks, and clumps of vegetation dug into his damaged back and head, urging the blood to continue to flow. It seemed like hours to him as he was dragged into rougher and tougher terrain. Finally, it stopped. Hands went through his pockets and over his wrists and neck, removing anything that could identify him. He was on the verge of losing consciousness, but he fought to stay focused on his plight.

He became aware of lying on the edge of a steep slope which dropped into a deep gulley, about 100 feet to the rocky and treed bottom. His tormentors spoke to him as they drizzled a jar of honey onto his hands, face, and hair.

"Well, Mr. Jamison McDougal, welcome to y'all's final restin' place, and welcome to Ozark justice. Remember Annie Leery when you hit the bottom." With that, Bucky Samuels rolled the nearly lifeless body over the edge. He stood watching McDougal rolling and bouncing off the rocks and tree limbs until he finally hung up on a large branch about twenty feet from the bottom. "The ants and bugs'll find him there," he said to his companion. "Honey'll make sure o' that."

"Thanks, Lynnes, for not trustin' this bastard to the law," Bucky said to nobody in particular. "I know'd ya was more like us hillbillies than ya let on. I also know'd ya was a real Army man."

"Let's git back to the road," he said to his partner. "We need to figger out where to take his fancy truck to and park it so the damn feds will eventually find it. A long friggin' ways from here."

"Right, Bucky," said Daisy Long. "This S.O.B. will be here a while. When he's found, if he's found, it will just seem like one more case of a round gone wild. Or, since my rounds don't go wild, maybe . . . . . Justice. Or, Murder in the Ozarks."

CHAPTER SIXTEEN: ANNIE

Sunday morning in Odessa found Annabel Leery awake in the motel the State cops had put her up in. Kathy was in a different room in the same motel. The two women were still key witnesses and the police wanted them available. The sense of excitement which Annie felt was mixed with a heavy dose of apprehension, since she'd found out that her husband, Izack, and nephew, Billy, were driving from Arkansas to see her and take her home when she was released. She assumed they would be coming separately since they shared an intense dislike for each other.

She had woken several times during the night, crying. The elation she felt at her first freedom in over two years was tempered by the still vivid memory of the horror and humiliation she'd had to endure at the hands of McDougal, Hank, Freddie, and a string of often brutal guests. Rape was too gentle a word to describe the torment that marked her daily determination to just make it through another day and remain alive. That had become her mantra, just stay alive. Just hope for the day when she might be freed.

Brushing her hair as she looked in the mirror, she found it hard to recognize the woman looking back at her. She had not seen her image even once during her captivity. Was the woman she had been still there? Could her old self return from the shell of a wretched likeness, that she was afraid she had become?

Washing her face would hopefully begin to remove the reddened, tear-stained eyes, and puffy cheeks which put her reality on display for all to see. Her life had been put on hold for over 700 days and nights. Could she ever get it back? The uncertainty of a future weighed heavily, even as she rejoiced at being freed from the predators.

Tempering her own reality, was the knowledge that her classmate and friend, Debra Trayner, was still missing without a trace. Would she ever be found? Right now, it did not look good. Maybe Debra would become just another of those statistics: still missing. Without a trace. Never solved. Annie looked in the mirror and said a silent prayer for Debra, followed by vowing that she would live the rest of her life in appreciation of what she had.

The phone call interrupted her soul-searching. It was from Bert Lynnes, her rescuer. He said he wished he could see her in person, but they were supposed to stay away so they would not influence her statements. This was only temporary, and he promised to visit in person as soon as that restriction was lifted. For now, he just wanted to know how she was doing. They talked for a few minutes, then Bert said something that moved her.

"You're going to be fine, Annie," he said. "All the mixed-up emotions you're feeling now will begin to fade away when you get back with family and friends. Not immediately, but over time you will get back to feeling normal again. I'm even going to predict that your marriage can be better than it was before. Of course, that's if you want it to still be?"

She really liked this man. Not just because his team had rescued her, but because he was just a good man. A man who genuinely cared. "Do you really think so?" she asked.

"Absolutely," came his reply. "You've been through an extremely hard and demeaning period. You're a good woman, though, so you'll come back. Just be patient."

She began to cry. "Thank you, Mr. Lynnes, for everything."

"I'll do my best to visit in person before you go," he said.

"Good-bye for now. You have my number. Call anytime if you want."

She said goodbye and hung up, feeling more upbeat than she had all day.

Annie decided to get a coffee in the motel dining room. Once there, the biscuits and gravy and sausage sounded pretty darn good, too. She ate more than she thought she could. As she was about to finish, she received a phone call from Billy.

Billy was elated to talk with her again. Over and over he told her how much he loved and missed her and could not wait to have her back home. Then he did something she did not expect. He handed his phone to Izack. They had driven separately but stopped about three hours away for coffee after driving all night.

Izack told her he was so sorry for her ordeal and could not wait to see her again. He told her that he knew she would have doubts about him, but he hoped she would be willing to give him a chance to prove himself to her. After a couple of minutes talk, they got off the phone so they could get back on the road.

As he began the last hours of drive to Odessa, Izack thought about what Bert had told him. He was told to search his heart now, so as not to break Annie's heart anymore. Bert said that he needed to know that she had been raped, often daily, by many men, while being held captive. "She was a sex slave," he had been told, and "you need to know how you feel about that. The last thing she needs is a husband who cannot or will not accept the hell she's been through." Bert told him to decide now, before he sees her, if he can accept her ordeal and help her recover. "If not, then leave her alone," Bert had said.

Izack drove in silence, following Billy's truck. As he drove, tears began streaming down his face. He was overcome with the realization that it was time for him to mature into whatever he had left with Annabel. There was no room and no excuse for his past behavior. If she let him continue their marriage, which he seriously doubted, then he had to be better than he was. Better than he had ever been.

Annie tried to sleep. Sleep just was not coming to her, though. She was too keyed up about seeing Billy Joe and her husband. Keyed up about the trip back to Mountain View and home. Her phone rang. Becky Thompson was calling. Annie had only met Becky the day she was rescued, but she remembered the pretty blonde woman who was so sweet and supportive.

Becky just said that she wanted to say hello and wish her good luck and much future happiness. She told Annie that her team was having coffee at one of the local shops, but wanted to take time to wish her well. Call anytime if you want to talk, she also told Annie.

Annie's tears had dried up and her eyes cleared by the time her nephew, Billy, arrived. The tears came again, though, when she felt her wonderful nephew's strong arms around her. Suddenly, she knew she was going to be safe, and going to be alright. Once again, she felt like a surrogate mother and an aunt, something she had not felt in many months. This time, though, her nephew was the strength and comfort that she needed.

After a long period of just holding his aunt, Billy gently moved her from his hug and told her he wanted her to see her husband now.

"He's a changed man, Aunt Annie. Whatever you do, I believe that, and I know you'll see it too."

He walked to the door and went into the hall, where Izack had been waiting. He nodded and motioned for Izack to go inside.

For the first time in two years, Izack Leery looked into the eyes of his wife. He could instantly see the fear, the pain, the torment, and the uncertainty etched inside them. If ever there was a time to be the man she needed, it was now.

"Annie, can I hug ya?" he asked.

She gave a slow and unsure nod. He moved slowly against her, wrapped his arms gently around her, and placed his head against hers, holding her warmly and firmly but not too tightly.

"I love ya, Annie. I've missed ya more than I can say. I'm glad you're safe now."

She could feel the difference in him. A gentleness that had rarely been there before. He was being genuine. She did not know if she could make a new life with him or not, but she had the feeling that she could at least give it a go.

"Nobody knows the future, Izack, and I can't give ya any guarantees. But I want to go home."

Back in Mountain View, the sun was directly above the mountains and blasting through the dense forest of pine, oak, hickory, sweet gum, and cedars, made nearly impenetrable by the brushy mix of greenbrier, Virginia creeper, and poison ivy. The quarter mile-wide and two-mile-long valley of Bobcat Hollow was nestled in the brilliance of this early fall day in September of 2018. Heavy dew, which initially covered the grasses and low shrubs of the valley, leaving telltale trails where the several whitetail deer had been grazing, had burned off. This Sunday, a few weeks before the start of deer rifle season, was a clear one, warm, without a cloud in sight.

Annabel Leery was going home.

CHAPTER SEVENTEEN: WIN-WIN

Sunday in Odessa, Texas, found Bert, Norah, and Becky spending several hours going on a walk with Missy before it got too hot, and then hitting a small privately owned coffee shop. The owners were friendly people and they did not mind Missy being on a leash and sitting next to Bert. She was happy to be in a relaxed atmosphere without the stresses of an investigation oozing from her masters. The people in the place were all interested in her and elated when Bert told them her story and allowed them to carefully pet and get to know her. Norah was in the background, conversing with Bert and enjoying the interlude, as well.

Following the fun of the coffee shop and two calls to Annabel, they decided to check out a few of the interesting sights in Odessa. They all got a big kick out of the 8-foot statue of the jackrabbit, Jack Ben Rabbit. From there, they checked out another dozen of the 37 Jamboree Jackrabbits scattered around Odessa. Missy was not sure what to make of the huge rabbits, though she was keenly interested in them at first, until she smelled them.

As they were leaving the twelfth rabbit, one of Bert and Norah's two daughters, Summer, called to see how they were doing. They had a good talk for about fifteen minutes, bringing her up to speed on the case and talking with their eight-year-old granddaughter, Hailey.

As they neared the end of the call, Summer began crying on the other end of the phone. "Daddy," she sobbed, "it's been two years since we lost Mom. It doesn't get any easier, because I miss her as much now as I did when it happened. Will the pain ever lessen?"

"Yes, Honey, it will lessen over time," he answered her. "But, it will never completely go away. I've found that it helps to just open your mind and listen quietly. Hear what is unspoken, and you can sense her still in your life. She is, you know."

"Thanks, Dad," Paige said. "It helps to talk with you. I always get the feeling that she continues to speak with you and live through you, even though she's gone."

"I do what I suggested for you, my sweetheart. I open my mind and listen. And, your mother speaks to me, every day. Her spirit has never left me, honey, so I can tell you that she misses you, too, every day."

Following the call, the team decided to continue sightseeing for a while longer.

Becky was quiet for the next couple of hours of exploring Odessa. Listening to Bert's call with his daughter had touched her in a way she did not expect. She could not express it in words, but it had touched her heart and continued to move her soul. Several times, she looked away and wiped tears from her cheeks.

The Presidential Archives and Leadership Library became an interesting diversion for a few hours. They saw the replica of Stonehenge at the University of Texas of the Permian Basin. They tried to see the meteor fragments at the Odessa Meteor Crater, but it was closed on Sunday.

It all passed much too fast. The sun was setting when they arrived back at the motel. Bert and Becky walked within arms-length, laughing about the day, while Norah likewise laughed with Bert. Missy took it all in, alternating between Bert and Becky for some lovin', then lying on the cool bathroom floor. Norah went over to her a few times and smiled at the twitching of Missy's ears and the shivering of her shoulders as she stroked and kissed her head. Missy always knew when her alpha female was with her in spirit.

An hour of talking passed, and the time was ticking away. It was after 9:00. Becky could feel a conflict and pull raging within her, and she felt like she was about to split in two. She looked at this good, handsome, and strong man, and sensed the beautiful and joyful spirit who shared his life. There was a love and bond between Bert and Norah which was undeniable, indescribable, and eternal. She could never come between them, nor did she want to. Her conscience would not allow her to take away what they had left of a wonderful life together. It was time to decide. The only choice she felt that she had. She stood up, struggling unsuccessfully to hold back her tears. They flowed down her cheeks and onto her shirt.

"I need to go," she said. She walked to the door, opened it, and hesitated for one last look at first Missy and then a stunned but silent Bert. Closing the door quickly behind her, Becky walked down the hall to her room. With eyes blurred by tears, she almost ran around her room, throwing her things into her suitcases. Not knowing where she would go, she just knew that she had to go somewhere. Her heart was breaking and she had to try to run away from the pain. She was in love with Bert but felt she could never have him. Even as she gathered her things to leave, she knew it would not stop the hurt which permeated every fiber of her being.

Forgetting that there was an outside door to the parking area, Becky drug her bags through the hallway door. She started toward the reception desk.

Having made her decision to leave, she now stopped twenty feet down the hall. She sensed someone behind her. Before she turned around, she knew that Norah's spirit had followed her. She felt the undeniable presence and heard the words, "please stop."

"What does Norah want to say?" Becky asked herself. "Can I somehow understand her without hearing her, and why did she leave Bert?"

Back in his room, Bert sat in a state of bewilderment, knowing the reality of what was happening. Not knowing how to deal with it. Becky was obviously leaving. Leaving him and leaving the business. His own guilt prevented him from going after her. How could he turn from his love for Norah? She was his first love and would always be so. He loved Becky but did not want to lose the connection to the beautiful spirit of his wife. The conflict in his heart seemed to paralyze him. He knew he should go and stop Becky from leaving, but Norah would then know the depth of his feeling for this other woman. Suddenly, he realized he was alone in the room. Norah was gone. Were his worst fears being realized? Were they both leaving? Was Becky, and now Norah, already gone?

Norah had followed Becky after several minutes lapsed and the dark cloud of breaking dreams was sinking over the room. Like Becky, she also knew that it was time to decide. She could no longer stay if it meant preventing the man she loved and adored from ever finding happiness again. If seemed to be time for her to turn to and follow the light. Not knowing where it might lead, Norah felt that she first had to try to communicate with Becky. She had to make Becky understand that her spirit would no longer come between a relationship with Bert. With all her spiritual strength, Norah asked Becky to stop

With tears streaming down her cheeks, Becky turned and looked where she felt Norah to be. She could feel what Norah was feeling. She could sense what Norah was saying, without hearing the words. "There is a way, Becky. It doesn't have to end like this."

Becky knew that she could not run away without at least trying. She spoke out loud to Norah.

"Norah, I've grown to love you as I've grown to love your husband. I want to try to make this work for all of us. I won't pretend it will be easy because it will probably be challenging. But, you and I both love this man, so we can make it work. I want him as I know you want him. You do not want to leave. I don't want you to leave us, Norah."

Becky set her bags down, paused, and listened for a reply. Though she didn't hear any, she felt it. The answer just came to her from Norah.

"Norah, I've read that spirits are sometimes able to jump, or move, into the body of the living. If that's true, do you think you could come into my body? Can your spirit join with mine?"

Again, Becky listened quietly and just opened her mind. As before, the answer just came to her. She knew that Norah was speaking to her subconscious mind.

"Norah, I want you to come into me. You have my permission and I want you to become a part of me, if only for a brief time. Perhaps, for the first of many times. I want to love your husband and I want you with me."

The answer came to Becky quickly this time. She relaxed and closed her eyes. She tried to feel every cell of her body. Then she felt a strange feeling, one of strength, as if she were somehow more alive and empowered. She knew that Norah had come into her. Their spirits were intertwined as one. Becky's tears stopped and she wiped her cheeks.

Becky returned to her room and placed her bags inside. She returned to and knocked at Bert's door. He opened it, and stood looking at her pretty blue eyes, reddened by the tears of emotion. There was a look he had not seen before. It was the look of a woman who finally knew with certainty what she wanted. He knew that this woman wanted him. She threw her arms around him and kissed him passionately. He kissed her just as intensely, sensing his dear wife's spirit in the lips of this other equally beautiful woman.

"Bert Lynnes," she said. "I love you sincerely and totally. I want to be with you always. Norah is also with me, Bert. Her spirit has joined with mine for tonight. We're going to make love to you. Still locked in passionate embrace, Becky moved tightly against him, toward the open door of his room."

Joined with Becky's living spirit, Norah had an inside peace she had not felt in a long time. She knew that she'd made the right decision when she found and chose Becky. Her decision was for her beloved husband, unselfishly made to help him find physical love again. From the minute she first saw Becky, Norah knew that this lovely blonde woman was right for Bert. What she did not know then, but was now finding out, is that the decision was also the right one for herself.

Becky walked Bert backwards into the room. "You might be the top dog in this company, Bert, my love. But tonight, Norah and I are on top."

She kicked the door closed.

I grew up on a west Nebraska cattle ranch, the oldest of four children. Hills and valleys were my playground; cats, dogs, and a raccoon were my playmates until younger brothers took their places; windmills, BB-guns, and haystacks were among my playthings; horses and cattle were my workmates. Like the hardy people I grew up among, I have many hours working cattle on horses, using heavy machinery, and learning about the flora, fauna, and geography of the region. My early education came by way of one-room country schools. I often rode horses the three-plus miles each way to school or drove myself in a little Jeep. Two-hole outdoor toilets, coal stoves, and kerosene lanterns are among my childhood memories. Because of Nebraska weather, no phones, and no drivers' license, I boarded out most of my first two years of high school. I was athletic, loved sports, and participated in all available sports throughout high school.

Growing up without a neighbor in sight or other kids of my age to play with, I learned to live in my head and developed a vivid imagination. That imagination serves me well in creating fictional mysteries. Work ethic came from being the oldest son and starting to work full-time, outside of school, at the age of eight.

I have a degree in Animal Science from the University of Nebraska, and I've loved nature and animals all my life. Coyotes were part of the ecosystem, though largely unseen. Their howls welcomed most sunsets. The coyote-wolf hybrid was a natural character for this story, and I wanted to introduce it to the reader.

I first learned of the coywolf hybrid from an Animal Planet documentary, "Meet the Coywolf." I felt I knew coyotes well and had almost no fear of them, only respect. Then, I happened to see another documentary named "Killed by Coyotes." This caught my interest immediately, because I knew of no adult human deaths by coyotes. However, an aspiring folksinger, Canadian, Taylor Mitchell, aged nineteen, was killed in 2009 in Novia Scotia by coyotes while hiking in a national park.

I feel that wolf DNA may have played a role in this tragic attack. Such behavior is not typical of the coyotes that I know. For this reason, I decided to introduce the coywolf to readers. While my female hybrid is a well-trained and domesticated fictional animal, the real hybrids are a blend of wolf and coyote and reflect the characteristics of both. The real animals are not necessarily pure coyote-wolf but may have varying degrees of DNA, to include dog.

Readers should understand that this hybrid is spreading across the United States as well as Canada, because of its resilient coyote blood. The wolf DNA makes it a larger, more aggressive, pack hunter, and therefore more dangerous than a coyote. The coywolf, like the coyote, can live and thrive in urban environments. It may be living and thriving in your city. With a typical weight of around forty-five pounds, it's large enough to be considered an apex predator.

I'm a retired Air Force officer and pilot, and I have traveled extensively across the United States, lived in three foreign countries, and have flown in about 40 different nations. I owned and operated a bed and breakfast in Cody, Wyoming for five years, during which time I was a freelance writer for the Wyoming Livestock Roundup newspaper. That experience developed my interest and love for writing.

I worked as a private investigator for two years, in Arkansas, conducting surveillance investigations in a variety of locales and situations. That experience is part of the background for the Bert and Norah stories. I've also had a lifelong fascination with psychic phenomenon.